Rose Alone

The Rose Garden Book 4

Casia Schreyer

Schreyer Ink Publishing

This is a work of fiction. All characters are the creation of the author and any semblance to people, living or dead, is coincidental.

ROSE ALONE – THE ROSE GARDEN 4
Copyright ©2018 by Casia Schreyer

Cover © 2018 by Sara Gratton

All rights reserved.
No part of this book may be reproduced, scanned, or distributed in any printed or electronic form without permission. Please do not participate in or encourage the piracy of copyrighted materials.

ISBN 978-1-988853-33-8
E-ISBN 978-1-988853-34-5

The Rose Garden Series is dedicated to
the Rooswinkle Family

Rose Alone is dedicated to
Betty & Jos

18th of Starfall, 24th Year of the 11th Rebirth
Dinas Rhosyn, Evergrowth
The Wedding of Princess Taeya Living-Rose & Francis Silver-Axe

Betha had lived in Dinas Rhosyn as the Evergrowth Princess for twelve years. She'd seen the wedding dresses of her predecessors, had eyed them from across the dressing room while the girls fussed over her, and had snuck in there a few times to finger the fine, delicate fabrics and imagine her wedding. Her dream had been a grand one. A dress with a sweeping skirt and lots of lace, music, lights, dancing, a feast, and a huge guest list. No matter how big the event became in her mind, she remained at the center of it all.

It stung a little to be sitting on the sidelines now, watching the Evergrowth Princess marry her soulmate.

Taeya and Francis held the places of honour today and Betha could barely keep her distaste hidden. Taeya was wearing a simple, undyed, linen dress, and had roses in her hair. *She looks like a peasant,* Betha thought. Francis was, at least, wearing something nicer than he usually wore. *But there's nothing to set this wedding apart from any other, nothing except some roses and some extra prayers. My wedding won't look anything like this.*

Not that any of the gathered nobles seemed to care what their new princess was wearing. In fact, they all seemed captivated by it, oohing and aahing, saying things like 'doesn't it let the natural beauty of the woman shine through?' And none of them paid any attention to Betha even though only weeks ago she'd been their princess. Hadn't she stayed in their homes, risking her life to travel this province and perform protection rituals? *Ungrateful louts. Dark Spirits take them all.*

She barely spoke through the ceremony or the dinner that followed. She snarled at the few nobles who did try to approach her and even snapped at her fellow princesses. The only one she refused to speak harshly to was the boy, James. She'd taken a real liking to him and happily let him fill the final seat at the dinner table, the seat that would have belonged to her prince.

Now I'm the last and everyone on the whole island will be watching me, waiting to see who the final prince will be. She looked around the table. Rheeya's prince was a common-born miner, Taeya's was noble-born but a younger son of a younger son with no lands or titles. Instead he'd been a carpenter. Betha strongly disliked Kaelen's smug attitude but at least the Metalkin prince, like Vonica's prince, was twice-named and came from a strong branch of a proper noble family.

It's a hodge-podge group. Nothing at all like our predecessors'.

Dinner had been served and mostly eaten and Taeya was beginning to feel nervous. She fussed with the dishes in front of her. Francis reached out and squeezed her hand. "I know," he said. "But it's time."

She nodded. Taking a deep breath, she stood.

Betha would have called for silence, or had one of the stewards do it, but Taeya just stood and waited. Conversations stuttered to a halt as people hushed their companions and silence settled over the hall. Betha's mood soured further.

"Twenty-four years ago, four infant girls were brought to the island instead of five. This was only the beginning of what is becoming the most unusual of rebirths." She paused and scanned the crowd. Her stewards had seated the familiar faces, the princesses and their princes, the Silver-Axe family, and the Edgefields, closest to the head table and Taeya felt reassured by their presence. "Perhaps the biggest upheaval came only weeks ago when we discovered that Princess Betha and I were given the wrong names at birth and sent to the wrong provinces twelve years ago. The next few months will be a time of change and adaptation as I learn how to be the Evergrowth Princess. But today is a joyous day, and there will be plenty of time in the coming weeks to discuss serious matters. Let's spend this evening celebrating a future of peace and prosperity."

Francis stood and escorted Taeya onto the dance floor as the music began. Conversations resumed, and other couples moved to dance.

Johann stood and offered his hand to Vonica. "Shall we?"

She smiled and accepted both his hand and his invitation.

"Excuse me," Kaelen said. "There are people here I should speak with while we're here."

When he'd gone Mallory sighed, her gaze lingering on the dance floor.

For a moment Betha's anger shifted focus. She waved down a passing servant. Softly, so her fellow princess wouldn't hear, she said, "Princess Mallory would like to dance but Prince Kaelen is unavailable at the moment. Find her a suitable partner."

"Yes, of course."

The next song was just starting when a young noble approached the table and bowed. "Princess Jewel-Rose, you look lovely this evening. Would you honour me with a dance?"

"I'm not really familiar with your …"

"Yes, she will," Betha said. "Go, haven fun."

Mallory smiled and took the young man's hand, following him to the dance floor.

"Do you want to dance?" James said.

"No. I'd like to get out of here. I'm not much in the mood for dancing and parties."

He hopped from his seat. "I can escort you back to your room." He stood with one hand out and the other behind his back.

She laughed. "I see you've been paying attention to your lessons."

He grinned at her.

"Are you sure you want to leave early and miss out on the food and excitement?"

He considered this for a moment. "You could ask them to bring food to your room. And besides, you have the best stories."

"You're right, I could get us some food," Betha said. "Let's go then. We'll find someone who can bring us food and tell Rheeya where you've gone."

Later that evening Betha was sitting in her room staring into the fire when a knock brought her to the door. She hurried to answer it and found Tomas in the hallway. "I've come to collect my charge," he said.

"He's asleep in that chair there," Betha said, stepping aside to allow Tomas in. "You know he told me a bit about his life before Rheeya. He's lucky he had you, and your father."

"It was a hard life," Tomas said.

"But he had family." She smiled at James as Tomas scooped him up and stopped herself from touching his hair.

"You had the other princesses," Tomas said. "I know they're not blood but family is what you make it. You'll find yours, just give it time."

"Do you think my stewards will be so patient?"

"No. But you know now, don't let them dictate where you search and don't let them cross anyone off your list without your permission." He'd made his way to the door. "Thanks for this," he said, meaning the boy. "You've made his evening."

"I always miss him between visits. Good night, Tomas."

"Good night Betha."

Betha turned and looked around the room. It felt empty now. After tonight she only had two more sleeps in this room and then she'd be northward bound. "Oh well," she muttered. "I never liked this room anyway."

19th of Starfall, 24th Year of the 11th Rebirth
Dinas Rhosyn, Evergrowth

Betha's latest attempt at packing was interrupted by a knock at the door. "I really don't need help," she said.

"Princess, I've been sent to remind you. There's a council meeting today."

Betha hadn't forgotten but she was pretending to. *No pretending now.* "All right. I'll be right there." She put the last of her undergarments in the open trunk and made her way to the study where the other four princesses and their new high priest were waiting.

"It's certainly been an adventure. He keeps me on my toes," Rheeya was saying.

"James?" Betha said.

Rheeya looked over. "Yes. I was just telling them about his latest adventures."

"I probably heard his side last night."

"I guessed as much," Taeya said.

Betha responded only with a cool smile and took her seat. She'd hardly spoken to Taeya since that day in the library when they had both been restricted, for the most part, to their rooms. In the end,

Taeya's actions had revealed a deeper problem, but Betha still felt the sting of betrayal when she thought about it.

"Let's begin," Baraq said. "Rheeya, tell me about current guild relations in your province."

"Improving. The mining guild has calmed down now that the iron guild has finished making reparations for the accident. The iron guild has calmed down some now that no one is hounding them for money. They did petition me to allow members of Jared's family to serve in the Stone Clan chapter of the Metalkin guilds and I refused."

"Given what we've learned thus far, it makes sense," Baraq said.

"Given what we've learned recently, they'll probably just change their names and come anyways," Rheeya replied with a shrug.

"Do you think so?" Mallory said.

"You could summon the entire family to Golden Hall and do a head count, compare it to church records," Betha said.

"This would have been easier where I'm from," Mallory said.

"Vonica, do you have anything new to report?" Baraq asked, keeping them all on topic.

"We're still sorting through records. We had guards seize everything they could find all at once so nothing more could be lost or altered."

"That's a lot to go through," Rheeya said.

"Johann helped select scholars who could be trusted to help us with the task. And Octavian, Johann's brother-in-law, comes to help when he can."

Baraq nodded. "These cultural scholars the Metalkin are sending out concern me. The Metalkin were never known for cultural open-mindedness, nor for scholarly pursuits. What are they up to?"

"I'd like to know how to stop them," Taeya said. "A lot of people were hurt. And two foals."

"They were spotted in the Animal People's province recently," Betha said.

"How could you know that?" Baraq said.

"I received a letter from a friend."

"May I see it?" Taeya said.

"I didn't bring it, it's in my room. And it's my problem to deal with now."

Taeya averted her gaze. "Of course. I only thought if there were names maybe I would recognize them."

"The two of you will have to share a lot of information in the next few months," Baraq said. "Historically our island is strongest when the provinces work together."

"Strength through unity and balance," Betha intoned. "I know."

"Good. Betha, I have instructed your stewards to go slowly with your suitors until you've had time to adjust."

"Balder would have had a ball arranged for two days after she was expected home," Vonica said.

Baraq shook his head. "And look where that got him, and us. Yes, you need a soul mate, but the pact needs you most of all, the five of you. Is it not my duty to see you five cared for?"

"It's just different," Taeya said softly.

There was a knock at the door and one of the serving girls peered inside. "I'm sorry. We've lost track of the Stone Clan boy."

"Try the kitchens, wherever your guards train, the stables …"

Betha cut Rheeya off and added, "Check my rooms. He was visiting me last night."

The girl nodded and went out.

"For his sake I hope she finds him before Tomas does," Rheeya said. "Is there anything else?"

"Travel plans," Taeya said.

"I'm leaving in the morning," Vonica said. "I've too many ledgers to read. Mallory, you're welcome to travel north with me as far as the temple."

"I'll inform my guard, and Kaelen, and we'll leave with you in the morning," Mallory said.

"I'll travel with you," Baraq said. "The priests here have everything well in hand. There's no need for me to linger."

Mallory's face brightened. "I have some questions about history and politics and such. Maybe I can pick your brain on the road."

Everyone stared at her, their expressions a mix of confusion and disgust.

"It means 'ask questions' or 'make use of your expertise'. No head splitting involved," Mallory said quickly.

"What a strange saying," Taeya said.

"I like it," Betha said.

"I'm leaving tomorrow too," Rheeya said. "We'll go north, check on the village that was destroyed in the landslide, and then take the central pass."

"Betha's staying a few days," Taeya said.

Betha glared. "I can answer for myself. I leave day after tomorrow. I'll come north and stay the night at the Temple."

"We'll have a room ready," Vonica said.

"I'd like to speak with Madam Olgam while I'm there."

Vonica didn't seem surprised by Betha's request. "I'll send word to her as soon as I arrive home."

Betha turned to Baraq. "How did this happen? Aren't there rituals? Traditions? Something in place so this doesn't happen?"

"Yes. There are five sacred items and the spirit of your people would have guided you to the right one."

"So, how did Taeya and I both choose the wrong ones?"

"I don't know yet," Baraq said. "But I'll be looking into the matter when I return to the Sun Temple."

Rheeya pushed back from the table and stood. "If there's nothing else, I should help find James."

Baraq nodded.

9

Taeya rose as well. "I need to check in with my stewards and then maybe I'll come down to your room, Betha, and help with any names your friend provided."

Betha frowned and said, "It looks like I'm going to pack."

"I should do that too," Vonica said.

"Me three," Mallory added. "Kaelen will insist on breakfast before we leave tomorrow."

"I'll insist on breakfast before we leave," Vonica said with a laugh.

"Oh. I don't generally eat until ten … er … midmorning."

"We'll pack something for you," Vonica said.

They all went out. Rheeya had already disappeared down the hallway and Taeya headed off the same way. Vonica and Mallory made their way to the guest wing leaving Betha to return to her room alone. She took her time, letting her gaze linger on familiar paintings and tapestries and statues in the halls. *Two more sleeps and then I might never see this place again.*

She'd always thought of Dinas Rhosyn as rustic and plain, had envied the grandeur of the Sun Temple and the splendor of Golden Hall. Now she was surprised to find she felt no eagerness to leave.

When she arrived at her room she found the door ajar. She pushed it open, her body tense and wary. There was a serving girl there, busy with Betha's trunks.

"What are you doing? I didn't request assistance with my trunks."

The girl turned and Betha realized she was actually middle-aged, her face set in a deep frown. "I brought your things up from the laundry and thought I'd do you the favour of putting them straight in your trunk. A good thing too."

"Leave. Now."

"Gladly. And I'll be taking these with me to return to Princess Rose of Roses." She reached for a pile next to the trunk, a pile of gems and jewelry, all of which Betha knew she'd already packed.

"You went through my things? Put those back, you thief."

"I'm not the thief here. These belong to the Evergrowth, which means they no longer belong to *you*. You're no longer princess here. I'm taking them to the captain of the guard, or straight to the princess, and we'll see what they have to say about this treachery." She tried to leave but Betha blocked her path.

"They aren't from the treasury, they belong to me and they are coming with me."

"I'll not stand by and let you rob the rightful Rose of Roses." She tried again to leave but Betha pushed her back. "Twelve years I served you and you were always an ungrateful, spoiled …"

Betha's temper, already frayed by the tumultuous events and the stress of leaving her home, snapped and she struck the woman across the face, startling her into dropping the disputed trinkets. "Don't you dare speak to me that way. I am still a Princess of the Isle of Light and one of Airon's chosen …"

"You make a poor princess," the woman said.

Betha shrieked and raised her hand again but a voice from the doorway halted the blow.

"What's going on here?"

Betha knew that voice without turning and lowered her hand.

"She struck me, Princess," the woman said.

"Convenient that you leave out the part about you stealing from me and insulting me," Betha said.

"You're arguing over these?" Taeya said. She'd joined them and was studying the scattering of precious things on the floor at their feet.

"Yes, Princess," the woman said.

"Josie, why were you in here?"

Of course she already knows everyone's names, Betha grumbled to herself.

"Returning Princess Living Rose's things from the laundry."

"Those don't look like laundry."

"I found them in her things. I was going to hand them to Captain Over-Field."

"Why? They belong to Betha, not to the Evergrowth Royal Estate."

"I … I …"

"You'll work in the kitchens until I can speak with you further about this incident. I need to seriously consider if a person who invades the privacy of my guests and attempts to steal from them has any place among the staff here."

Josie bowed her head. "Yes, Princess." She left without further complaint or argument, closing the door behind her.

"You shouldn't have struck her," Taeya said. She knelt and began gathering the fallen jewelry.

"How did you know I wasn't actually stealing these?" Betha knelt to help.

"I saw them in your desk when I came to find Talia's letter, about the poisons. They reminded me of my window box back home. Besides, I've never known you to lie before, not even to be tactful."

"A few days ago she wouldn't have tried something like that. She wouldn't have spoken to me that way."

"I know this is hard for you."

"No, you don't. You came here, liked everything, and decided to make a home here. Yeah, maybe it was all divine will, but you knew what you were getting, you got to see it all before things changed. I didn't always like being the Evergrowth princess, but I was raised to rule here. It's all I know."

"It won't take you long to get your feet under you once you're settled into your new home."

"I'm not looking forward to leaving here."

"Betha, consider this your grand adventure. Take the long way home. You're restless in a way the rest of us never were."

"The guards won't agree and my new stewards won't be happy."

"Betha, stop. We've all been so concerned with making everyone else happy all these years. I didn't come here because of the Dark Spirit attack, that was just my excuse. I came because I wanted to see the gardens and I was tired of waiting for your wedding. Rheeya made a lot of people angry when she went to the mine, and when she brought James home with her. Vonica crossed all the guilds and hid from all her suitors."

"They both had good reasons to cross their stewards, and the guilds, and so did you. What's my excuse? Restlessness?"

Taeya sighed. "What else needs packing?"

"Not much. Most things in here belong to you now."

"Is there anything here you've always loved? Since it's mine now I can give away whatever I like."

"No," Betha said as she turned in a slow circle, her gaze sweeping over paintings and pottery. "No, nothing here ever really called to me. It's almost as if this was never really home." She was studying the shelves against the far wall. "Actually …" She crossed to the shelf.

Nestled between books about halfway up was a finely wrought silver rose about three inches tall and exquisitely detailed. She brushed her finger over the petals.

Taeya came up behind her friend. "Take it. It's probably the only rose you've ever been fond of."

Betha picked it up, holding it close as she took it to the open chest. Once it was nestled safely among the clothes she took one more look around the room. "An adventure," she said.

"You'll find everything you're looking for, just have patience." Taeya settled into one of the chairs. "Do you have that letter?"

Betha nodded. She produced a folded piece of paper. "This was the list included with the letter." She settled into the other chair while Taeya read.

"Can I make notes on this list?"

"No."

Taeya glanced up, her eyebrows shooting up in surprise.

"It's just that I should keep that as it is now, right? As a record. I don't want to edit it in any way just in case I need it as evidence of something."

"Makes sense. I'll need a pen and paper then."

Betha rose to fetch them, relieved that Taeya wasn't insisting on editing Joseph's words. This was just the list, she hadn't even shown Taeya the letter, but the thought of someone else adding to it, changing it, when he'd written it just for her, made her uneasy.

She handed Taeya the requested items then sat to wait. Finally, Taeya handed the papers to Betha. "That's all I know, off the top of my head. If you have any questions once you're in the midst of things, just write me. Or ask the stewards."

"Thank-you. Now, if you'll excuse me, I want to see James before he leaves. I'll see you at dinner."

20th of Starfall, 24th Year of the 11th Rebirth
Dinas Rhosyn, Evergrowth

Betha ate breakfast in her room, her need to avoid Taeya for as long as possible outweighing her desire to spend time with the others before they left. She was halfway through her meal when a knock interrupted her.

"Yes?" Her voice was sharp.

"Princess? It's James," came the reply, slightly muffled by the heavy wooden door.

"Come in."

"You're dressed?" He was peering around the door.

"Yes."

He bounded in, remembering to close the door behind him. "Oh, you're eating. Good. We missed you at breakfast."

"Oh, did everyone dine together?" She already knew the answer.

"Yes, except Mallory. She just had tea and kept complaining about something called coffee."

"What's coffee?"

"Apparently it's a hot drink, like tea, but different."

"I see." His description didn't tell her much and she added it to her mental list of things to ask Mallory about later.

James settled in the second chair. "They let me eat as much as I wanted this morning, and no one told me I was being rude."

"Are you ever full?"

"Sometimes, but it doesn't last long."

"Do you want a biscuit?"

"No, it's okay. When are you leaving?"

"Tomorrow morning."

"Are you scared? I was scared when we left the village with Rheeya. I was excited too."

Betha handed the boy some apple slices. "I don't know that I'm scared but I am nervous. I was scared when I first came here twelve years ago."

"We'll still be neighbours."

"Yes. And now there won't be a mountain range between us. You'll come visit me when I get married."

"And after that?"

"Keep up your studies and maybe Rheeya will send you with important messages."

There was a knock at the door. "Pardon the intrusion, Princess," the serving girl said as she entered. "We're looking for Princess Stone-Rose's charge."

"Yes, I have him with me."

"They're preparing to leave."

"I'll bring him."

"Yes Princess."

Betha finished her tea and stood. "Let's get you to your carriage."

They went hand-in-hand to the courtyard where the customary hustle and bustle of people coming and going had already settled and the only people still milling around were the guards riding escort.

The Evergrowth stewards were waiting under the old oak with the princesses and their princes. Betha and James joined them.

"Are you sure you don't want to keep him?" Tomas joked.

"I've enough changes in my life right now. I don't need to learn how to take care of a child too," Betha replied. "But he is always welcome to visit."

One of the guards came over. "Everything is ready."

"Then we will go," Vonica said. "We all have long journeys ahead of us."

Hugs, handshakes, and farewells were exchanged and those leaving boarded their carriages, leaving Betha with her former stewards and the new Princess and Prince of Evergrowth.

"We already have a line of petitioners today," Master High-Oak said.

"One hour," Taeya said.

"I need to see to the applicants from the Carpentry Guild," Francis said. "I'll see you later. He gave Taeya's hand a squeeze before heading across the courtyard.

"I'd like to speak with you before court," Taeya said to Betha. "Have you eaten?"

"Yes."

"Then come walk with me." Taeya led Betha through the gardens, down paths Betha had hardly set foot on in twelve years except to hide from her duties, to the rose covered gazebo. "This is my favourite place in the gardens. There was only one place I liked better, and that was the workshop."

"I don't see it," Betha said. "It's just flowers."

"Tell me about court, and the guilds."

Betha started slowly, unsure of what to say to such a general inquiry, unsure of where to start, but as she spoke she shed the awkwardness and the words came easier. Taeya asked some questions but for the most part she just listened, getting a feel for the political climate she as walking into and what was important to the people she now ruled. When their hour was almost up they returned to the castle where Master High-Oak was waiting for them.

"We're ready," he said.

"Then let's begin," Taeya said.

There were two chairs set up at the front of the hall. As Betha expected, Avner High-Oak spoke almost exclusively to Taeya, offering her suggestions and asking her questions. What surprised her was how often Taeya turned to her for advice or deferred to her recommendations, even though Avner frowned eat time.

They sat in court until after midday. The list of petitions was not over long but each one took longer to address than it would have taken Betha on her own on a normal day. When every petition had been dealt with Taeya stood to address the room.

"This rebirth has turned out to me more complicated than the past nine," she began. "Princess Jewel-Rose did not grow up with us at the Sun Temple but rather was discovered earlier this year. Our princes have been found in unexpected places, the Stone Clan prince survived an assassination attempt, corruption was discovered within the Merchant Bank and multiple guilds, and the High Priest of Airon was replaced by divine appointment." She paused and scanned the nobles and wealthy merchants and guild members who had come to observe her official day in court. "We do not yet know how or why any of this has happened. How has this corruption spread so far? How did Princess Betha and I wind up in the wrong provinces? We don't even know if that was a mistake or deliberate, and if it was deliberate, what motivated the deception. High Priest Silver-Cloud will be investigating the matter. I have my own matters to look into, matters connected to the involvement of the Metalkin meddling in trades they had no business learning. I know the other princesses will be conducting their own investigations.

"Going forward your cooperation will be required, whether that is a summons to court, or a request for records or information. Believe me when I say that a refusal will be seen as extremely suspicious behaviour and will result in the guards getting involved.

"I have much to learn about my new role, I know that, but I will not let that stop me from setting right anything that is threatening the Evergrowth people."

There was a polite spattering of applause as Master High-Oak dismissed court for the day.

21st of Starfall, 24th Year of the 11th Rebirth
Dinas Rhosyn, Evergrowth

Betha rose early after a restless night and dressed without assistance. Her trunks waited by the door. There was nothing left in this room to make it hers. She felt disconnected, adrift. She rang for an early breakfast but when it arrived she sat and stared at it, the smell of the sausages making her nervous stomach do backflips. She poured a cup of tea with shaking hands. The tea settled her stomach enough that she could eat the bread and honey. She ignored the sausages.

Servants came and collected her things. She left the remains of her breakfast on the tray and made a slow pass around the room, running her fingers over carvings and vases, her gaze lingering on paintings of fields and flowers. She collected her shawl and made her way down to the courtyard where an escort of guards was preparing for the journey north.

Betha, watching the preparations, didn't notice Taeya standing just behind her until the other girl spoke. "I'm going to miss you."

Betha glanced over her shoulder just long enough to confirm it was Taeya speaking and that the other princess was alone before turning her attention once more to the scene before her. "Where are your stewards?"

"I told them to stay inside. Francis too."

"Told? Or asked?"

Taeya shrugged. "If you want to say good-bye to them I can …"

"No. It's fine. I just want to get this whole thing over with."

"You'll find your prince sooner than you think."

"Perhaps."

"Betha, I'm sorry about the way things played out. I didn't come here with the intention of falling in love with an Evergrowth man."

"I know."

"Of all the others, I always felt closest to you."

Betha didn't particularly feel like being kind right now. "When everything has settled, and I've found my prince I'm sure this will stop hurting."

The strain in Taeya's voice eased a little. "Don't forget to write Talia," she said. "And James. And me, if you can spare the time."

And Joseph, if I ever find out where he is. "I'll try," she said.

Taeya put a hand on her friend's shoulder, wishing she could hug her instead. "Good luck." She turned and went back inside.

When the guards called that all was ready Betha walked calmly down the stairs, leaving her home behind for the second time. *I am not twelve anymore. I will not cry this time. This is a grand adventure after all.*

26th of Starfall, 24th Year of the 11th Rebirth
Sun Temple Complex, Sun Temple Province

"Princess, the carriage and escort have arrived."

Vonica looked up from her reading. "All right, thank-you. I'll be right out."

"It's raining," Johann said.

"Then I'll wait inside the door, but I've been sitting here since midday, I need a break."

"I'll see you at dinner then."

Vonica stretched and looked over at her husband. He was seated in one of the tall-backed chairs by the fire place, one ankle on his knee, a ledger book open on his lap, and a cup of tea in one hand. His gaze was on the page, his face and body relaxed. She smiled. "Yes, I'll see you at dinner. Remember to move at some point."

"I'll have to get up to grab a new ledger soon." He still didn't look up.

Her smile widened and she left shaking her head.

She ended up not having to wait. Betha had just come in as she reached the front hall. "You made it. I expected you yesterday."

"I stopped at one of the estates in Northern Evergrowth," Betha said.

"And no point writing, the bird wouldn't arrive that much before you did. It looks like you didn't get too wet."

"One of the advantages of the covered carriages. I'm sure the guards are soaked."

"You're in your usual room. Are you going to want a bath?"

"Please. Though I suppose it would be quicker to stand out in the rain."

"And colder."

"It was actually refreshing. It was so hot the other day."

"I'll go find someone to run your bath and bring up your trunk. And we'll be having tea with Madam Olga after dinner tonight."

Betha bit back a protest. She had wanted to go alone. "Thank-you. I look forward to it."

The bath was far nicer than the rain and she took her time soaking the road dust from her weary body. When she was clean and dressed she took a walk down the corridors she'd occupied as a child. She could almost hear the laughter and the patter of slippered feet on stone, racing the length of the hallways, sliding around corners, the shouts from teachers and servants at their recklessness, and the fits of giggles when they caught each other. *If I feel I could just turn the corner and see us there, ten again, and full of mischief.* But it was quiet now, still and empty. Betha sighed and walked on, her sedate footsteps echoing off the stone walls.

Dinner that evening was roast duck, garden fresh summer vegetables, and warm bread. The princesses were joined by Johann and Johann's brother-in-law, Octavian, who had arrived while Betha was off exploring.

"...and all that just since the fire," Octavian was saying.

"I'm glad things turned around for him. He's a good man," Johann replied. They were talking about some blacksmith at the Sun-Song estate; Betha was only half paying attention.

"How's Ioanna?" Vonica asked.

"She misses you. She sent me with a list of books I'm to bring back. Oh, and this." He fished a note out of a pocket and handed it to Vonica. "She regrets not being able to come to tell you in person."

Vonica quickly read the note then passed it calmly to her husband but Betha could tell that whatever was in the letter had sparked an impressive emotional response in her friend. *She can hide it from them but not from me.*

Johann dropped the paper in his gravy. "I'm going to be an uncle?"

Octavian nodded.

"You're going to be a father?"

"That's how it works, yes," Octavian said, chuckling.

"Congratulations! I'll have to ride down as soon as time allows to congratulate Ioanna in person. Oh, I can just imagine my mother is beyond excited right now."

"It's all we could do to keep her quiet about this until we could inform you."

"This certainly is a big step," Vonica said. "You're so lucky."

"We'll see if that luck holds. If the child is anything like me he'll be quiet, intelligent, and a quick study."

"And if the child is anything like my sister he'll be trouble from the day he gets his feet under him until … well you'll have to let me know when she stops being trouble."

"A toast," Vonica said, raising her glass. "To the father-to-be!"

Betha reluctantly joined the toast and offered a dry, "Congratulations to the skinny, tousled man sitting across from her.

Octavian set his glass down and cleared his throat. "Princess Betha, perhaps you'd tell me a bit about Dinas Rhosyn. I should very much like to visit one day."

"You're are more than welcome. I doubt I will ever return there."

Octavian tried again. "How large is the garden?"

"I'm sure Vonica or Johann could tell you. They visited just recently."

"But you lived there."

"And now I don't," Betha said. She pretended not to see Vonica shake her head. "I'm sorry. I'm not very hungry. I'll return to my room for a while. You'll fetch me for tea this evening?"

"Of course," Vonica said.

"It's good to see you again," Johann added.

Betha forced a quick smile and went out. Behind her she heard Vonica say, "I'm sorry, Octavian. She's always been very direct and she's not happy with her current situation."

I don't even have the door closed and she's already apologizing for me. Betha hurried to her room, desperate to reach privacy before the tears started.

When Vonica knocked on Betha's door a few hours later the sound started her awake. "Yes, what is it?" She was suddenly grateful everyone expected her to be in a bad mood. *They'll mistake sleepiness for irritation.*

"If you're still interested in tea with Madam Olga, it's time."

Betha yanked the door open and nodded to Vonica. "I'm ready." As they walked together Betha said, "I didn't realize it would be so late."

Vonica shrugged. "That was her request."

They retraced Betha's steps down little-used halls and turned down a side-passage. "She stays here? Alone?" Betha said, looking around at the obvious state of neglect. These rooms and halls would be cleaned, top to bottom, only when Betha and her fellow princesses were nearing the end of their lives, to prepare for the next rebirth.

"Also her request. I've offered her other rooms, but she refuses. She's more stubborn even than you." Vonica took a deep breath. "I used to visit her often until my stewards said I had to stop hiding in my childhood and put a stop to it. They wouldn't let me see her until Johann helped me put my foot down on that matter. By that time, she … well, you'll see." Vonica stopped and knocked gently on one of the doors before opening it. "Madam Olga it's Vonica. And I've brought Betha with me."

The room was dimly lit but cozy with comfortable furniture arranged around the hearth and tapestries in warm colours hanging on the walls. Someone had brought a fresh tea tray and left it on the side table.

An old woman sat in one of the chairs with a blanket over her legs. Betha remembered a round-faced woman with bright eyes and dark hair. This woman was too thin and her hair was stark white.

"Oh, my Sunny Girl, there you are. I was hoping you hadn't forgotten." Even her voice was wrong, too thin and small, nothing like Betha remembered.

Vonica went and hugged her. "Of course, I didn't forget. I'll pour the tea."

"And you, you're not too surly to give me a hug, are you?"

"Of course not," Betha said. Even if the tone was wrong Betha recognized the blend of no-nonsense gruffness and absolute caring that had been the hallmark of Madam Olga's character. "I'm sorry we came so late."

"I don't sleep much anymore. I don't do enough in a day to make me tired, and soon enough sleep will become my permanent state."

"But not yet," Vonica said. She handed Betha and Madam Olga each a cup of tea and then went back for hers, which was empty. The girls sat.

"You're looking well," Madam Olga said.

"Well enough. But how are you feeling?"

"Old. Stiff. Useless. My eyes don't work so well anymore, and I can't knit because of my hands. But the girls take good care of me.

They always told me I was foolish for not having a family. You'll have no one to take care of you when you're old, they told me. But I'm doing just fine. How many old ladies can say they get to grow old in the comfort of a castle?"

"Not many," Betha said.

She looked over at Vonica who was standing again. "Where are you going?"

"Oh, I'm finished my tea already and I have a few things to do this evening. I'm sure Betha will stay."

"Of course," Betha said.

Vonica patted Madam Olga's hand. "I'll see you again soon."

"Bring that husband of yours next time. I like him."

Vonica laughed. "All right."

When Vonica had gone Madam Olga said, "Now you can talk about what's troubling you."

Betha set her tea aside and placed her hands in her lap, leaning forward. "Did you know about the mistake?"

"There's no way I could have known something like that, but I always did wonder about Airon's plans for the four of you. What benefit was there in sending a young girl with such strong convictions to a province built on compromise? Was it wise to send one so outspoken to rule a people accustomed to gentleness? But my job was to keep you fed and washed and presented to the proper places at the proper times, not question the infinite wisdom of the priests. Balder made that quite clear to me any time I protested. I like this Baraq Silver-Cloud much better."

"I don't want to go to Caranhall."

"My sweet stubborn girl, you are as much bound by duty as I was."

"You should have protested louder. You were right."

"Right or wrong I had no proof. I couldn't fight the priests with their traditions and their rituals. Now, there is proof."

"Proof of where Taeya belongs, but what about me? I feel I'll never belong anywhere. What if they got the wrong baby? What if I was never meant to be here?"

"You can't think like that. All you can do is move forward with your life, wherever it takes you, and keep looking for proof."

"Proof of what?"

"Of where you belong."

27th of Starfall, 24th Year of the 11th Rebirth
Sun Temple Complex, Sun Temple Province

Betha joined Vonica, Johann, and Octavian for breakfast, ignoring their looks of surprise. "I'm very sorry about yesterday," she said. "I was tired from the road. Octavian, you really should consider visiting Dinas Rhosyn. You and your wife would love it. There's an early harvest festival with music and dancing."

"Thank-you for the recommendation."

"Vonica, I've been feeling a little lost lately. I was wondering if I could stay a few days to do some research and reading about the Animal People."

"We have the ledgers …" Johann started.

"I know you're busy. I grew up here. I don't need a babysitter, and I'll be so busy I won't need someone to entertain me."

"I don't mind," Vonica said. "No one else needs the room. But you should talk to Honourable Silver-Cloud and inform your stewards."

"Thank-you. I won't be any bother."

Betha didn't like to read. As a child this had been a point of contention between her and her various teachers and tutors. Fortunately, Taeya and Vonica had loved reading and were more than willing to explain things to Betha and Rheeya, who both preferred to learn from spoken stories. Rheeya had also enjoyed getting her hands dirty, something discouraged as beneath any of them.

I wonder what our old teachers would think of Rheeya digging at a mine. I wonder what they would think of Tomas and James?

She hovered in the foyer of the library. She'd been here a few times as a child but mostly she and the other girls had used a smaller, private library in the nursery wing for their studies.

This library was certainly grand in scale if boring in décor. The stone pillars were finely carved, as were the legs of ever table and desk. The stone floor was bare between the shelves and beneath the work areas, but here in the foyer woven rugs had been laid out. Torches were hung from the pillars in ornate wrought-iron holders, but nearer the shelves it was dangerous to leave such large open flames unattended. Candles were set out on every table and desk, to be lit when someone was working there and four giant chandeliers hung over the various work areas, each set with over two dozen candles.

A man in a plain linen robe and a sash that marked him as a scholar approached her and bowed, his actions jumpy and sharp. "Welcome to the Great Library, Princess Rose … Living Rose. Do you require any assistance?"

What I really want is to go and explore, but I told Vonica I was here to study. I should at least make a show of it. "I'm looking for information on the Animal People."

"Of course. If you'll follow me. We have an entire section on your province's history and culture."

With no other option, Betha followed him. Around them other men in linen robes worked, some at the tables, some searching for books, others still putting volumes away. Their voices, when they spoke at all, were hushed.

"Beginning at this shelf here," the scholar said. "The books you're looking for go all the way to the wall there. Historical texts are at this end, followed by studies in culture, things like art, music, et cetera, and then some literature and poetry against the wall. Is there anything else I can help you with?"

"Not at this time," Betha murmured. Her eyes were on the shelves and she didn't even notice him bow and take his leave. He'd brought her to a section that was easily as large as her bedroom back in Evergrowth had been and it contained hundreds of volumes. *I don't even know where to start.*

She walked down the first aisle, trailing her fingers over the spines of the books. She pulled a few free and examined their titles but they were all boring. "A History of Animal Husbandry in the Third Era". She wasn't sure breeding horses had changed so much that they needed to write a book on its history. "King Adolf: His Life and Legacy". She didn't even know who King Adolf was or how long ago he'd ruled. She left the ancient, dusty books behind and moved on to newer looking ones until she started coming across titles that dealt with the pact.

"A Biography of Taeya Living Rose, First of her Name, Chosen Rose of Airon." She paused at that one and flipped to the author's introduction.

"History is so often written so long after the event has happened, often because we do not realize the historical significance of an event until much later. There is no denying the historical impact of what has happened this past year which gives me the chance to write the biography of historical figures while they are still alive.

"Airon in his wisdom has selected five young women to rule the island. Princess Vonica Bright-Rose, Princess Ashlynn Jewel-Rose, Princess Taeya Living Rose, Princess Rheeya Stone-Rose and Princess Betha Rose of Roses. In this volume I will describe these remarkable young women, their personalities, and their achievements."

Book open in her hand, eyes on the page, Betha made her way to the nearest table and settled in to read. She'd heard stories of the pact, dry, dusty accountings of prayers and rules, duties and responsibilities, but no one had ever bothered to teach her anything about her past lives. Now here was something about her, about who she had been, at that precise moment when her soul had been bound to the pact, written by someone who'd been alive at the time, someone who might have even met the original princesses before the cycle of rebirths had started.

She managed two chapters, one on the pact itself, and one on the first Princess Taeya Living Rose, before admitting boredom and giving up. She could find little similarity between herself and the first Princess of the Animal People and therefore little to interest her. She left the book on the table since she couldn't remember exactly where she'd found it and went searching for others.

In short order she had a stack of unread or partially read books on the table and no more idea about who she was supposed to be or how she was supposed to act than when she'd entered the library. She wandered the last row of shelves, examining books of pastoral poetry and old journals, ready to give up and call it a day. *There's nothing here. I need to find something interesting or there's no point in staying, and I am not ready to go to Caranhall.* She wasn't even ready to call it home yet.

With a heavy sigh she turned her back on the shelves and wandered aimlessly about the library. It was peaceful here and she could understand how Vonica could find solace in a place like this, away from prying eyes and the busyness of the day. For Betha, however, it was nothing but boring. Empty aisles and too much quiet. She craved people, more importantly she craved the attention those people would pay to her.

For a time, just before Vonica's accident, there had been other girls living here at the Temple. They were the daughters of scholars and guild representatives, sent here to be educated at the finest school. *And no doubt attempt to build a friendship with their future rulers, a friendship that would benefit their family or guild.*

Betha hadn't paid much attention to the politics of the grown-ups back then and while Taeya was her dearest friend Betha had loved those brief excursions when she got to meet the noble girls. Then the accident had happened, and those visits had been put on hold. They'd turned twelve so soon afterward and had been sent to their own provinces, so the visits had never resumed. *And the girls in Evergrowth were so boring!*

There were voices just ahead, hushed but obviously young. They were talking about something, Betha couldn't yet make out the words, and someone kept laughing softly. She approached on near-silent slippered feet, her ears straining to catch what they were saying before they noticed her.

At first she'd thought there were two voices, now as she got closer she picked up a third, softer than the others, with a whiny quality. Someone laughed again and there was a scuffling noise. Something hit the floor followed by more laughter and that whiny voice again.

"You'll damage it."

"You'll damage it," one of the other voices said, mockingly. "What do you care? You're not one of us."

"I came here to study. I have my student's robes."

"You think that makes you one of us? You think you'll actually become a scholar?"

"Scholar of horse shit," the other voice said.

Betha peered around the shelf. Two young fair-haired men stood in the aisle, their backs to her, their bodies blocking her view of the third.

One of them kicked something and it skittered across the stone.

"Stop it," said the third man, the one Betha couldn't see, the owner of the whiny voice.

"Stop it," the one on the left mimicked while his companion laughed.

"You're supposed to care about the books."

Betha stepped fully past the end of the shelf. "He's right. I thought all of Airon's followers cared about books."

The two men spun around and Betha could see from the rapidly changing expressions on their clean-shaven faces that they had intended to tell her off before seeing the expensive dress and the tell-tale red hair. Whatever crude thing they had intended died on their lips and they stuttered for a moment before remembering their manners and bowing.

"Princess, we didn't see you there."

"Forgive us," said the other.

"Me? You haven't done anything to me."

"But he's just an …"

His friend, the taller of the two, elbowed him sharply in the ribs and he stopped talking.

"No, please, continue. I'd love to hear your rationale."

"I'm sorry Princess, it was inappropriate of me, I should not have said it."

"You haven't said it, but I think you should."

He looked down, his foot scuffing at the floor. "He's not a real scholar, he's just a student from the Animal Province."

"Perhaps it's time for some scholarly input from someone who actually cares about the subject. I just came from the Animal People section and the books there, written by previous Sun Temple scholars, were greatly lacking."

"But Princess, it's just not …"

"I am the Princess of the Animal People. If you can't write a book, about my own people, that can hold my interest, you're not doing it right." She glared at them but neither man would meet her gaze. "You sound like a pair of children, picking on him like this. I thought Sun Temple Scholars were responsible for recognizing the value in all cultures. How can we trust you to record *our* history or write about *our* culture when you don't see us as intelligent? How can we trust you to teach our children?"

"We're sorry, Princess, we weren't thinking."

"No, you weren't, and you're lucky I don't report the both of you to a senior scholar for your behaviour. I would advise you both find somewhere else to work for the remainder of the day. If I see either of you again, I may change my mind about reporting you."

"Yes Princess," they said, hastily bowing. They hurried past her, one on either side, careful not to bump her.

With them gone she finally got a clear view of the young man she'd been protecting. He looked young, soft in the face and wide-eyed, the type to be easily excitable, framed with brown hair that was tinged with copper. While she'd been arguing with the bullies, he'd managed to collect the books they'd knocked to the ground. He nodded a few times, swallowed hard, and managed to say, "Thank-you, Princess Living Rose."

"Does that happen often?"

"I'm afraid so. And they're not the only ones. I'm a bit of an oddity, a Carainhithe who likes to read. Oh, I know I'll never become a Master Scholar or anything grand like that, but I want to know things, things that would be useful to our people. When I return home, I can find a job with one of the guilds."

"What's your name?"

"Michael Mares-Grace."

Betha forced herself not to roll her eyes. She still found most Carainhithe double-names ridiculous sounding. Instead she smiled. "It's a pleasure to meet you. I wasn't sure I'd meet anyone from my province here, outside of the stables anyways."

"I know many of the young men working in the stables here. I can take you to see the horses if you'd like."

"No!" she said, a little too quickly and a little too forcefully. When he gave her a strange look she smoothed her skirt and cleared her throat. "It's just that I can spend all the time I want in the stables when I return home. I only have a short time to spend here in the library."

"What are you looking for?"

"Information on our people. A nice man showed me the proper section but all the books I found were so boring." She smiled sweetly at him. "I'm sure you'd be more interesting and I'm sure you know lots about the history and culture of our people."

"Yes, I do, actually," he said. "I was supposed to be working on some papers for one of my teachers but I'm pretty sure you outrank him."

"Yes, I'm pretty sure I do. If we're going to be talking wouldn't it be best for us to go elsewhere? So that we don't interrupt the scholars who are studying?"

"I know a wonderful little spot," he said, offering her his arm. He set his stack of books on the first table they passed and led her out of the library.

After several hours of feigning interest in Michael's stories Betha stretched her arms wide and said, "Oh, I could use a walk."

"Yes, that's one of the marks of our people," Michael said. "A restlessness, a need to move and do."

Great, maybe I am their princess after all. I never felt I could just settle in somewhere. She pushed the thought aside. "Maybe you could take me on a tour of the scholar's wing."

"You grew up here."

"We weren't allowed in the scholar's wing, our caretakers always told us 'the masters don't need little girls underfoot, making noise, asking foolish questions, and touching things'," she sighed. "I'm sure you think it's very plain compared to everything else here, but I'd still like to see it."

"A quick tour then," Michael said. "The masters aren't very welcoming of guests or tourists, no matter their age."

"Are you the only person from the Animal Province studying here?"

"For the most part. There are some younger men and a few women, sons and daughters of the guild representatives in town, who make use of the school here. I'm the only one my age."

"Do you have many friends?"

"A few. Not everyone here is stuck up and rude like those two you saw earlier."

"Not everyone, but some?"

He nodded.

"Have you told the masters?"

"Why? I'm a grown man, not a child in a school yard scrap."

"You're very strong to deal with it on your own," she said and watched him preen a little at her words. "I should very much like to meet your friends," she said. "I'm sure they all have wonderful stories."

"I'll see who's around. Most are in class or in the library or off studying. Everyone here is so serious about their studies."

"And you're not?"

"Oh, I love being here, and I love the books and reading, but this isn't my place. I'm eager to finish what I came here to do so that I can return home. I'll miss having access to this many books but I miss home already." He shrugged and opened a door. "This is where we eat. It's simple but the food is decent and filling."

She nodded, and they walked on down the hallway together. "Did you know Johann, before he became the prince?"

"Not really, no. He's an illuminator, and already fully trained in his craft. I'm just a student, and a foreigner. Though I heard from some of the others that that wouldn't have mattered to Johann … to the prince, rather."

"No, he doesn't seem to be the type to discriminate based on something as simple as the place of your birth."

"I've heard he was exceedingly patient as well. An asset when dealing with the senior scholars to be sure. Ah, here, this is the room I was looking for." He opened another door and peered inside. "Yes, he's here. Come inside."

She followed him through the door into a study so crowded she wasn't sure how Michael could locate anyone. Not that there were a lot of people here, but there were books and scrolls on every available surface. A face popped up from behind a stack of books. Curiosity turned to a wide smile and the owner of the face came around the table. Like Michael he was young, but his hair was an almost colourless blonde, pin straight, and long enough that it fell in his owlish eyes. They were dressed in matching linen robes tied at the waist with a simple cord as neither had earned their scholar's sash yet.

"Michael!"

"Julius, good to see you."

"I thought you were in the library on some errand."

"I was. I got side-tracked. Julius, this is Princess Living-Rose."

Julius frowned at Betha. "You're not quite what I imagined based on what was described to me. No wait, I remember, I did hear about the whole ordeal. News does trickle down to us here eventually, even to lowly students."

"A pleasure," Betha said stiffly. If he was going to go on at length about 'the whole ordeal' or press her for details about it then she wasn't going to enjoy the afternoon at all.

"She's looking for stories," Michael said.

"And tea," Betha put in. "I'm famished."

"Won't be much in the scholar's mess at this time of day," Julius said.

Betha smiled brightly at them. "Why don't the two of you join me? I can have tea and cake brought up to one of the studies in the guest wing."

Michael and Julius exchanged a glance and Julius shrugged. "I've never been in the guest wing," Michael admitted.

"Then you are both my guests today," Betha said. "I will order tea and you will tell me stories. Fair?"

"More than fair," Julius said.

"We're not interrupting?" Michael said, glancing around at the messy room.

"Interrupt me, please," Julius replied, heading for the door. He yanked it open and then bowed. "After you, Princess."

It turned out that once she got Michael and Julius away from the books and scrolls and scholarly duties, they were both full of entertaining stories, about the historic past and about more recent exploits. More than once during tea Betha found herself genuinely laughing.

"Tell me, what were you doing in that study anyway?" Betha said, pouring herself more tea.

"Oh, I managed to upset a particularly grumpy scholar and got assigned to several hours of copying manuscripts. We make copies when the original is decaying, or when another library somewhere on the island needs one."

"Do you have to copy all the pictures too?"

"Oh, heavens no. Illuminations can be added later, if the recipient of the manuscript wants them. If it's a text with technical drawings, like healing manuals, then someone far more qualified than me would take care of the copying. I have no ability to draw, at all."

"Neither do I," Betha admitted. "Though I haven't been allowed to really try since I was a child."

"Would you want to?" Julius asked.

"No."

"Julius, we should get back," Michael said.

"No one has come looking for us," Julius replied.

"No one would even know where to start looking. I agree this is far more fun than our work, but we do have things to do and I'm sure Princess Betha has other things to do today as well."

"You haven't interrupted my day at all," Betha said. "But I shouldn't be keeping you from your work. I will be returning to the library tomorrow and I would love a little assistance, and to meet more of your friends."

"Then perhaps we will see you tomorrow," Michael said. He stood and tugged Julius to his feet. While Michael bowed, Julius snuck a few extra cookies.

"Until tomorrow, Princess!" Julius said as they went out.

Betha finished her tray, rang for a servant to clear the dishes away, and then headed for her rooms. She had just enough time to write a few letters before dinner.

"And now, if Vonica asks me what I learned today, I'll actually have something to tell her."

28th of Starfall, 24th Year of the 11th Rebirth
Sun Temple Complex, Sun Temple Province

Betha settled into the chair in her room with a warm cup of tea and some warm biscuits and smiled. It had been a wonderful day.

She'd met Michael in the library in the morning. Julius wasn't available, but Michael introduced her to Kenneth, a future banker, and Nathan, a young Metalkin man whose family worked minting coins for the bank. He and Kenneth had become fast friends in the few years they'd spent studying economics together.

The four of them took morning tea in a small, high-walled garden off the library. After a little prompting, they slipped out of 'economics lecture' style and into a more casual, and interesting, story-telling. They filled Betha in on local gossip, told her stories about their families, and even managed to make the economic intrigue of the island interesting.

She'd managed to pick up enough useful, and boring, facts to satisfy Vonica's questioning at lunch.

After lunch, Michael was no where to be found, so Betha slipped into the scholar's wing, heading for the stuffy study where they'd found Julius the day before. He was still there, digging through piles of old manuscripts, when she walked in. He couldn't leave without severe penalty, so she spent the better part of the afternoon perched on the edge of a dusty chair, listening to his stories.

He was far more animated than the others and often waved his arms so wide as he spoke that he sent books tumbling from their piles. He'd blush and scramble to set the books to rights, still talking at a dizzying pace. He frequently jumped subjects as well, his mind following a path Betha sometimes found difficult to follow.

On her way out, she ran into Michael again and the two of them had a quiet dinner together. In softer tones he told her of Caranhall, what it had been like to grow up there. His happy memories made her smile, made her feel the first inkling of excitement about eventually seeing the city for herself.

"You miss it," she said.

He nodded. "It's a warm place, not the temperature, the colours, the people, the smells. I miss my family. I miss my mother's cooking."

"How long until you've completed your studies?"

"Another year or two. But I'll go home for Holy Week."

"That's not too far off now."

"Not close enough."

She'd met with Vonica afterwards and managed to put enough of Michael's stories together into something that sounded like research to put her friend at ease.

"I was worried you'd just sit and daydream," Vonica said. "Or hide somewhere. But it sounds like you're actually learning something."

"I'm trying to," Betha said. "Most of the books are dreadfully boring. Honestly, your scholars don't know how to write about the other provinces. There's no life in those books."

"Didn't we all complain of that as children?"

"You don't complain about it anymore?"

"There are still a lot of boring books out there, and sometimes I'm forced to read them. The rest of the time I read what interests me."

"The Animal People are supposed to interest me, but I've yet to find a book about them that does." She opted not to tell Vonica that she'd stopped looking after that first day.

"Well, keep at it. I'm sure you'll find something. In the meantime, I'm pleased you're finding something useful."

Betha wasn't sure how useful the stories would turn out to be in the long run, or how long she'd be able to keep this up. But it was fun, listening to the young men's excited ramblings all day. *I wonder what tomorrow will bring.*

29th of Starfall, 24th Year of the 11th Rebirth
Sun Temple Complex, Sun Temple Province

Betha had breakfast in her rooms and then went straight to the library. There was no sign of Michael but she found Kenneth at a table, reading a book that had to be three inches thick, and convinced him, quite easily actually, to walk in the garden with her.

Arm in arm they strolled through a garden that was nearly as grand as the one in Dinas Rhosyn. The Sun Temple was one of the wealthier provinces and though they could not tend the gardens themselves, they had an eye for beauty. Golden Hall, though wealthier, was more elitist in its views and had almost no garden to speak of at all.

Betha didn't care much about the garden one way or the other, except that it reminded her of Dinas Rhosyn. Currently she viewed the Evergrowth capital with a mixture of homesickness and distaste. Her twelve years there came in handy today as she was able to name various plants for Kenneth as they walked.

"I've never spent much time out here before," he said. "I'm good with numbers and facts, not so much with painting."

"What does painting have to do with gardens?" Betha said.

"The only people who come out here regularly are the poets, painters, gardeners, and guests. Apparently, gardens are inspiring."

"They never interested me either," Betha said. "Which should have been the first sign that something was wrong. I guess I tried too hard, hid it too well." That was a complete lie, and she knew it. She'd outright refused to go for walks just for her own 'pleasure' and had refused to meet scholars in the garden gazebos. When they lunched there, the young men always rambled on and on about the flowers around them, as if Betha would care.

"It's hard not to be impressed, especially by something you cannot do yourself. Great art impresses me because I have no hope of creating anything like it. Music impresses me because I have no talent to produce it. I look at these plants and I think of the immense care that went into growing them, the patience and the knowledge, and that impresses me."

"Yes, I suppose," Betha said.

"I …" He stopped walking cleared his throat. "I'm impressed by you, Princess Betha."

"Oh?"

"I could not imagine having to leave my home, not once, but twice. Your courage in the face of this life-changing upheaval is inspiring. I'm nearly finished my schooling, you see, and there's a chance I'll be sent to another province for work for a few years, possibly for the rest of my life."

His words warmed her immensely. "I was nervous too, both times," Betha said. "But think of it as a great adventure, one very few people actually get to experience."

"That's a lovely way to look at it. Thank-you."

Betha looped her arm through his and they continued on their way through the garden.

Upon their return to the library they ran into Michael. He seemed more flustered than usual.

"Thank-you for the walk, and the advice," Kenneth said with a bow. He nodded to Michael and disappeared among the shelves.

Betha turned to Michael. "You seem upset. More trouble with the Sun Temple students?"

"No. I had an examination this morning. I had to recite some work for the master scholars."

"How did you do?"

"I knew the material, but I know what they'll say, my presentation was lacking. They intimidate me, and I always feel like they don't want me here, like they're waiting for me to fail."

"It's nearly midday. Why don't we have lunch together and you can tell me all about whatever it was they were testing you on."

"I need to work."

"It is work. We're working on your presentation. And if the Princess of your own province isn't an intimidating enough audience …"

"Okay. Food would be good. I didn't eat this morning, I was too nervous."

She hooked her arm through his and led him towards the palace wing. "I'm more than happy to be of service."

Lunch went long and then when Michael insisted that he had to return to his studies she spent a few hours in the dusty old study with Julius, laughing at his stories and antics. She had dinner with Kenneth and Nathan, instead of with Vonica.

They ate in the guest wing in a small study and filled the space with laughter. Nathan and Kenneth had a friendly rivalry that kept them passing insults back and forth as well as trying to outdo each others' tales.

The sun was setting when the young men decided it was time to return to the scholar's wing. On their way out, Nathan stopped in the doorway.

"I have a little something for you," he said. "A token of friendship and good will." He produced a nugget of raw gold, about the size around of a minted coin but thicker.

"He means, he's trying to secure prosperous political relations between his family and the Animal People Crown," Kenneth quipped from the hallway.

"It's not my fault you didn't think of a gift first," Nathan said. He smiled at Betha. "Don't let his jealously ruin this for you."

"Oh no," Betha said. She took the lumpy bit of metal in her hands. It was cool, having been in a pouch on Nathan's belt through the meal, but it warmed quickly. "Nothing will spoil this gift. I thank you. This was most thoughtful. I will always treasure it."

"You honour me deeply," Nathan said, with a flourished bow.

Kenneth rolled his eyes and grabbed his friend by the back of the robe, hauling him out into the hallway. "Enough already. You look like you're courting. Good-night, Princess, and thank you for dinner."

"Yes, sweet maiden. Our deepest thanks," Nathan said with another bow that nearly got him kicked by his friend.

Betha watched them wander down the hallway, their voices and laughter carrying back to her, making her smile.

The gold made her smile more. She rolled it in her hand, watching the way the light gleamed off the smooth bits, making it look almost liquid. She tucked it in her pocket, summoned the servants to clean the room, and made her way back to her own room. She had to make sure the trinket was secure. And she wanted a bath.

While she was in the tub she heard a knock at her door. The girl who was assisting her went to answer and came back with the message.

"It was Princess Bright-Rose. She was concerned because she hadn't seen you all day. I told her you'd just returned from dinner with some scholars and were in the bath."

"Thank-you. I'll try to visit her tomorrow."

33rd of Starfall, 24th Year of the 11th Rebirth
Sun Temple Complex, Sun Temple Province

"Have you seen Princess Betha?"

Vonica shook her head. "I'm sorry Master High-Oak, she didn't join us for dinner last night or for breakfast this morning. In fact, I haven't seen her since the twenty-eighth or so. Is there a problem?"

"Most Honourable Silver-Cloud is looking for her."

"I'll see what I can do after court. She's probably in the library or her room."

"Of course," her steward said though he didn't sound convinced.

Court was a brief affair. Summer was moving on towards autumn, people were busy in the fields, food was plentiful, and all of the guilds were on their best behaviour because of the ongoing investigation. Afterwards she met briefly with Master Royal-Gold of the Jeweller's Guild to ask some questions about the guild's accountants. He was more than willing to share names with her.

"All right let's find Betha," she said to Avner when her meeting was done.

"I've had someone check her rooms already," Avner said.

"I'll speak with the library scholars. Oh, she may have gone to visit Madam Olga again."

"I've said it before, she shouldn't even be here. She should be sent to live with family or …"

"She has no family, no children of her own and no surviving siblings. She will stay here because she is my family."

"No, she's not. She's a servant who was given the job of tending to your childhood needs."

"She is the only mother any of us ever had. She will stay here until she dies, and I will visit her as often as I like. This conversation is over."

"Yes, Princess. I'll send one of the girls to check Madam Olga's room. Is there anywhere else we should look?"

"She said she wanted to learn about her people. Try the aviary or the stables, try any of the scholars who specialize in the history of the Animal People, oh, and try the chapel in the old wing as well."

"She doesn't strike me as the praying type."

"She's not. But she is the private type."

"I'll send word if I find her."

"As will I." Vonica made her way to the library.

It was nearly midday, but the scholars and students were still hard at work. Most had to be herded to the Scholar's Mess at meal times. If left to their own devices they'd often forget to eat. There was no sign of Betha among the tables and searching among the shelves could take days if she didn't know where to look. Instead she went to the library scholar on duty at the scholars' doors.

"Pardon my intrusion," Vonica said.

"Nonsense, I am here to help," he replied.

"I'm looking for Princess Betha."

"Hmm. I've not seen her, and I've been right here most of the morning. But let me check with a few of my colleagues. She may have come in a different set of doors. Hold on." The wiry gentleman slipped away from his desk.

Vonica didn't mind waiting. The library was still, by far, her favourite place. She loved everything about it, from the worn rugs on the stone floor to the smell of the books, to the whispery sounds of the scholars at work.

The library scholar returned. "I'm sorry Princess, unless she slipped past all of us, she isn't here."

"Considering that I often slipped past all of you, I wouldn't rule that out, but she was looking for specific information, so I doubt she'd come without speaking to someone." She was about to thank the man and leave but a new thought gave her pause. "Have you seen her at all these last few days?"

"I haven't seen her at all. I only knew she was visiting because word travels among the scholars. I know one of my colleagues showed her to the Animal People section a few days ago, though."

"Thank-you. Why don't you point me in that direction and I'll see if she's there?"

She returned to her study, expecting Avner to meet her there soon as he'd likely sent servants off to check the list of suggested places. Sometimes she wondered if he ever lifted a finger himself but then he was a steward and it was his job to organize and delegate. *And he is very involved in the court. He's a very busy man.*

Sure enough, she didn't even have time to ring for a pot of tea before Avner arrived. He entered without knocking and stopped short when he saw her. "No luck then?"

"None I'm afraid," she replied. "You?"

"The same. This isn't so big a place that she could go missing."

"Send word to the kitchens. If Betha rings down for any form of refreshments or a meal they're to send someone to me and let me know where the food is headed. She has to eat sometime, even if she is avoiding me at meals."

"You plan to confront her?"

"Not yet. I want to know what she's up to so that I can plan accordingly."

"Very well. What about your lunch?"

"Something simple. I'll have it here. There's still work to be done before that baby comes."

35th of Starfall, 24th Year of the 11th Rebirth
Sun Temple Complex, Sun Temple Province

It was raining today which put a halt to the little garden soiree Betha had been planning for lunch. *At least for today. It can't rain forever. I'll have it tomorrow.*

Not even the rain could spoil her mood today. She hummed as she combed her hair and pulled on a simple dress then slipped from her room before the servants arrived. It had been a week since she'd last spent any time with Vonica and she didn't feel like answering questions about her activities this last week. She was having far too much fun and didn't want to stop now.

Word must have travelled around her little circle of admirers because Kenneth had a gift for her this morning, a palm-sized painting of a rose that his sister had done. The details were exquisite, even if she found the subject overdone and boring. Still, she thanked him profusely and promised to display it in her room in Caranhall.

If it had ended there, she would have considered it part of their friendly rivalry, and thought nothing else of it, but Michael had a fine pair of leather gloves for her. They were soft and well-fitted with the tiniest stitches Betha had seen. "I can't take these," she said. "They must have cost you a fortune," she'd protested, though a part of her wanted the gloves very badly and that same part was preening at the attention.

"They are a gift, and the cost of a gift is of no importance," he said. "Truly, I want you to have them. I could be here a few years yet, and I don't know if I'll ever have the chance to see you again, after you leave here."

"Then I thank you for these."

She was in the kitchens that afternoon, making arrangements with the cook for her garden party the next day, when a boy came down with a parchment tied in fine ribbon.

"What's this?"

"A letter for you," the boy said.

Curious, Betha untied the ribbon to reveal a short note and several lines of verse.

Dear Betha, the Metalkin are not known for their artistic abilities but your beauty and patience have inspired me. Nathan

The poem that followed was not very good and likely hastily written to compete with the painting Kenneth had given her. Badly written or not, it was the first poem anyone had dedicated to her and she intended to keep it.

When she'd finished with the cook she returned to her room to store the poem with Joseph's letters and the bit of gold. From there she went to the scholar's wing where she had tea with Julius who was still locked in that study transcribing old manuscripts.

She had tea brought in, against the scholars' rules, and when she took her first sip she looked at her cup in surprise. "You can't get this tea outside of Dinas Rhosyn," she said. "The flowers used are grown in a small region of the southeast coastal area. It is very expensive." Her words received no answer. She looked at Julius who was staring at his shoes, his hands behind his back. "Julius?"

"I have a friend in the Healer's Guild. He has family in Dinas Rhosyn. When I mentioned that I'd met you, well, this sort of came up and I got some for you. I thought you might be missing home."

"There is little about Dinas Rhosyn that I miss, but this is one of them," Betha said. "You must come and have some. You'll never taste it again."

He smiled. "You're not angry?"

"I'm honoured by your thoughtfulness."

Michael came in just then. "Ah, here you are. I was hoping to find you."

"Will you join us for tea?"

"No, I can't stay. I just wanted to thank you for the invitation for tomorrow. I will see you then. I have to run. One of the master scholars is searching for me and if I don't make myself known he'll have some punishment for me tomorrow."

"Best hurry then," Betha said.

He nodded and went out again.

"Tomorrow?" Julius said.

"Yes. Lunch tomorrow in the garden. You're invited as well, if you can get away."

"I might be able to join you for a short time. I have a lot to get done here."

"Do you break the rules often?"

He laughed. "There are an awful lot of rules and it's not that I try to break them, I just find interesting things to do and they end up being against the rules."

"Yes, that would be a problem."

"This isn't even so bad a punishment. I find very interesting things in these manuscripts."

"But it's so dusty in here."

"Yes, I sneeze a lot." He shrugged. "A small price to pay."

"Have some tea and tell me some of the interesting things you've found."

3rd of Cloudfall, 24th Year of the 11th Rebirth
Sun Temple Complex, Sun Temple Province

Betha rolled out of bed smiling. The day was full of possibility. *Maybe tea with Michael today?* She hummed a little. None of the men she'd met here interested her at all, some of them weren't even from the Animal People, but she'd found their quick and seemingly limitless devotion to her, whether driven by the chance at being her prince or the allure of accruing political favours, entertaining.

There was a knock so soft Betha thought she had to be hearing someone knocking on the door across the hall. A moment later there was another knock and a timid voice. "Princess, are you awake?"

"Yes, I'm up."

The girl came in and curtsied. "I'm to help you dress. Princess Bright-Rose has requested your presence at breakfast this morning."

"Fine," Betha said. She hadn't seen much of Vonica this last week and a bit, but then she *had* promised to stay out from under foot during her visit.

Once dressed she headed for the door but paused when the girl didn't follow. She looked back. "Is there a problem?"

"I must see to the laundry," she said. "The bedding needs washing."

"I recently had a servant attempt to steal from me …"

The girl curtsied deeply. "I've no interest in losing my position here. Not a slip of paper or scrap of cloth will go missing, my word on it."

Betha nodded and made her way to the private dining room where Vonica and Johann ate their meals.

She found Vonica at the table where a simple breakfast had been laid out, but the Sun Temple princess was the only other person in the room.

"Where is Johann and his brother-in-law? I thought they'd be joining us."

"They left yesterday for the Sun-Song Estate to see Ioanna"

"I thought you would have gone with them."

"My duties keep me here at this time. I will go visit when the baby arrives. Nothing will keep me away from meeting my niece or nephew."

"It must be nice to have a family."

"You won't find yours here."

"I've been meeting with some suitors," Betha said. She'd dished herself some fruit and bread and reached for the honey pot.

"And young men from every other province as well, even though there is no chance any of *them* could be your prince."

So much for being discreet. "I was making political connections on behalf of my province."

"Betha, you have been here thirteen days now. You've barely set foot in the library. You haven't met with anyone who could teach you any of the things you were here to learn. It's time you went home."

"That's easy for you to say! You've never left your home. Twice now I've been uprooted, pulled away from places I've lived for years to be tossed to some other place, some other province. This is more my home than Caranhall."

"It was your home. It hasn't been for twelve years now and it can't be again. You need to complete your journey to Caranhall. You can't hide from this."

"I need to pack."

"It's being done."

Betha felt tears welling up and tried to blink them away. "Can I at least say good-bye to Madam Olga before I leave?"

"Yes, but I will accompany you."

She doesn't trust me. It's not fair. She said I could stay. Betha finished eating in sullen silence. Afterwards she followed Vonica to Madam Olga's room.

"I'll wait here," Vonica said after opening the door.

"You're not coming in?"

"I can, if you like, but I thought you'd like to do this alone."

"I do. Thank-you." She took a deep breath and entered the room.

A thin voice rose up from one of the chairs. "I'm not done with my tea, but you can take the rest."

"It's Betha," she said, still moving across the room.

"Sorry dear, these eyes just don't work right anymore. You're so early."

"I'm leaving today."

"I can hear the uncertainty in your voice."

"I don't want to go to Caranhall." Betha could hear the tremble in her own voice as she tried not to cry.

"Duty is most difficult when it clashes with desire. Betha, you are strong, perhaps the strongest of all the girls. For whatever reason you are needed now in Caranhall."

"I'm so tired of doing what everyone else wants me to do."

"There are no answers for you here. If you want answers, go to Caranhall, and start asking questions. Maybe you'll find what you seek. Maybe you'll find something to point you in the right direction."

"Maybe I'll find nothing but horse dung."

"Betha, you don't believe that."

"No, I guess I don't. I should go before Vonica comes to drag me away." She rose and hugged Madam Olga. "Thank-you."

9th of Cloudfall, 24th Year of the 11th Rebirth
Caranhall, Province of the Animal People

    Princess Betha's first glimpse of Caranhall was through the carriage window as they passed through the outer gate. The wall was made of felled trees, just larger than a double hand-span round, lined tightly against each other. Betha frowned at this. There had been no war on the island for eleven generations and no one really knew how well walls would keep the Dark Spirits out, but this crude wooden wall just reinforced to Betha how backwards this province was.

    Her view was limited by the small windows of the carriage made smaller by curtains she barely parted for fear of everyone she passed staring back at her. She recognized training grounds and a long, low building that was likely the guards' barracks. Everything here felt rustic at best. When they passed by the stables she frowned again.

    Why didn't we stop?

    They continued up the mud track and around the corner where they finally stopped. Only to continue on again after a moment's pause and a deep creaking grumble. They passed through a second gate, this one no hinged log door, but an iron-reinforced wooden portcullis raised by a gear and chain and set into a proper stone wall.

    There was a bump as the wagon moved from mud path to cobble road. The houses they passed were modest if she was being generous and it was obvious to her that this was the common district, and yet, each house had a wide fenced in yard. The crowding of buildings side-by-side that Betha had seen in every other capital city on the island wasn't present here.

They passed through a market district that made her crinkle her nose in disgust at the smell of the animals, then through a line of quaint shops, then guild halls and on to the city manors of the major noble houses, both of the Animal People, and of nobles who ran the various guilds from other provinces.

Somewhere along the way Betha realized that the road they followed meandered left and then right and then back again and was on a gradual but noticeable incline. After the manors there was a stretch of empty road that ended at yet another gate.

This one opened into the courtyard of the castle proper and the carriage soon came to it's final stop in front of a smaller, finely kept stable. Several men and a handful of boys came out of the building and started freeing the horses from their harnesses. The carriage door opened, startling Betha, and a young woman in a simple linen dress stared up at her.

"Welcome Princess. My name is Keren. Ms. Hartley has assigned me to assist you today with anything you require: a bath, meals, unpacking, directions or a guide, anything at all. There are three other girls, plus Ms. Hartley, who will be working directly with you to take care of your personal needs." She held out a hand.

Betha gathered her skirts and allowed Keren to help her down from the carriage. "I'll need to find my rooms, and I'll want a bath and a hot meal and a clean dress. I suppose I'll be meeting with my new stewards this evening."

"Master Wise-Ranger did mention that. The boys will bring your trunks." Keren paused, flagged down one of the passing servants, and said something softly to them. When they'd hurried off she continued, "They're heating water for your bath now. Why don't I take you to your room the long way round for today so you can see some of the castle."

Since the alternative was likely sitting in her new room staring at the walls until her bath was ready Betha nodded. "All right, lead on."

Until now her full attention had been on the girl. As she turned and got her first proper look at the castle her eyes went wide. She'd been imagining a glorified manor house, maybe two-stories in places, if she was being kind, and made mostly of wood with a thatched roof. Even Michael's stories hadn't much changed the mental image she'd built as she'd passed his descriptions off as nostalgic exaggeration. But the Caranhall castle was nearly as grand as the one in Golden Hall and was perched gloriously atop the hill they'd been steadily climbing since entering the city. True it was only two-thirds the size of Golden Hall, but this was not the hovel she'd feared.

She followed Keren to the large double doors and into her new home.

Her room here was similar to the one she'd left behind in Dinas Rhosyn, not as fancy as the rooms in Golden Hall, but bigger and better furnished than the family estates she'd visited around Evergrowth on her tour of the province. There were new-to-her paintings, tapestries, books, and statues around the room, but she wasn't interested in studying them yet. She had the rest of her life to stare at them.

After her bath and dinner Betha followed Keren to a simple study where her new stewards were waiting for her. "Just ring for me when you're finished if you need help back to your room," Keren said before curtsying and heading out.

Betha felt a tightness in her chest as she faced the two men she'd be working with to run a province she knew little to nothing about.

"Master Wise-Ranger, Master Bright-Star," she said, nodding to each of them.

"You've made it safely," Adalard Wise-Ranger said. "You've eaten dinner?"

"Yes, I just finished."

"There is tea here if you would like." He gestured to the table.

"Not right now, thank-you," she said, taking a seat in one of the chairs.

When they were all settled she said, "I don't know where to begin."

"We thought that might be the case," Dritan Bright-Star said. "We've set tomorrow aside as a day of rest so that you can get your bearings. I've also arranged for a historian to come in for a short time each day to help you learn more about the province and the people."

Adalard jumped in. "Several of the guilds have expressed a desire to meet with you, informally, so you can get to know the representatives. We weren't sure if you're prefer a series of small meetings or a large dinner."

"You're asking?" Betha said.

"You know how you want things done," he replied.

"There is the matter of your suitors," Dritan said. "Most Honourable Silver-Cloud recommended letting you set the pace for those meetings. While I agree with him, and with Master Wise-Ranger, that you know how you want things and that you need time to settle, if is my job to assist you in your search for your prince."

"I know. I won't run from it, I just need time to figure things out first."

"We're always available if you have any questions or concerns," Adalard said.

"I'm sure I'll have lots of questions going forward."

"The last pressing matter I have is your correspondence," Adalard said.

"I don't have any letters to send right now."

"If you do, ring for a servant and they'll take it to the hawk master for you. Of course, you are welcome to go yourself once you know your way around. Several of our past princesses have been quite comfortable around the birds. Your official seal is in the desk in your rooms. I was talking about a letter that was left here for you." He produced a folded piece of paper with a simple wax seal.

"Who left me a letter?" she said as she broke the plain wax seal.

"A Master Rose-Gold. He was here on guild business from Golden Hall. He left about the time we expected you to arrive. He returned to Golden Hall."

Betha's breath caught in her chest as her steward's words sunk in.

"He mentioned you two had already met," Dritan said.

"Yes, briefly," Betha murmured. She was staring at the page, taking in the now familiar curve of his writing and the scrawl of his signature, but not really reading the words. She wanted to wait until she was alone for that. She reluctantly folded the paper and laid her hands over it.

"Not bad news I hope," Adalard said.

"I'll read it later," Betha replied. "Why don't you walk me through court and some of the current issues that have arisen? And I'll take that tea now."

The tumble of emotions she'd tucked away through the remainder of her meeting came bubbling to the surface again as soon as she was alone in her room. After dismissing Keren for the evening, Betha settled into a chair near the hearth to read Joseph's letter.

Dear Betha,

I had greatly hoped to cross paths with you in Caranhall before returning to Golden Hall. Sadly, I cannot wait any longer as I must report in person to Princess Jewel-Rose.

I did not find any other information about Academic Diplomats during my travels in the Animal People's province. I hope the information I sent earlier proves helpful.

I will be staying in Golden Hall for a while, partly to meet with Princess Jewel-Rose, and partly to visit my family. My father is not well, and I must help my mother and sisters make arrangements so that they are prepared should the worst happen while I'm in Stones Shore. I am hoping to travel through Caranhall on my way southwest to Stones Shore. It's a little longer to travel west and then south over the river than skirting the northern edge of the mountains where the four provinces meet, but I'm certain I can find an excuse to justify the detour. I would very much like to see you again.

I'm sure things are difficult for you right now. Know that if you need a sympathetic ear that you can always write to me.

Joseph Rose-Gold

She raced through the letter the first time, devouring the words, delighting each time he referred to Mallory by her title rather than her first name, the way he had her.

The second read-through she forced herself to slow down, to make sense of every word. When she'd finished she went to the desk and rooted through the drawers until she found paper, ink, a pen, and the promised Living Rose seal.

Dear Joseph,

I'm sorry that I missed you. I was held up at the Sun Temple for a few days. I should be glad that there is no further news of the Academic Diplomats in the province but it makes me suspicious. Where have they gone? And what are they up to? Are they really gone? Or is someone here hiding them and the harmful results of their actions? I suppose it is up to me now to figure that out.

I thank you for your concern, it means a lot to me, especially in the face of your own personal difficulties. I hope your father's health does not fade too quickly and that you are able to spend some time as a family when all your work for Princess Mallory is complete.

I look forward to your visit, however brief it may be.

Betha

She set the sealed letter aside to send to the hawk master in the morning with whomever brought her breakfast tray and got ready for bed. Before tucking in to her new bed she retrieved Joseph's letter and slipped it under her pillow.

16th of Cloudfall, 24th Year of the 11th Rebirth
Caranhall, Province of the Animal People

It hadn't taken Masters Wise-Ranger and Bright-Star long to make dinner arrangements with the various guild representatives living in Caranhall. It wasn't as fancy a gathering as her wedding would be, but it was nice to put on a prettier than normal dress and entertain a group of wealthy men and their wives.

There were candles in silver holders on the table and silver threads woven into the table cloth. The dining room was a modest size, but the furniture was beautifully crafted. After twelve years in Evergrowth Betha could recognize fine woodworking craftsmanship.

Everyone who came was dressed in fine clothes and the women wore lovely shawls and gemstone pendants. The meal was a summer vegetable soup followed by a mixed salad and a roast goose so tender, Betha had never tasted anything like it. Afterwards they had nut cakes drizzled with honey.

The conversation during the meal was friendly and everyone was happy to share a bit about their guilds and how business was without turning the conversation overly political. That was a feat akin to magic since Betha was hosting guild representatives from all five provinces at one table at the same time and they rarely got along for any great length of time.

"Now what about you, Betha?" one of the ladies asked. "What do you think of Caranhall so far?"

"It's not what I expected," Betha answered truthfully. "So far my stewards have been very helpful and I'm glad it's summer so there's not as many petitions to hear."

"What were you expecting?" asked the representative from the Equine Guild.

Betha's cheeks flushed pink. "Honestly, our schooling was very in depth when it came to our own people but lacking when it came to the other provinces. We only learned what we needed to deal with the political situations we encountered. So, I really didn't know what to expect. My only experience with the Ani… the Carainhithe has been guild representatives, people who worked at the castle in Dinas Rhosyn, and Princess Taeya."

"And Princess Taeya was not even Carainhithe," he said.

"No, but she was raised to be. Just as I was raised to be Evergrowth."

The Silver-Guild representative smiled sweetly at her over a glass of wine. "I suppose it's a good thing the two provinces have so much in common. It shouldn't be too big of an adjustment."

And just like that the friendly atmosphere in the room shattered.

"There are very few similarities between the Evergrowth and the Animal People," the head of the Weavers' Guild said. Her face was very red, and her husband was nodding emphatically beside her.

"And the similarities are all positives," agreed the resident historian. "As a scholar I would know. Strong work ethic, a love of the outdoors and open spaces, a deep sense of empathy and a strong nurturing instinct."

"Right," said the Gold Guild representative. "Like he said, they're all farmers and cooks, spending their days out in the dirt."

"We're generally cleaner than the iron workers," said the palace healer. "In fact, most farmers and even stable hands are."

"Iron is cleaner than horse dung," said the Iron Guild representative.

"But stable lads don't come home covered in dung," the Equine Guild representative shot back.

"Everyone needs to stop talking now," Betha said, standing. Silence descended quickly. "The one thing every princess from The Pact on through all the rebirths, regardless of their provincial heritage, has drilled into their heads from a young age is 'strength through unity and balance'. This," she waved her hand, "Is not unity. This does not promote balance."

"Having people sticking their noses in only the Metalkin Guild affairs is not balance," the Gold Guild representative said.

"Neither is the way the Metalkin guilds have been mistreating everyone else," the Stone Miners' Guild representative replied.

"That was one man at one mine," the Iron Guild representative said. "You can't blame us all for his mistakes."

"It goes deeper than that," protested the resident historian. "And much further back, to."

Before they could get too far out of hand again Betha rapped her knuckles on the table and said, "Enough. I see now that calling you together was futile. The guilds have clearly forgotten how to work together. We are dependent on each other. We all know this. This petty behaviour is not becoming of men and women of your political and official standing." She paused and let her gaze find each and every face around the table before continuing. "It is clear to me that this province has a long way to go before it returns to a place of prosperity and peace, and I don't think my finding a prince will be an instant fix."

"Speaking of your prince," the Equine Guild representative said, "When do you plan to start meeting with suitors? You've already been here a week."

"And I've spent that week in court and in meetings, as well as educating myself and meeting with many officials, including all of you. We are currently considering the best way to hold these meetings. My stewards will inform the necessary people when we are ready to begin."

The conversation thankfully returned to friendly, if tense, conversation and everyone tiptoed around subjects that would spark disagreements. Eventually the guests excused themselves and left for home in pairs and small groups until Betha was alone again.

She poured herself another glass of wine and sighed. Around her servants were already clearing plates from the table. It wasn't long before her stewards came in and pulled up chairs on either side of their princess.

"How was dinner?" Adalard asked.

"The provinces don't actually get along with each other, do they?"

Adalard and Dritan exchanged a look and Dritan said, "It depends on who you speak with. You and your fellow princesses get along just fine. Most commoners get along with their neighbours, sheep farmers with wheat farmers, iron workers with stone miners, artisans of wood and stone and cloth. It's only when you get to the higher ranks of the guilds, and the twice-named families, that you find the sort of better-than-thou attitude I'm sure you encountered at dinner tonight."

Betha looked down at her lap and fussed with her dress. *I'm just as guilty. I even looked down on the people I thought I belonged to while I thought I belonged among them. Strength through unity and balance. I say the words, but have I ever really supported them before?*

"But with things sorted out now with you and Taeya, everything will improve for everyone," Dritan said.

"And when the corruption investigations end and the guilds and bank are cleaned up tensions will ease, and we can begin repairing relationships between the provinces and the guilds."

She shook her head. "I think you're far too optimistic, Master Bright-Star. I don't think the twice-named families will be so easily swayed into being bosom companions with people they've bickered with for so long."

"I'm sure with you and the other princesses setting an example …" Dritan started.

"No, she's right. This goes deeper than the current political turmoil and will take longer to heal."

"It's getting late," Betha said, setting her empty wine glass on the table. She didn't want to sit and listen while even her stewards bickered. "And I'll be busy again tomorrow. I should turn in now." She pushed away from the table.

"Of course," Adalard said. "And Betha?"

She stopped and looked at him.

"You're doing a good job so far."

"Thank-you." Betha returned to her room, her face carefully neutral. She felt restricted, restrained, forced to be on her best behaviour and make a good impression while fighting the urge to rail against everyone around her, to force everyone and everything around her to fit the way she wanted things to be. Only she wasn't entirely sure how she wanted things to be.

**28th of Cloudfall, 24th Year of the 11th Rebirth
Caranhall, Province of the Animal People**

Betha mentally reviewed her schedule for the day as she dressed and had breakfast. She had court this morning, and then a session with her tutor. After the midday meal she was meeting with her stewards to plan for suitors. The rest of the day was hers for exploring, reading, or relaxing.

She was still relying heavily on Adalard during court but more and more she was voicing her opinions on matters and while he sometimes advised for or against a specific course of action so far, she hadn't faced the disapproving scowls Master Avner High-Oak was famous for, nor did he criticize her for not delivering all of her pronouncements with a smile. *It seems Dritan was not the only one willing to work with me in spite of my temperament. Either that or he's biting his tongue raw to stop the reprimands.*

After court she was whisked off to the cozy little study for a history lesson. She'd hated her classes as a child and so far, these were just as boring. Names, dates, rituals, traditions. *Why is it that nothing exciting ever happens in a history lesson? I wonder what they will tell future princesses about us?*

"Princess Living Rose, are you listening?"

"Of course," Betha lied. "Continue."

"This book contains the last written record of our historic language, along with meanings and pronunciations." He handed her a small volume; not much bigger than the journals she often saw the scholars toting around.

"And you're entrusting it to me?" she squeaked.

"It's not the only copy of this title, Princess."

"Oh, that's good." She accepted the book. "I will read from it every day."

"I hope so. Much of our individual culture was lost, or changed, when we accepted Airon as the chief spirit guide. Most historians agree that it was the best choice and given the stories that are told about the prophet, Abner, the miracles were quite convincing."

"Did this happen with the other provinces too? This cultural shift?"

"I believe it did, but at a much earlier time. It's strange, given the geography of the island, that the Stone Clan didn't retain their culture the longest, being farthest from the Metalkin and isolated by the mountains, but they always had the closest trade relationship with the Metalkin."

"So, why did we hold on to ours then?"

"Perhaps because we were a bit wilder, like the animals of the forest, uninterested in what the others were doing. By the time Prophet Abner began spreading his message our culture was already starting to blend and change as we traded more. It started with the upper classes as they sought to imitate the wealthy traders, make themselves more appealing I suppose."

"Taeya told me the sun priests erased most of this."

"They did. They rewrote the holy books and the prayers and the rituals, said it was because they needed to add Airon to everything, but when it came back to us, it was in the common tongue and our language faded from use."

Betha took the book back to her room before the midday meal. She could hear Taeya's voice, remember her words so clearly. *"It's a private, sacred thing, but you are their princess now. You need to know."*

When the book was carefully stowed she made her way to a small dining room where she could eat when she didn't have company and didn't want to dine in her rooms. Some days her stewards joined her and she assumed this would be where she entertained suitors, when the time came, but today she ate alone.

Beside her plate there was a scroll with the familiar Jewel Rose seal. Betha served herself and then opened the letter.

Dear Betha,

My investigator, Master Rose-Gold, has brought it to my attention that not only are there some suspicious dealings within the Metalkin guilds in your province (Taeya said there was a special word for it but I can barely remember how to say it and have no idea how to write it) but he also discovered evidence that the Academic Diplomats were asking questions.

This concerns me greatly. My Metalkin steward is useless. He refuses to let me do anything or talk to anyone, says it's not a problem, that I'm blowing things out of proportion because I don't understand. But he won't explain anything to me! How am I supposed to learn anything?

My Sun Temple steward is a kind man and patient. He has taken much time to teach me some of your history and traditions. Without him I'd be completely lost. Unfortunately, he holds little political sway either in court or in the province and cannot help me much.

My concerns, before I get too side-tracked. I cannot figure out who these people are, why they are visiting the other provinces, or what they are doing with the information (and supplies) they are acquiring. No one will talk about them. I fear they have ties within the wealthiest Metalkin families. I fear my steward is too afraid to anger them to stand up to them, even if it means leading me towards ruin.

My investigator has been helpful, I believe you met him once. There again, though, there are short-comings. I hired him to investigate the guilds, as an accountant basically, to look over the books for anything suspicious. He's loyal to the throne and not to the twice-named families that hold the highest influence in this province, which I'm learning is a rare thing in this province. But these cultural scholars or whatever they are calling themselves are operating outside the guilds and the guilds are denying all knowledge which makes it difficult for him to learn anything either.

I wish I knew what to do. I feel so helpless. I feel like all the answers are here, I just don't know how to bring them to light. I wish I had some help, someone who understood how your politics worked, how to talk to these people so they'd offer up some answers. But I'm an outsider to them and they refuse to trust me.

I'm sorry, I only meant to update you and here I am rambling on about all my problems. I know you're very busy, and probably feeling as lost as I am right now, learning a new culture and all.

If you learn anything about these cultural scholars and what they were doing in your province, please send word. Any information I can get my hands on will be helpful.

My thanks, and best of luck,
Mallory Brock Jewel-Rose

Betha mulled the letter over while she ate. There was no explicit request for assistance from Betha in the letter, aside from a request for information about a problem they were both attempting to address. At the same time it felt like Mallory was reaching out to her, not just as a fellow ruler, but as a friend and confidant. There was much in the letter that suggested Mallory was struggling, that she needed someone with more knowledge and experience to help her, someone who wasn't afraid of the twice-named families, or worse, in their debt in some way.

Well, I certainly angered enough nobles back in Evergrowth. I don't see why I can't do the same in Metalkin. And since I don't really want to be here, this is a lovely excuse to leave for a while.

Her stewards were waiting for her in the study when she marched in, her shoulders back, chin raised, the picture of confidence and leadership. The men stood as she came in.

"Ah, good," Master Bright-Star said. "We can begin. I've brought the lists of twice-named suitors and …"

"It will have to wait," Betha said.

"Wait?" Dritan Bright-Star stammered. "Wait for what?"

"Until I return?"

"Return? Return from where? You've only just arrived."

"I've been here three weeks now. I know it's not much, really, and I am sorry. But this is a trying time politically and I am needed in Golden Hall."

"What happened?"

"Something has come up in the investigation of the Academic Diplomats." She produced Taeya's list of names and information. "I need you to look into the following people, their families, and their guild connections, and send everything you gather to me in Golden Hall. I will be leaving in the morning, before breakfast."

Dritan was spluttering but at least he hadn't raised his voice yet. "You can't. The suitors. Your duties. We need you here."

Adalard finally spoke up. "Betha, until now I have tried to be patient and understanding. Master Bright-Star told you when we were at Dinas Rhosyn that he was not afraid of butting heads with you, and neither am I. Right now, you need to do a very good job of convincing me why this is necessary, why it cannot wait, or why you cannot send someone in your stead, because if I am not suitably convinced, I will stand against you on this."

Betha appreciated his honesty at least, but she fully understood that 'because I said so' was likely to get her locked up in her room for several days and that they'd contact Mallory to get any answers she was not willing to give them. *And since Mallory doesn't actually know I'm coming, that would be disastrous.*

"Shall we sit?" Betha said, giving herself a moment to think.

They settled around the table and Betha set her papers down.

She started by handing Adalard Taeya's list. Taeya hadn't recognized all the names from Joseph's list so Betha had added those to the bottom herself. "These are the people Master Rose-Gold implicated, or suspected, as being involved with the Academic Diplomats. Princess Taeya was kind enough to review the list and make any notes she thought would be helpful. I need to know how deep their ties to the Metalkin run."

"Seems like an important job," Adalard said. "One best tackled by the Princess of the Carainhithe. I'm assuming there is an even more important job awaiting you in Golden Hall?"

"Yes. The missing foals," Betha said. "At least one foal that we know of was purchased by the Metalkin and transported away from the Evergrowth province."

"Mallory has information about the missing animals?"

Betha went on, choosing not to answer over lying outright. "Then there is the matter as to why they were studying horses and fish in the Evergrowth province and then came here to visit a slate mine, among other things. They claim they want to know about horses or mining, but they aren't going to the source of the knowledge. Why? Mallory has a few ideas but it would be more effective if I were to speak to the Carainhithe guild representatives in Golden Hall myself. It appears Mallory's late arrival has made it difficult for her to build trust and rapport."

"How long would you be gone?"

"I'm not entirely sure, but not long."

"Define, 'not long'."

"What do you consider too long?" Betha countered. She didn't want to trap herself into a trip that was shorter than she might otherwise get away with.

"Besides the obvious answer of 'a year'?" Adalard said. "If you're not back in Caranhall by the end of the month, I'd send someone looking for you."

"Then I will limit my stay to the end of Cloudfall," Betha said. "In the mean time you can make arrangements for a dinner party with dancing, but nothing as big as a royal ball. Invite the twice-named suitors and some of their sisters or cousins so everyone has someone to socialize with. When I return I we will set the date."

"You're giving us permission to do everything except set the date?" Dritan said.

"Yes. Guest list, menu, music, program, have the girls pick out a dress, all of it."

Dritan nodded. "Very well. At least that will keep the noble families satisfied while you are running this errand."

"Then I will leave you so I can pack. I also need to send a Sun Hawk to Golden Hall to inform Mallory that I'm on my way. See to it that a carriage and escort are ready at full light. I don't want to be kept waiting." She breezed out without waiting for a reply.

Dritan & Adalard watched her leave and then looked at each other. "We're really letting her do this?"

Adalard shrugged. "You saw what happened in Evergrowth. Avner fought against her so often that she was prepared for every interaction to be a fight. I thought that if I only fought her when she was actually leading us astray or endangering someone maybe she'd be more willing to listen."

"You won't change her direct nature."

"Firm and direct are both traits of our people."

"Not like her."

Adalard shrugged again. "She's going. You work on the dance, I'll work on this list of names. If we need her back we send a Sun Hawk and tell her to come back. Maybe she and Mallory will be able to solve this together. We keep the girls so far apart. Maybe as a pair they'll succeed."

"I hope you're right. Because we're taking a big risk letting her run about like this."

Betha hurried straight to the hawk master. "I need to send a Sun Hawk to Golden Hall," she said.

"Of course, Princess. You have a letter?"

"Not yet. Do you have paper?"

"Of course. The desk is there, help yourself. I'll go fetch the bird." He went through a door at the back of the office. While the door was open Betha could hear the hawks calling to each other. He came back with a beautiful golden bird. It was smaller than she expected. "The letter?"

"Ah, yes." Betha quickly signed her name to the bottom and handed it to the hawk master.

"Do you want to see her fly?" he asked.

Betha nodded and followed him out onto the balcony. He stroked the bird's chest and then tied the letter to her ankle.

"Keep close watch on her," he said. "They're the quickest animals on the island. And one of the cleverest." He leaned in closer to the bird. "Golden Hall," he said. The bird screeched in reply.

He held up the hand that was holding the bird and she stretched, flapping her wings and straining a little against his hold. With an upward bump he released her.

Betha expected her to take off due east but she did two lazy circles around the balcony.

"She's showing off," he explained.

She shrieked again, set her nose to the east, and shot forward with two powerful thrusts of her wings.

"Beautiful," Betha said. "The way the sun almost glints off their wings."

"Yes, the shine of the feathers is quite stunning. The other hawks are darker and a little larger, but beautiful in their own way. I could give you a tour if you'd like."

"Perhaps another time," Betha said. One bird in flight was beautiful, a whole flock in cages was messy and noisy. "I have to pack. Thank-you though."

She managed to keep her pace even and her face neutral until she reached her rooms. She glanced over her shoulder to make sure the hallway was empty before shutting the door. She took a deep breath and then let out a joyous whoop. She spun around, arms wide, laughing.

With a deep and contented sigh, she dropped, dizzy and delighted, into the nearest chair. "Freedom."

32nd of Cloudfall, 24th Year of the 11th Rebirth
Golden Hall, Metalkin Province

Betha stepped out of the carriage and looked up at the castle of Golden Hall with a contented smile. *It's good to be back.* Her last visit here had been short, only three and a half days, but she'd fallen in love with every part of it.

"Princess Betha, what are you doing here?"

Almost every part. She turned and shot Kaelen, Prince of the Metalkin, a frosty stare. "Kaelen. So … *nice* to see you again. Where is Mallory?"

"She was caught up in a meeting and told me to come down to meet a guest. She didn't mention it was you." From his voice he was as excited to see her as she was to see him, which was not at all.

"Well, I will wait for her. I'm eager to see her. If you'll excuse me, I need to oversee the unpacking of the carriage and getting my escort settled."

"You're doing servant's work?"

"No, I'm doing your work since I know you won't be bothered to do it."

"And what do you mean by that?"

"I can't expect you to show the proper courtesies, now can I? So, I'll see to it myself. Excuse me." She turned her back on him, something she knew he hated, and walked away.

Servants had finally started to come out, likely alerted by the stable boys, and they approached the carriage with caution.

"There are trunks that need unloading," Betha called. "Princess Jewel-Rose should have a room prepared for me, they can be placed there. Have someone run a bath, a hot bath, we travelled fast, and I need to get the dust off of me. Have someone else show my escort where they will be bunking while we're here."

The stable master made his way over and bowed deeply before Betha, taking off his cap to reveal a bald spot framed by wispy, greying hair. "Princess Living Rose, it is an honour to meet you. The stables here are not as impressive as the ones in Caranhall of course, but I'd be honoured to show you …"

She stopped him with a hand. "If you were hired on as a royal stable master then I know you are the best of the best and that our animals will receive the same care and attention that they would back home. I have explicit trust in your abilities. For now, I am going inside to wash up."

"Of course, of course," the man said much more quietly. "It just that I was hoping to speak with you about another matter." He was twisting his cap in his hands and glancing past her with wide, worried eyes.

Betha peered over her shoulder and saw Kaelen was still hovering on the edge of the courtyard, a deep scowl on his face.

"All right," Betha said. "A quick tour."

"Thank-you, Princess. It is a great honour." He bowed again and put his cap back on.

She followed him into the stable, a long, dimly lit building that smelled of horses and hay. Betha crinkled her nose. "What's your name, stable master?"

"Jeremy White-Hart, Princess. I've been stable master here some twenty years. And before you ask, this isn't about suitors. I'm too old and my only boy is too young."

"I assumed, based on your behaviour, that this is about Kaelen or the Metalkin more generally."

He nodded. "I … you have to forgive me. My family and I are well cared for here, we want for nothing, but we aren't paid much. I always thought it a fair trade off, not having to buy clothes or food, what did we need so much money for? But now we don't have enough to move away from here, or to survive on if I can't find another position."

"Why would you need to leave?"

"That's the thing, he threatened me. He said if I ever told anyone else what I saw that I'd be out of a job. So, I didn't tell. I should have written you, should have trusted the hawk master to understand, but I had to think of my family."

"What did you see?"

"Some foals came through here. Prince Kaelen had me check them over before moving them north. They were skinnier than I like to see and a little wild-eyed, but otherwise healthy enough. I don't know where they are now. I didn't really think anything of it until word reached me of what happened in Evergrowth. Looking back, I never saw any of the Carainhithe in the group that was transporting them."

"Thank-you. That helps more than you know. Continue to do what you need to do to protect your family, but if things get too difficult here, write my stewards immediately and they will help you."

"Thank-you Princess, that is most generous."

When she stepped outside again she saw Kaelen and Mallory on the far side of the courtyard engaged in a heated discussion that ended with Kaelen storming off. Betha saw Mallory take a deep breath.

"Everything all right?"

Mallory turned, a too-bright smile on her face. "Sure! Everything's fine. Let's get you settled in." She turned, and the two women fell in step beside each other. "I received your letter and burned it as you instructed." She lowered her voice. "I really didn't intend for you to drop everything and ride down here."

"Your letter sounded desperate."

"Things have not been going well here, I'll be honest about that. But how will they view me if I go running for help at every turn?"

"I'm your friend and ally. And this is a common problem we share. And I already know the foals we are looking for passed through Golden Hall."

"What? When? How did you learn that?"

Betha glanced around. "Maybe that's a story for another time. Once I'm settled we can plan a course of action."

"Oh, by the way, this arrived for you a few hours ago. Apparently, it arrived in Caranhall a few hours after you left there." She produced a letter and handed it to Betha. "I'll go see about dinner, a private affair for just the two of us."

"Thank-you." Betha took the paper and let a servant usher her into the guest room where a warm bath awaited her.

Betha,

It seems I'll be in Golden Hall longer than planned. My father's health is fading fast and he likely won't see year's end. My mother and sisters are greatly upset and I feel my place is with them during this time. Luckily Princess Jewel-Rose agrees.

I hope to see you before month end,
Joseph

Betha made her way down to the dining hall. She'd had enough time to bathe, change, and write quick notes to Talia and Joseph, letting them know she'd arrived in Golden Hall. Now, she was only paying enough attention to the hallway in front of her that she didn't walk into anyone or anything, her mind eagerly imagining the replies she'd receive, and what invitations they might contain. As it was, she didn't notice Prince Kaelen leaning against the wall outside the dining room until he stepped forward, directly into her path.

"Princess Betha, my apologies for my less than gracious behaviour earlier. Your appearance caught me unaware."

Betha scowled. "You can drop the act, Kaelen. What do you want?"

"It's a question of what you want, Betha. Why are you really here? What are you after?"

"Answers," Betha said. "And to help Mallory in any way I can. Is that going to be a problem?"

"Oh, no, no problem," Kaelen said. "I just thought that perhaps you were here to expand your collection."

"My collection?" Her heart was starting to pound a little too loudly, she could feel it all down her arms and in her throat, the force of her pulse in her veins.

He was smiling in an overly charming way but there was a hint of something darker in his eyes, something dangerous and seductive. "Yes. I heard that you have exquisite taste. I was looking forward to accommodating that with some tours of the markets and such. But of course, if you're here merely for the sake of duty, you'll have little time for such frivolous things." He bowed. "I will leave you ladies to your dinner, you have much to catch up on, I'm sure, but perhaps I will see you later."

"I'm sure our paths will cross," Betha said, putting more confidence in her voice than she felt. She was relieved that her full skirts hid the slight tremor in her knees. Aside from Taeya and a few servants she hadn't thought anyone knew about her jewelry collection, and she didn't like the idea of this man knowing something so personal about her.

He walked past her, his stride calm and confident, purposeful but not rushed. The heels of his boots clicked on the stone floor, eventually fading away. Betha took a few deep breaths to calm herself and then walked the final dozen steps to the dining room.

Mallory was waiting inside, her eyes on a scroll, one of half a dozen on the table before her, but she looked up when Betha came in. "Do you feel better now?"

"Yes, much better, thank-you," Betha said with a forced smile.

"Oh dear, I know that look. What happened?"

"I passed your lovely husband just now. He has a way of disrupting my good mood without trying." Betha caught herself and went on, "I'm sorry. He is your prince, after all. I should be more respectful."

"No, it's all right. I …" She shook her head. "Later. I'll ring for dinner and we'll catch up. I didn't have much time to speak with you in Dinas Rhosyn."

"Your pronunciation is getting better," Betha said.

"I'm lucky you speak a language I understand, for the most part," Mallory said. She finished gathering her papers and moved them to a desk against the wall. "The paperwork never ends, does it?"

"Never. And if it's not paperwork, it's some ritual or ceremony."

"You know, I don't mind those. They sort of remind me of home. I mean, this is home now, but my home before, where I grew up."

All of Betha's cares disappeared beneath the intense, burning curiosity and she leaned forwards. "Tell me about growing up in the outside world."

"Oh," Mallory said, laughing uncomfortably. "I wouldn't know where to start."

"Anywhere," Betha said breathlessly.

"Then I'll start with dinner." Mallory rang for the servants and waited for them to finish setting the table with dishes and food, thanking each of them as they passed her. "The food where I grew up was similar to here. I grew up in an embassy in India and in India they don't eat cows. You don't have cows here, just goats and pigs and sheep and that's what we ate there too."

"At least some things were familiar."

Mallory nodded. "But I miss the seasonings, the curries and spices. If you went outside, you knew when you were passing a kitchen because of the smells wafting out of the windows. There's nothing else like it, nothing to really compare it to. The food here is plain, almost bland, in comparison. And you don't have coffee. Gods, I miss coffee."

"What is coffee?"

"It's like tea, but instead of being made with dried herbs and leaves and fruit it's made by passing hot water through ground coffee beans. But coffee beans come from far away. You can't grow them here, not in this climate. It was stronger than tea, a little bitter if you got a dark roast, but you add milk and sugar and it's hot and strong and full of caffeine."

"Caffeine?"

"The thing in coffee that wakes you up." Mallory sighed. "I wish I'd had more warning before coming here. I'd have spent my life savings on coffee to bring with me."

"What's an embassy?"

Mallory paused, mulling over the best way to explain. "In a way it's similar to your guild halls, but it's for politics, not a trade or profession. When two countries are allies, they often have politicians, diplomats, living in each others' countries. The place they live and work from is called an embassy, it's like a piece of the United Kingdom in India, or a piece of India in the United Kingdom. If you're visiting a country and run into trouble you go to your country's embassy, or the embassy of the nearest ally."

"So, you don't have guilds?"

"We did. In some places I guess we still do. We have other professional organizations, especially for doctors." At Betha's puzzled look she added, "They're healers." Betha nodded and Mallory continued. "The universities, where our scholars study, have organizations for different professions, like engineers or architects. And we have commercial organizations for farmers. Oh, and we have unions, they replaced the guilds, I guess. They protect workers' rights, making sure the people get paid fairly and have days off with their families and such so the businesses they work for don't abuse them."

"What was the biggest change for you?"

"The culture, I guess. Learning a new religion, with magic and monsters, learning about your guilds and your politics and your history. We aren't assigned a profession based on where we were born. I mean, kids who grow up on farms tend to be farmers, but I wasn't going to be a diplomat like my father. I was studying to be a veterinarian."

"I don't know that word."

"An animal healer."

"Oh."

"The clothes and books and the rest? It's strange, sure, but really, it's just like stepping back in time. I miss my underwear, and my jeans, and my coffee, but I studied civilizations like yours in my history text books."

"You learn about us?"

"Not you. I never knew a place like this existed. People like you, people who lived like this," she gestured to the room around her. "With castles and servants and no electricity or cars."

"Every time you answer a question, I end up with a dozen more questions," Betha said, laughing. "Electricity, cars, I've never heard of these things before. But I want to know. I want to know what I was taken away from. I'll never know my real mother and father, I'll never hear their names or see their home, or know what they did for a living. I ... do you think they wonder what happened to me?"

"Yes. Just like I'm sure my parents are frantically looking for me. I wish I could have left a letter, something about 'travelling the world, exploring, don't worry, be back eventually'. At least then they wouldn't worry right away."

"But you'd never come back."

"I know. They'd worry eventually. When they took you, what did they do? Just kidnap you? Did they fake your deaths?"

"I honestly have no idea. No one talks about it. It's a huge mystery that only the priests know anything about."

"I thought there were a lot of secrets here in Golden Hall, but I think the whole island has too many secrets."

"I think you're right," Betha said, nodding. She tried to put her parents out of her mind again and focus on the here and now instead. "Secrets like what the Academic Diplomats are doing, and where they come from. Who is funding them? What do they want?"

"And why won't anyone here talk to me about them?"

Betha nodded. "Where did the foals end up? What do they want with them? Why go to Evergrowth to learn about horses and fish, then go to the Animal Province to learn about slate quarries?"

"And the gems that the black smith at the Sun Song estate saw. Why were the Metalkin transporting gems that the Stone Clan knew nothing about? Where did they get them? Where were they sending them?"

"Where did they get them is a good question since it came to light in Vonica's investigation that the Gem Stone Guild is concerned about a shortage in gems."

"Well, precious stones are a finite resource. There's only so many to be found. On an island this size, it's only a matter of time before they run out. But that's part of what makes them valuable. If they were easy to find, or if there were more gems than people, they wouldn't be as valuable."

"I think the Gem Stone Guild is aware of that. They're probably mourning the decline as a natural thing. But if it is a natural thing, the question remains – where did those gems come from? And was the fire at the forge a result of him seeing something he shouldn't have seen?"

"A deliberate fire? Who would do that?"

"Who wants to keep the transport of gems a secret?"

"You remember you said that my answers left you with more questions?"

"Yes."

"Well, your questions are leaving me with more questions."

Betha couldn't help but laugh and Mallory was soon chuckling along with her.

"I'm glad you're here," Mallory said. "I've been feeling overwhelmed by everything. I thought I was coping, thought I was adjusting, and then Rheeya's letter arrived about the mine and the Iron Guild and since then everything's just snowballed into a giant mess."

"We haven't had snow since your arrival."

Mallory smiled. "It's a saying, it means that the problem keeps getting bigger, like when you roll a ball of snow along the ground and it picks up more snow."

"Oh. I like it. The saying, not the growing problems."

"At least we have a list of questions," Mallory said. "We know what we need to find out. The next step is figuring out who to ask."

"That's a difficult one," Betha said. "Because the people who have the answers might not be willing to share with us."

"Oh, you can count on that. That's what makes it secret."

"We're going to be busy," Betha said.

"How long are you here for?"

"My stewards would like me home in a week, maybe two, but if we find something useful, I'm sure I can stay here as long as you need me."

"I don't want to cause problems for you or your people either."

"You won't," Betha assured her. *I might, but you won't.* "What were you and Kaelen discussing in the courtyard earlier?"

"Oh, he doesn't like it when I make 'big decisions' without consulting with him. I'm not sure how having you visit for a week or two is a 'big decision'."

"Mallory, do you …"

A knock at the door silenced her. The door opened before Mallory could issue an invitation and Master Black-Kettle, her political steward, came in. "Excuse me, Princesses, I know you asked not to be disturbed. A hawk arrived, the message was marked urgent."

"That's all right. Things come up," Mallory said, holding out her hand.

"Actually, it's for Princess Betha."

"Oh," Betha said. "Thank-you." She took the scroll.

Master Black-Kettle bowed and left again.

Both girls stared at the scroll. "Who sent you an urgent scroll?" Mallory wondered allowed. "And how did they know you were here? You only just arrived."

"It's from Taeya, judging by the seal, and it likely arrived in Caranhall after my departure." Actually, the seal was so familiar it made her chest ache. Until the middle of Starfall that had been her seal.

"Open it. I won't think you rude. My father often had important documents at the table with him. My mother hated it."

"But not you?"

"I resented being ignored as a girl but now that I'm ruling a whole province? I'm realizing it's necessary."

"Then let's see what Taeya thinks is so urgent." She unrolled the scroll, glanced over the content to ensure there was nothing private or embarrassing therein, and began reading aloud:

Dear Betha,

I hope this letter finds you well and I hope you are finding life in Caranhall easier than your years in Dinas Rhosyn. I wish this letter could be all cheer and good news but I'm afraid it is a dire emergency that moves me to write.

It started a week or two after you left, and I honestly dismissed the first report as tragic but nothing suspicious. By the third report I knew this was not natural and when I put the pieces together, the conclusion I reached scared me.

We've had a terrible sickness spread through several herds. As I said, at first I didn't think much of it. I provided what aid I could to help bring the situation under control. We no longer believe this was a natural illness. For one thing, I've been assured that the living conditions of the affected herds were as close to ideal as possible. For another, the illness did not spread from herd to herd in a predictable pattern, cropping up seemingly at random. It took me longer than it should have to realize that the farms affected were owned by or tithe to families that testified or provided evidence against the Academic Diplomats. We now believe someone deliberately poisoned.

I don't know what those men were really doing here, or what happened to those foals, but we were never meant to find out. It appears they do not like the fact that we know even as little as we do. Please, be cautious as you continue your investigation and prepare for some form of retaliation as you search for answers. I think we are dangerously close to something, if only we had that one key piece that would make everything else make sense. It's frustrating, not being able to figure out their motives.

I wish I could end this letter with some good news to balance out the bad. I suppose the best news I can offer is that this is the only bad news to come our way since you left.

Please send my warmest regards to Masters Wise-Ranger & Bright-Star.

Taeya Living-Rose

"I suppose it's a good thing I decided to come here," Betha said. "The problem is far more serious than we thought." She looked up to see Mallory sitting tight lipped and still. "Mallory?"

Mallory gave her head a sharp shake. There was something bright and dangerous in her eyes. "How is this even possible?" she said, her voice remarkably calm. And then she exploded upwards, out of her seat. She slammed her hand down on the table, catching the edge of her plate and sending her dinner tumbling. "How is this even possible?!" It came out a roar. She sucked in a great heaving breath and continued to yell. "Who are these people? Who is hiding them? I'm going to find them and I'm going to hang every last one of them. The animals? What sort of heartless, spineless, cruel, cowardly monsters am I governing? *These* are *my* people? No, oh no, this is not going to fly here. This ends here and now." She wound down, breathing hard.

Betha sat pressed back in her chair, her hands meek on her lap and her eyes too wide. The woman who stood before her was like nothing Betha had ever seen before and she could imagine that this was what the first princesses of the pact looked like standing up to their fathers in the Great Temple of Airon, their eyes full of defiance and fury.

A moment of silence passed and then Mallory cleared her throat and sat down. "I'm sorry."

"Why?" Betha said. She picked up her fork and resumed eating as if nothing had happened. "You should ring for someone to clean that up." She pointed her fork at the mess on Mallory's side of the table.

Mallory blushed. "It's fine." She quickly swept everything back onto the plate with her fork. She closed her eyes and took a deep breath, holding it until she felt calmer, steadier. When she opened her eyes again she leveled her stare at Betha. "What are we going to do?"

"This evening? We are going to sit somewhere comfortable and talk. You can tell me everything you've been feeling and dealing with and we will outline everything we know and everything we think we know. Maybe we'll see something we've missed. At the very least we'll be able to start tomorrow with a clearer idea of what we don't know."

Mallory nodded. "Okay. That's reasonable. I can do that. Do we need to invite anyone to join us?"

"No. I want to know what you're thinking and feeling and seeing without you hiding things from your stewards or Prince Kaelen."

"Oh. Prince Kaelen is …"

"I don't trust him and I'm beginning to think that you don't either, not fully, but you're scared and trying to keep up appearances. I don't care about appearances at this point."

Mallory nodded slowly. "All right."

When Betha joined Mallory in her rooms that evening she started automatically towards the chairs by the fire.

"Why don't we sit on the bed," Mallory said. "It's big enough and it's far more comfortable."

"Oh. I don't know. I'm sure it is more comfortable, but it's your bed."

"This is something we used to do when I was a little girl and I'd have friends over for a slumber party. We'd all sit in the bed together and talk until very late and we all just fell asleep where we were."

"You know, Taeya and I used to do that when we shared a room. I don't think I've done this since I was eight." Even with the invitation, even with Mallory waiting expectantly for her, it felt awkward, crawling onto the bed. She sat near the foot of the bed, a little stiffly, and tried to smile.

Mallory tossed her a pillow and hugged a second one to her chest. "Thanks. I guess I'm just tired of being treated like I'm unapproachable, with all the bowing and 'yes princess' and stuff. I'm sure the staff here likes me, but none of them are my friend, you know?"

"Yeah. It was like that in Dinas Rhosyn, though I don't think they actually liked me very much."

"Why wouldn't they?"

"I wasn't very nice. I was very angry all the time. I guess it's because I wasn't their princess." She sighed. "Tell me about your parents. I didn't grow up with parents. Madam Olga was wonderful, and she did love us, she still does, but servants and nannies isn't the same as parents."

"No, it's not. A lot of my needs were met by the staff at the embassy too. I had private tutors and I rarely saw my mother cook. But we ate together and went on trips together and my mom always asked how my school work was going. My father was from England. He was a slender man with fine dark hair. He always shaved, he never had stubble, not even on a day off."

"Where is England?"

"England is an island off the coast of Europe. My mother was from Ireland which is a smaller island off the coast of England. England took over Ireland so they're actually both part of the United Kingdom but there's a lot of violence in Ireland right now. The people there, especially the Catholics, don't want to be ruled by England anymore. There are bombs going off and sometimes fighting in the streets. It's sort of good thing I grew up in India because my mother's family didn't like my father at all."

"Wait," Betha said. "There's something in our history books, about why we made the pact with Airon. Apparently, people came over from across the Narrow Water. They said there was an island there, like ours, and beyond that, more lands than we could imagine."

"Ireland, England, Europe and the World," Mallory murmured. "It certainly fits. That means the strangers that chased you out were the early Celts. That would have been a *long* time ago though."

"Longer than eleven generations?"

"Yes." Mallory gave her head a shake. "It's getting too late in the evening for questions like that. But one of these days I will figure out how the pact works and why we were born in the Wide World, as you call it."

"Why didn't they find you when you were a baby?"

"Oh, that's an easy one. My mother got pregnant on a trip to Ireland, but I was born in India. I had dual citizenship and everything, though I guess that doesn't matter much now."

"That means the rest of us were likely born in Ireland."

Mallory nodded. "That would make sense. I never heard about a bunch of missing babies though. I mean, I was just a baby myself, but even as a child or a teenager, there was no talk of some weird, unsolved baby-napping."

"Napping?"

"Oh, you know what kidnapping is, right?"

"Of course."

"If you steal a baby that's baby-napping. If you steal a dog, that's dog-napping."

"That is so strange."

Mallory shrugged. "There were a lot of strange words back home. I think Carainhithe is strange. And Dinas Rhosyn. But we said things like 'groovy' and 'funkadelic'."

"That last one isn't a real word!"

"We call it slang – silly words that teens use to express things like how cool something is, or how attractive, or how much they like or dislike it."

"I'm assuming cool doesn't mean chilly?"

"Oh, it does. But it also means 'interesting', 'entertaining', or 'popular'."

"That's not confusing at all."

Now Mallory laughed. "I know. It was so weird for me, having to learn all the slang when I moved back to Ireland. The embassy in India was a very serious place and slang in Hindi is very different."

"Hindi is another language?"

"Yes. You're picking this up quickly. People keep looking at me like I'm from another planet or something because I keep saying words they've never heard before."

"It's not actually possible to be from another planet, is it?"

"Not that I've seen proof of, but there's stories. People say they've seen lights in the sky, or that they've seen aliens … er, people from other planets."

"Do you believe it?"

"I don't know. I didn't believe the Isle of Light existed and now look at me."

"I heard a rumour from a friend of mine that when you came through the gate you were wearing men's clothes."

"I wasn't … oh, wait." Mallory took a deep breath. "I wasn't wearing men's clothes, they were definitely for a woman, but after decades of fighting for more equality, women are allowed to wear pants if they choose."

"Really?"

Mallory nodded.

"Any time they want?"

"Well, some people think we should still wear a skirt or a dress for church or weddings or things like that. Some women have to wear skirts as part of their work uniform. Otherwise, yeah, for the most part, we can wear pants whenever we want."

"I can't imagine the uproar I would cause if I walked down to breakfast one morning in pants," Betha said, shaking her head.

"Yeah. They let me keep the clothes I came in, but I can't really wear them anywhere. I take them out sometimes and hold them when I feel homesick."

"Does talking about it like this make you homesick?"

"Actually, it doesn't. This is kind of fun. Did you want a snack?"

"Isn't it kind of late?"

"Maybe. But I want a snack. Something sweet."

"Nut rolls?"

"Sure. Let me ring down for some."

When the snacks came they curled up in the bed together, munching and laughing as Mallory tried to describe cars, airplanes, and electricity.

In the morning the serving girls would find the two princesses asleep in a jumble of pillows and blankets in Mallory's bed.

33rd of Cloudfall, 24th Year of the 11th Rebirth
Golden Hall, Metalkin Province

In the morning Betha had to hurry back to her own room, disheveled and slightly embarrassed. There she changed out of her wrinkled dress and brushed her hair. A girl brought in a tray with breakfast and a message from Mallory.

"Princess Jewel-Rose has called a meeting this morning for you and someone else. She said it was very important."

Betha nodded. "Good. We need to get this underway as soon as possible."

She ate quickly and then had a servant show her the way to this meeting Mallory had quickly thrown together. Mallory was not there yet but there was a man, broad shouldered and dark haired, standing at the window.

Betha squared her shoulders and collected herself, ready to do verbal battle with Kaelen. "Good morning," she said, her voice politely cool.

He turned and smiled at her. "Betha."

Her whole body relaxed so quickly she thought her knees were going to give out on her. "Joseph. I didn't expect …"

"Good, you're both here," Mallory said, coming in behind Betha. She had two books and a pile of papers in her hands. She set everything down on the table. "I'm sorry for the short notice, Master Rose-Gold, but we had some disturbing news from Evergrowth last night and we need to get a handle on this, now. Sit, please, both of you."

Joseph and Betha glanced at each other and Joseph shrugged one shoulder, a silent apology.

The letter from Taeya was quickly read aloud and the three of them settled down to gather all the information they had between the three of them about the Academic Diplomats, the iron mine incident, the bank corruption, and whether or not it all tied in together.

Gems discovered in the collapsed mine, gems being transported by the Metalkin, a smithy burning down, an archivist poisoned, too many accounting errors from too many guilds, and young Metalkin men studying everything from gardening to fishing to horse training.

"Master Spirit-Light has been assisting me with the archives," Joseph said. "We've confirmed that many of the last names these cultural scholars are using are fictitious. There are no families bearing those names."

"What of those men who claimed to be cousins or relatives in order to gain access for them among other nobles?" Mallory said.

"Any family members I've spoken to here in the capital claim they have no knowledge of their relative's actions."

"And we've no way to prove who knew what," Mallory murmured. "I don't suppose you have a magical polygraph test, do you?"

"Considering that I don't even know what that is," Betha said.

"A lie detector. It's a machine that tells police when someone is lying. You don't have a magical way of telling when someone is lying, do you?"

"No," Betha said. "But that would make life easier."

There was a knock at the door and a servant stuck their head in. "Excuse me, Princess Living-Rose, but there are some men here from the Gold Guild to see you."

"Yes, I was expecting them. I'll be right there." She nodded to Betha and Joseph. "I have to go. If the two of you think of anything, make note of it for me."

"Of course," Betha said. "Duty calls."

"Does it ever stop?" Mallory smiled apologetically and slipped from the room.

For a moment Betha and Joseph just sat in silence. Finally, Betha said, "It's good to see you."

"And you. Your letter yesterday was quite a shock to me. I didn't expect you here in Golden Hall. I can't say it's an unpleasant surprise. I thought our time of crossing paths had pretty much ended and I'm glad to find I'm wrong on that count."

"So am I. I received your letter, about your father, when I arrived here. My stewards sent it over."

"If I had known you were coming I could have waited and told you the news in person."

"I didn't write ahead because I thought you'd already be visiting Princess Rheeya."

"That was the plan. How was the trip east?"

"Blissfully uneventful and short. And you? Your stay in Caranhall and your trip home went well?"

"Well enough. I find that families who support the Academic Diplomats in some way are less than hospitable when I come to call on them. But they listened to my questions and offered answers. No way to know how honest those answers were though. How long are you in Golden Hall?"

"I'm not sure. As long as Mallory needs me and my stewards do not."

"Then perhaps we'll have time for tea, or a meal, while you are here."

"I'd like that."

"My family lives at the far southern end of the city but the boys here at the castle know the way so if you need to send a message, they can run it for you."

"All right."

"I should get home. We have a meeting with the healer again this afternoon. My father will want help washing up." He sounded tired.

Betha smiled and laid a hand over his. "This must be difficult."

Joseph shrugged.

"I'm sorry that there's nothing I can do to help."

"It means a lot that you even want to." He stood. "I will see you soon?"

"Yes. I hope so."

He bowed and went out as a boy came in with a letter in hand. "Princess Living-Rose, a letter for you from in the city."

"Thank-you." She recognized Talia's seal so she opened it immediately.

Betha,

You're in the capital? How exciting! I can't make it up to the palace right now, but you must come and see me for tea today, or tomorrow after lunch. You mustn't refuse. And don't let your guards keep you cooped up in the castle for your entire trip! You'll be perfectly safe here. We haven't had a single attack in the city and we even have private guards at my father's estate.

Oh, I just have so much to tell you. I don't know how I'll sleep for the excitement. Write back so I know when to expect you.

Talia

Talia's enthusiasm was contagious and Betha could feel the energy building in her as she read on. Late night or no she was looking forward to a lively afternoon with her friend. It had been over half a year since she'd seen Talia in person, and the last time they'd met it had been so brief!

"This time we'll make the most of it," Betha said. She tucked the note, and the unread one, out of the way and called for a servant.

When the girl arrived Betha said, "I need to speak with the head of my escort as soon as possible. And ask one of the scholars or stewards for directions to the Gold-Haven's estate here in the city."

The girl curtsied. "At once, Princess."

"And have someone bring lunch to my rooms at midday, I'll dine there," Betha added just before the girl disappeared.

Betha spent the rest of the morning making plans with the head of her escort, one General Martin Wild-Hart. Since she had to go into the city to see Talia she planned to visit the local Equine Guild on her way there. "I have the most questions for them," she said.

"Are they expecting you?"

"Not yet, I haven't had the chance to write to them. I plan to write those letters this afternoon. After tea with Talia I want to stop at the Farmers' Cooperative. Other animals may be involved, and I want to know if they've had any reports."

"You could just write them, have them meet you here."

"I'll be going into the city tomorrow," Betha said. "Mallory does it all the time. Vonica went down to the city to visit the guild hall too. It's daylight, I'm safe. Make the arrangements, we leave after the midday meal."

Sir Wild-Hart bowed. "Yes, Princess."

After a long and boring afternoon writing letters to guild halls and noble families Betha joined Mallory for dinner. Unfortunately, Kaelen was also dining with them this evening.

"I haven't seen you all day," Mallory said when Kaelen entered. "You weren't at court. You hardly ever miss court."

"I only missed because of your delay this morning. I was expected elsewhere and couldn't wait any longer."

Betha gritted her teeth. She couldn't imagine Tomas, Johann, or Francis speaking to their wives with such a snide tone. It wasn't Mallory's fault this investigation had to happen, it wasn't Mallory's fault there was an emergency in Evergrowth, but after her conversation with the stable master upon her arrival, Betha was beginning to suspect that some of the fault would eventually be laid at Kaelen's feet.

"I won't apologize for that," Mallory said.

Kaelen harrumphed. "I don't like you spending so much time with this Master Golden-Rose."

"Rose-Gold," Betha said. "Named for a metal, not a flower."

Kaelen frowned at her but said, "Of course, how careless of me." He turned back to his wife. "Still, I don't like it. I don't like that tracker hanging around either. What business does he have in the castle?"

"He has been employed by Master Spirit-Light, to what end I don't know, but I see them deep in conversation on a regular basis."

"You should send him away."

"To what end? He's doing a job for one of my stewards. The priests and both of my stewards trusted him enough to send him on the expedition to find me. Doesn't that make him trustworthy? What has he ever done to you?"

"Just because they are priests of Airon doesn't make them trustworthy. That prophet who claimed to be performing miracles in Airon's name, the one that chained the other provinces to the sun temple? He was a political tool, a weapon used to cripple the other provinces and force us all to submit to the Sun Temple."

"That's not true," Betha said.

"You were raised at the Sun Temple, of course they taught you something different," Kaelen said. "My point is, the priests are a tool of politics, they have their own motives."

"I'm fairly certain their motives for sending a search party into the Wide World was to find Mallory and bring peace to the island," Betha said. "Isn't that what you wanted too?"

Kaelen stared at Betha for a moment and then said, "Of course. We had so many years of relying on the priests and stewards for guidance and judgement. We are lucky our princess was found."

The last line sounded off to Betha, hollow, like how she recited the words of the pact without emotion or conviction. Betha studied Kaelen carefully.

Mallory was talking again. "I don't know enough about your history and traditions yet to have an opinion on this prophet, but I do know that Master Spirit-Light has been extremely helpful and kind since I arrived. Master Black-Kettle has been far more difficult to deal with."

"He's younger," Kaelen said. "It was never meant to be his job."

"So, where were you?" Mallory said. "What was so pressing that you missed court?"

"My father required my assistance," Kaelen said.

"How honourable of you," Betha murmured.

Kaelen shot her a dark look but went on. "There were no troubles in court today?"

"No. I'm getting the hang of this."

"I knew you would," Kaelen said. "I have a meeting in the city this evening."

"Again?"

"People are concerned," he said.

"About what?" Betha said.

"There are a lot of questions, with the mix-up in your placement, the Dark Spirit attacks, the investigation that the five of you insist on carrying out – all that makes people nervous. They want to know things will get better, that stability will return, that this investigation will end."

"It would end a lot sooner if people were more forthcoming with information," Betha said.

"Perhaps you are looking for information that does not exist and answers that are more complicated than you need them to be," Kaelen said.

"Perhaps people are keeping secrets and lying through their teeth," Betha shot back.

"You are young, passionate, and misguided," Kaelen said with a sneer.

"You are just as young as we are," Betha shot back. "And stubborn and …"

"Enough," Mallory said. "I'm finished eating. I'm retiring to my room. I strongly suggest, Kaelen, that you leave for your meeting, sooner rather than later. And Betha, stay out of trouble."

"Always," Betha said, her gaze still locked with Kaelen's. She broke the stare with a haughty flip of her hair. "I have letters to write so I will retire as well. Good-night, Mallory." She pushed away from the table and headed for the door, nose in the air, and without another word to Kaelen.

**34th of Cloudfall, 24th Year of the 11th Rebirth
Golden Hall, Metalkin Province**

The Equine Guild was tiny, not at all what Betha expected. She'd envisioned a stable attached to the building and teaching space, and space for equipment. This little building held four offices, one meeting space, and the archives and nothing else. There wasn't a single living, breathing horse in sight, except for the ones she'd left harnessed to her carriage.

The young man sweeping the front room took one look at Betha and his eyes went as large as tea saucers. He rushed from the room and didn't return. Instead, an older man in brown leggings and a linen shirt entered. Except for the fact that his clothes were spotless and his vest was embroidered in gold thread he was dressed exactly like a commoner.

He bowed. "Princess, your presence here is welcome, if unexpected. How can we help you today?"

"I came to Golden Hall to assist Princess Mallory with her investigation into the foals that went missing from the Evergrowth province."

"Foals? I was under the understanding that one of the two animals was purchased. It's not missing, it's simply in the hands of its new owner."

"You have the records of the sale?"

He blinked at her. "Uh, no, Princess. I don't."

"Neither does the Equine Guild in the Evergrowth province. If the foal was purchased, no one knows by whom. Doesn't the Equine guild keep records of every foal born for lineage purposes?"

"No, Princess. That's an exaggeration. We keep extensive records of the Sun Mares and several strong breeding lines which are often bred to those mares. The common work and riding horses, no, we don't have records of them at all, just rough numbers provided by the farmers."

"Hmm, that may complicate matters. What about suspicious deaths?"

"Often deaths are reported if illness is suspected so we can track and prevent the spread of diseases in the herds. Deaths are also reported in cases of abuse or mishandling. In those cases there is a hearing against the stable master or stable hand involved. They lose their association with the guild if they're found guilty and they can't get a job in a stable without that association."

"I need all records of such deaths from the last two years sent to the castle promptly," Betha said.

"Illness? Or Abuse?"

"Abuse is more important, abuse and neglect. If any illness cases stand out as odd or suspicious I want to see them as well. Have your most attentive and concerned representative search the archives. I'd rather have too many cases to read than too few."

"Uh, yes Princess. We can take care of that for you. Is there anything else?"

"Is there? I mean, are there any complaints or concerns I need to deal with while I'm here? Is there any other information you have about the missing foals?"

"No and no. I'm sorry we can't be of more assistance."

"Just ensure those records are sent today, and that nothing is missing."

"Of course," he said with a bow.

She nodded sharply and went back out, her escort for the day close on her heels.

From the Equine Guild they went on to Talia's house. Nothing in Golden Hall sprawled, the buildings were packed in too close for that, even the castle was built tall instead of wide.

It made sense in a way that the Equine Guild was so tiny here. This was only their office space. The boys learned their trade in the stables, and there were few stables in the city proper. There were few horses out on the streets at all. Most people walked though Betha saw a few litters, draped in expensive fabrics and borne on the shoulders of servants.

The streets were narrow and most people had to crowd off to the side to make space for Betha and her escort. That meant her presence was stirring up quite a bit of attention. Betha stared right back at the people lining the street, her interest in them every bit as intense as their interest in her.

Talia's house was larger than the guild hall but less than a third the size of the castle. The property was surrounded by an elegant chest-high wrought-iron fence. In the narrow space between the fence and the house someone had planted some flowering shrubbery. The house was stone but the wooden front door had elaborate metal fittings that were as much art as they were function. In the center was a black, metal door knocker. It was heavy in her hands but warmed by the sun.

She knocked three times, impressed by the solid sound of metal against wood, and then waited, her escort at her elbow, his eyes darting everywhere. A servant opened the door and bowed. "Princess Living-Rose, we were expecting you. Please, come in."

Talia and an older woman were approaching from down the hallway as Betha entered. The older woman stopped a respectful distance back and curtsied deeply, but Talia just pushed forward and wrapped her arms around Betha. "It's good to see you again."

"And you," Betha said, returning the hug.

"This is my mother, Madam Gold-Haven," Talia said, turning and gesturing back towards the older woman.

"Welcome to our home, Princess Living-Rose, this is an honour beyond measure."

"Thank-you for the invitation. My days are most often filled with dry but necessary tasks. It's not often I have the chance to relax and visit like this."

"Tea is ready and being served in the sunroom," Madam Gold-Haven said. "I'll leave you ladies to your visiting. I have my own engagement that I'm already late for."

"I'm sorry," Betha said. "I had to stop at the …"

"No, don't apologize. My hostess will be more than understanding."

Talia took Betha by the hand. "Come. We have so much to discuss."

The house was decorated much the same way the castle was, with fine portraits in the halls, silver vases on end tables, and rugs with elaborate patterns, highlighted with gold and silver threads.

The receiving room had tall shuttered doors that were open, revealing a little flagstone courtyard and letting in a breeze sweetened by the flowers planted around the courtyard. The furniture here was of the highest quality, all with metal legs and brocade fabrics that combined rich colours with gold accents. The mirror above the mantel was framed in brass.

The tea service, set on a little table between two chairs, was silver. There was steam rising out of the teapot's spout. A tray of cookies and cakes sat next to the fresh tea.

"You're looking well," Betha said, pulling her gaze from the room around her to the friend who now sat opposite her.

Talia laughed. "And you're looking tired. You haven't been sleeping well, I can tell."

"It's hard to sleep in carriages and guest beds."

"How was your stay at the Sun Temple? I've never been you know."

"It was absolutely delightful. I met four young students while I was there and they were wonderful."

"Ugh. Students and scholars are all so boring."

"They can be, but once you get the younger ones past all the stuffy, formal, education-speak they can be entertaining. And generous."

"Oh! Did you get gifts?"

Betha nodded. "Trinkets, really, nothing overly expensive or impressive."

"At least someone else picked it out and gave it to you. I got a new necklace but I had to buy it for myself."

"Is that the one you're wearing?"

"Yes." Talia leaned forward. "Do you like it?"

"May I?" Betha said. When Talia nodded she reached out and touched the pendant. It was a small emerald, simply cut and simply mounted, but the stone was impressive in its clarity. "It's lovely. It must have been quite costly."

"It wasn't costly at all, actually. There was this jeweler in the market near here who was had all these beautiful pieces for a very reasonable price. I've never seen a necklace like this so cheap before."

"And you couldn't pass it up?"

"I really couldn't."

"I hope things aren't going horribly wrong with your suitors."

"That's the thing. I thought they were going well. I had half a dozen young men coming around. Three just stopped, no warning, I haven't seen them in weeks and they haven't responded to any of my notes. Another one announced his engagement to someone else."

"Oh, Talia, I'm sorry."

"That wasn't so bad, actually. I wasn't sure I really wanted to marry him."

"What about the two that are left?"

"They're a little older and they have connections with my father and my uncles. Honestly, I think my father chased the other three away. I don't know why. They're from good families, all twice-named, all have family ties to the royal guard and high-ranking guilds." She sighed deeply. "I'll never get married at this rate."

Betha reached out and patted her friend's hand. "You will. And it will be a beautiful ceremony and you'll be very happy."

"I hope you're right."

"Of course I'm right. So, which of your suitors got engaged and to whom? And who else is getting married before Holy Week? And who is engaged to be married next year?"

Now Talia laughed again. "Don't worry, court has been full of juicy stories lately, and I know everything about everyone!"

The Farmers' Cooperative looked like a barn after an afternoon spent in surrounded by the finery of the Gold-Haven's household. Like the Equine Guild it the cooperative was housed in a small building in a densely populated part of the city. At least it didn't smell of animals.

Several representatives met with her but none had anything suspicious to report. She informed them of Taeya's warning, her words causing obvious distress among them.

"Princess, we work closely with the Evergrowth. Farming grain and farming livestock is closely entwined, we live and work in the same communities. More than most professions from most provinces, we understand the need for cooperation and balance.

There are few squabbles over land, or labour. Not once in all my years with the Cooperative have I ever heard of an Evergrowth farmer attacking or harming an animal in retaliation for a slight, real or imagined."

"I agree," another said. "I simply cannot imagine Evergrowth farmers being a part of this."

"What about healers?" Betha said.

The men around the table exchanged cautious glances. "Princess, you would be hard pressed to find a healer who lives and works in a farming village who would endanger the livelihood of so many people, even for money."

"Could they have paid for the poison elsewhere and hired someone completely unrelated to the matter to administer it?"

"In my experience, healers are extremely guarded about anything they make that could cause harm. You'd have to find a healer who was far more concerned with money than human life."

"I understand. And getting them to admit as much? Next to impossible. Even if they did not fear criminal charges from the crown they would certainly face severe repercussions at the hand of the guild, as well as being ostracized in any community. Thank-you for your time."

2nd of Thornfall, 24th Year of the 11th Rebirth
Golden Hall, Metalkin Province

Betha retired to her room after dinner. She was tired of Prince Kaelen, her suitors, and the guild representatives. She was tired of not making any progress on the investigation. And she was tired of Mallory being too busy to discuss the Wide World with her more often.

Maybe after a short rest I'll go visit her in her rooms again. There's so much more I want to know.

The last few days had been full, from sun up to sun down, with meetings Betha did not want to attend. Unfortunately, refusing to attend meant agreeing to return to Caranhall and she wasn't ready to do that just yet.

I haven't even gone to visit Joseph yet.

There was little to do in the guest room aside from studying the few Carainhithe history texts she'd brought with her. That didn't interest her at all, even if these books were written by Carainhithe scholars and were *more* interesting than the ones in the Sun Temple. *But only marginally more.*

Instead she made her way through the guest wing to the private wing where Mallory and Kaelen had their rooms. She knocked on Mallory's door.

From inside Mallory said, "Come in. You can put the tray on the table."

"I hope you requested extra," Betha said.

"Oh, it's you. Come in. There's always too much on one of those trays anyways. It should be hard to get an extra tea cup. What brings you to my end of town?"

"That's just a saying, right?"

"Yes."

"I was bored."

"Well, that's good. Better than an emergency. I don't thing I could handle any more bad news or emergency meetings."

"Me either. I want to know more about your world."

"All right, but we can't stay up nearly as late as we did the last time," Mallory said, laughing. "Come sit by the fire. I find it so relaxing. We didn't much need heating in India, it never dropped below freezing except for up in the mountains."

"What about Ireland?"

"Oh sure, you needed some heat for a few months of the year, but it's all natural gas or electric now. Most homes don't have fire places anymore or only use them for recreation."

There was a knock on the door and the girl came in with Mallory's tray. She saw Betha and paused. "I'm sorry. I didn't know Princess Living-Rose was visiting you. I've only brought one cup."

"I'm sorry, I didn't know Betha was coming to call this evening or I would have requested two cups."

"I'll leave the tray and be back in a moment."

"Thank-you."

Betha accepted a nut roll from Mallory. "I can't even imagine a way to stay warm without fire," Betha said. "Or to cook."

"The rest of the world moved on," Mallory said. "People discovered things, like electricity and nuclear power. We have democracies and unions instead of monarchs and guilds. We have so many different cultures and religions." She sighed. "That's where you have the right of it and we don't. Out in the wide world, people hate other people for the stupidest reasons. There's none of this 'strength through unity' stuff."

"We don't always get along, but we understand that we need each other. If even one province breaks the pact it will be disastrous."

"Yeah, I know. We've had two global wars out there. Millions and millions of people dead. The land torn up. Families shattered. All for hatred and greed."

Betha shuddered. She couldn't imagine what a million people looked like, *Probably the entire population of the Isle of Light,* and she couldn't imagine all those people and then some all dying. "I'm glad you're here to repair the pact," Betha said. "So that another million people don't have to die."

Mallory nodded. "Yeah. Once I figured out that you were all serious about these Dark Spirits and the threat to your island, I stopped trying to go home. I didn't want to be the one to cause a million more deaths."

For a moment they stared into the flames, listening to the crackle of burning wood and the soft, steady beat of their own hearts.

The girl returned with a second cup and stopped to pour the tea before leaving again.

"That's not what I meant to talk about," Mallory said. She shook her head and tried to smile. "There are so many beautiful things out in the world. We don't need to discuss war right now."

"Tell me more about your family," Betha said. "And I will tell you more about Madam Olga and growing up in a temple."

"It's a deal."

3rd of Thornfall, 24th Year of the 11th Rebirth
Golden Hall, Metalkin Province

Betha woke slowly and stretched. The bed here was wonderful and she'd had a delightful evening with Mallory exchanging childhood stories. She still wasn't quite sure what an elephant was but from the size of it, she was sure it was terrifying. They hadn't talked until collapsing like the last time, but they had stayed up later than either had intended.

There was a knock at the door and Betha got out of bed, wrapping a robe around her as she crossed the room. She yanked the door open, upset at being disturbed so early, to find a girl with a breakfast tray.

The girl curtsied, no small feat considering how much was balanced on the tray. "Your meal, early as requested."

An early breakfast because you're spending the day in the city with Joseph today. "Yes, thank-you. Just there on the table please."

The girl nodded. "Is there anything else?"

"I'll need help with my hair as soon as I'm done eating."

"Of course. Just ring. I'll be sure to bring a few extra girls with me to assist you this morning."

"Thank-you." She ate quickly, the excitement bubbling inside of her. *How could I have forgotten, even for a moment? What if he introduces me to his family? What if it gets awkward? What if his family doesn't like me? I'm just one of the Animal People, and the Metalkin often look down on us. No, I'm a princess, they wouldn't do that.*

Still, a nervous energy accompanied her excitement as she ate. She rang for the girls and then went to the wardrobe to select a dress. She hadn't brought many with her, and most of them were simple day dresses. The two formal dresses she'd brought wouldn't do either, they were for important dinners, not for travelling about the city visiting and sight-seeing.

In the end she settled on the only dress that fell somewhere in the middle, sturdy enough and simple enough to survive a busy day and not be in her way, but nice enough to show this was important to her and that she was putting in the effort.

The girls arrived and helped her dress, twisting her hair up into something fun and semi-formal. A shawl completed her outfit and she was ready by the time her escort arrived to take her down to the carriage.

She already seen enough of the city on her previous travels to know that it all looked very much the same. Some buildings were larger than others, but they were all packed in tight against each other on both sides of the narrow streets. Shop keepers called from the stalls, offering everything from bread and eggs to fish and smoked deer to dresses and necklaces. Shoppers moved from stall to stall with baskets in their arms. The noise and smell was as overwhelming as the tightness of the crowd and the buildings.

And yet, while the whole thing should have suffocated her, the Animal Princess who should have longed for open air and open fields, Betha was fascinated, captivated, and delighted at every turn.

The castle was located in the eastern corner of the city, so they had to travel southwest to the southern edge of the city to find the Rose-Gold household. It wasn't as grand looking as Talia's house, but the fence and gate were in good repair and the home was just as large as its neighbours.

Betha stepped out of the carriage and up the walk to the door, which opened before she could knock. A dark-haired woman, easily a few years older than Betha, stood in the doorway. Her face was somber, and her clothes were conservative.

After a moment's pause the woman curtsied. "Princess Living-Rose, you honour our home. Please, come in."

"I suppose Master Rose-Gold informed you I was coming today?"

"Yes, my brother did mention it. He's not down yet. Our father …"

Betha waited a moment but the woman didn't continue. Betha cleared her throat. "I'd heard that he was ill. My condolences. I hope the healer can …"

"No. There is nothing except making him comfortable now and waiting for the end."

"Oh. I didn't realize. I'm sorry."

"It is what it is. Would you like tea while you wait?"

"No, thank-you."

"I see she's here," came another female voice. Betha looked up as another dark-haired woman came down the stairs. "I'm Huberta Rose-Gold. You've met my daughter Maria."

"A pleasure," Betha said. "And I thank you for welcoming me into your home at such a trying time."

"What choice did we have?" Maria muttered. A stern look from her mother silenced her.

"It is a difficult time. Please, come and sit. Joseph is assisting his father at the moment and will be down as soon as possible. And I'll take some of that tea."

The drawing room was small but finely decorated with warm coloured rugs on the floor and airy curtains over the single window.

There was a lantern on the side table, unlit, and brass candlesticks placed strategically around the room.

Betha and Huberta sat in the only two chairs while Maria went to fetch her mother's tea.

"Excuse my daughter. My husband was a younger son, not far down the line of inheritance but not high enough that Joseph has any chance at a lordship, not even high enough that we're welcome to live at the Rose-Gold manor with Lord and Lady Rose-Gold. We live comfortably but with the healer's expenses we've let go all but one servant and she only does the cleaning and the laundry."

"I didn't realize …"

"No. Joseph doesn't like to speak of it. And I'm not telling you so that you'll pity us. The work Joseph does pays well enough. When my husband is gone and we no longer have to pay the healer we'll return to our former comforts. Of course, Maria is eyeing a suitor from a nearby estate and our expenses would be lessened if she married him, or anyone. I don't approve of the man but the way my eldest daughter carries on I don't think that will stop her." Huberta stopped talking and smiled as her daughter came in with a small tray. "Thank-you my dear. Could you go upstairs and inform your brother that his guest is here."

"Of course, Mother."

"Seems strange to me," Huberta went on, "To see the Animal People's princess in a Metalkin home wanting to spend time with a young, unmarried, Metalkin man."

"Joseph and I became friends over the course of the investigation he's been conducting for Princess Mal… Princess Jewel-Rose. Sine I was in the city assisting Mallory I thought it would be nice to see my friend for a day. I don't see a problem with that."

"Problem? No. I suppose not. But traditionally like has kept to like. There isn't much socializing between the provinces."

"Not between the nobles, no, but between the commoners? Oh yes, all the time. And besides, one of my dearest friends is a young Metalkin noble woman. We write each other all the time and I've already had tea with her since my arrival in Golden Hall."

"Ah, Betha, you're here," Joseph said as he came in.

Huberta cleared her throat, loudly.

"Uh, I mean, Princess Living-Rose. Welcome to our home."

"Thank-you. It's a lovely place."

"My father is insisting on seeing you."

"I would be honoured to meet him," Betha said.

Next to her, Huberta was rushing to her feet. "No, that won't be possible. He doesn't walk so well anymore, he can't come down the stairs, not even with help."

"I can go up to him."

"We haven't cleaned up there, it's not fit for company."

"I can overlook linens in the hallway and dust on the cupboards," Betha said. "You've all had a very stressful and emotional time. It's understandable."

"He's in his room, my room. It's private. My clothes, my belongings …"

"I can bring Father to my room then," Joseph said. "He's insisting."

"It wouldn't be proper for her to be in your room," Huberta said.

"She and I won't be alone," Joseph said. "And besides, she's from a different province, the princess of another province, there is nothing romantic between us and there never will be. It's simply impossible. Neither of us would endanger the pact by acting inappropriately."

"Exactly," Betha said as her heart ached in her chest.

"Fine. In your room, not mine, and just for a moment. And I'll be in the hallway the entire time."

Joseph nodded and led Betha up the stairs, his mother close on their heels. The man Joseph brought to meet her looked like a coat on a wire hook. He'd been a larger man, Betha could see it in the skin that hung around his face, but now he was slender and hunched over.

He offered Betha a trembling hand. "Princess," he said. "Princess, welcome."

"Thank-you," Betha said. "Your home is lovely, and your family is kind and welcoming."

"You have brought us honour," he said.

"The way your family cares for you has brought them honour. I'm glad I had the chance to meet you while I'm in the province on business."

He frowned. "Where would you go?"

"Home," Betha said. "When my work is done, I have to go home."

"Back to the castle, of course," he said, nodding. "Of course."

"I need to go out for a while Father, I need to help the princess with her work today."

"You're a good lad," he said.

Betha followed the two men out of the room then hurried down the stairs to wait while Joseph got his father settled again. Huberta followed after her at a slower pace, her steps stately and calm.

"I thank you for visiting us. I'm sure your work will keep you busy for the remainder of your trip to Golden Hall and I doubt we will see you again."

I doubt I would be welcome here again.

Joseph came down the stairs at that moment, saving Bethan from having to respond. "I'm sure your escort and carriage are waiting."

"Yes. They are."

"Then we'd best go." He went to the door and held it open for her.

123

She paused in the opening. "Thank-you again for welcoming me into your home during this difficult time."

Her knees trembled a little as she walked to the carriage. Joseph offered her a hand up into the carriage and she was surprised to see her own was shaking.

"I'm sorry for my family's behaviour," he said once they were moving.

"This is a difficult time," she said.

"Yes, it is that, but it's more than that. My father was a difficult man in life and my mother resents how long it is taking him to die. And my mother is not fond of you or the other princesses."

"I gathered as much but I've no idea why."

"When I was young, apparently, I said things and did things, odd things. And then there was my affinity for the castle when I first stepped foot inside its walls. I suppose, like all mothers, she hoped I would be the chosen one, the prince, and then Mallory was found, and she married Kaelen and then I decided to stay and work for her anyways."

"It is so odd. You seem like you'd be a much better prince for Mallory than Kaelen. Forgive me for speaking ill of him, but I sometimes wonder if he's entirely honest with her. You are honourable and sincerely wish to help and support her."

"I do. But I could never marry her. I don't love her, I feel nothing special for her. And to be honest, I find there are times she frustrates me. She stares out the window, lost in daydreams, when I speak with her about serious matters. I know she has a lot to adjust to, but she longs for something that isn't here and I don't know how to feel about that."

"What of your other sister? You mentioned in one of your letters that you had more than one."

"Yes, Maria is the eldest. I have a younger sister as well. She's been staying with some cousins and second cousins at the Rose-Gold estate."

"Where the Lord Rose-Gold lives?"

"Exactly. Lord Rose-Gold has several daughters and now that the business with Princess Mallory is over, they are attracting many suitors. My father had hoped that by sending her there, she'd find a husband."

"This was before he fell ill?"

"Before his illness progressed to such a state."

"And your older sister? She wasn't sent?"

"No. My mother insisted she stay to help with the house. It's … complicated."

The carriage stopped and Betha looked to the window. "I haven't been paying the least bit attention. Where are we?"

"At our first stop. This is the headquarters of the Jeweler's Guild."

"A guild meeting?"

"No. A tour. I've arranged for you to meet some of the artists and craftsmen, to see the workshops and watch them work. Is that all right?"

Betha nodded.

After the Jeweller's Guild they went to a tea house to dine. They sat at a semi-private table near the back but from the way necks craned it was obvious they were the topic of every conversation. After their meal, Joseph took her to an artisan's market street to watch the men work in brass and silver.

It was fascinating and she returned to the castle at the end of the day with a small bag of shiny trinkets to add to her collection. They took dinner together in a small sun-room near Betha's room in the guest wing.

"That was a wonderful day," Betha said. "I've never had the opportunity to just shop and explore, not anywhere."

"Not even in Dinas Rhosyn?"

"I'm sure if I had asked I might have been able to, and I did some 'exploring' after the fire, if you could call it that. It was all work, not just a relaxing afternoon in the market."

"I suppose you had little interest."

"None."

"Will you do this in Caranhall?"

"I don't know. Caranhall is a curious place, not at all what I expected. I imagine there would be much to explore."

"I enjoyed my stay there, but I was glad to return home."

"Joseph, tell me about your father," she blurted out. She blushed and looked at her plate. "I'm sorry. You don't have to. I've been thinking about it all day, but you probably don't want to talk about it. About him."

"I don't speak of him much."

"I know. I'm sorry. It's just …" She sighed. "I didn't have parents. I mean, I have parents, somewhere, but I never met them, I didn't grow up with them. And I didn't really think much of it until Mallory. She's been telling me stories of her childhood and I was wondering what yours was like."

"He was a hard man. He worked hard, harder than anyone I know. He cared about us, he must have, why else would he work such long hours to clothe and feed us? But he didn't show that care, never really showed that he loved us at all. He had a temper and he took it out on me more than once. But at the same time, I have seen him stand up to other nobles, seen him testify on behalf of wronged salesmen and artisans, even those from other provinces. He believed in balance and unity. My mother did too. Some of her views were simply scandalous as far as the other nobles were concerned."

"She really believed you were a prince?"

"I guess so. I think it's just too much for her. With Maria threatening to marry this man with a shady reputation, to my father's illness, to my less than royal social standing … she's tired, emotionally and physically."

Betha reached out and squeezed Joseph's hand. "I won't judge her based on today. Perhaps, if I ever meet her again, things will be different."

"I hope so. Because I miss her, the woman she was when I was young. I miss her vibrancy and her energy, and I hope that returns."

Later that evening, as Betha was tucking her new treasures away in her trunk, her fingers brushed against the bundles of letters from Joseph and she smiled.

Whatever else happened, she could now say that this trip was well worth her time.

5th of Thornfall, 24th Year of the 11th Rebirth
Golden Hall, Metalkin Province

The meeting was supposed to be short and simple, as far as Betha was aware, but it didn't work out that way.

After the fire in the Sun Temple Province which the princesses all strongly believed was linked to the gems the blacksmith had seen in the packs of a Metalkin trader, the Gem Guild had been working closely with Mallory to track and monitor the gemstone trade. Two guild representatives arrived, as scheduled, to deliver the latest report.

"Currently we've noted no thefts from any mines and all deliveries have arrived on time, with the entire shipment accounted for," said the elder as he wrapped up his report.

His younger companion said, "We are currently conducting a review of every mine on the island. We're looking for evidence of unreported gem banks in metal mines."

"I for one must commend you," Betha said. "With all this uncertainty you've still managed to lower the cost of the stones you are providing to the jewellers."

"Lowering?" the elder gentleman said. "No, Princess, I'm afraid you are mistaken. With the current shortage and the ongoing investigation, costs are rising."

"That makes sense," Mallory said. "Supply and demand and all that."

"But a friend of mine just purchased an emerald necklace for the lowest price she's ever seen."

"Might be it wasn't a new piece, but something being resold. Might be that the setting was new, but the stone was taken from an older piece. Sometimes jewelry is sold when people go through times of financial troubles."

"We often cannot track those gems," the younger went on. "They are sold directly back to the jewellers."

"Yes," Betha murmured. "That must be it."

"Thank-you, gentlemen," Mallory said. "I will see you again in a few weeks."

They bowed and headed on their way again.

Mallory turned to Betha. "What's this about your friend's new necklace?"

"Talia. I had tea with her the other day. She was showing off a new necklace. The way she went on about it I was certain it was new, not just new to her. It wasn't a large emerald but clear and beautifully cut."

"Perhaps an off-cut of a larger stone? Would that account for the lower price?"

"The Metalkin don't see the world that way. You charge the same for every usable piece, you don't offer discounts just because you've used a piece already. No, it makes more sense that it was an old piece of jewellery and the stone was simply placed in a new setting."

"That seems odd to me as well. Aren't fine pieces generally passed down through the family? Wouldn't you take it and request a new setting, to update a piece? And if so, wouldn't you intend to keep the new piece?"

"Yes on all counts. But if they hit upon hard times?"

"I'm told the economy here in Golden Hall is flourishing. There seems no need for such a thing, at least not among those who could afford such a piece in the first place. And no need for discounting prices either."

"You suspect this has something to do with the whole mess?"

Mallory shrugged. "There's really no way to know at this point what is a part of the web we are attempted to untangle and what is not. I need to think on this and figure out the best course of action."

6th of Thornfall, 24th Year of the 11th Rebirth
Golden Hall, Metalkin Province

Betha hurried through the halls to the Great Hall where Mallory was holding court. She watched from Mallory's private doorway, out of sight behind the throne, as Mallory finished dealing with the day's final petition.

When Master Black-Kettle dismissed the court Mallory strode purposefully towards the doorway, and Betha, her skirts gathered in her hands.

"I received your note," Betha said.

"Good. I'm on my way to an important meeting. You can come."

Betha hurried after her friend, her heart hammering in her chest. "Did you discover something new?"

"No, but I've made up my mind about something."

They arrived at a small study where Joseph Rose-Gold was waiting. He bowed. "Princess Jewel-Rose, Princess Living-Rose. What can …"

"You'll leave for Shores Stone today," Mallory said.

"My father …"

"The crown will pay for all of his medical expenses while you are away, in return for your services. I can't delay this any longer. I'm sorry."

Joseph nodded. "I pledged my services to you, so if you have need of me in Stones Shore, I will go."

"I have need of you in the mountains," Mallory said. "I need you to arrange visits with some of the mines as well. We've had conflicting information. The Gem Guild claims prices are rising but we've had reports of inexpensive jewelry available in the city. New items, not items being resold."

"I understand." He nodded. "I will pack and be gone before day's end."

"I will have a small escort ready to ride with you and the necessary letters and papers that you will require to do your job."

"Thank-you."

"Betha, you mentioned that a friend of yours had recently received one of these inexpensive necklaces as a gift?"

"From one of her suitors, yes. She showed it to me. She was quite impressed with it."

"What I'm about to ask you, it's something that would have been considered inappropriate in my world. Can you visit her again and find out more, without letting her know that you're interrogating her for the investigation?"

"You want me to use my friendship with her to gain information?"

"Yes."

"Easily done. I will send her a letter this afternoon and hopefully see her tomorrow or the next day."

"Just like that?"

"I'm curious about this matter as well, and deeply concerned." She glanced at Joseph. "We all have to make sacrifices. I'm sure, should Talia ever learn of it, that she will understand why it is necessary. If not, well, I'm not sure a princess should be friends with someone conspiring against the pact."

"Then it's settled. I will be meeting with several guilds today and tomorrow to see what I can learn. It hasn't gotten me anywhere in the past but maybe this time I will learn *something*. Excuse me. I have a very busy day."

"Of course," Betha said.

Joseph bowed as Mallory left and then straightened and looked at Betha. "I guess this is good bye again."

"Yes."

"How much longer will you be here?"

"As long as I'm needed. Honestly, I'm surprised my stewards haven't sent someone looking for me yet."

"I will send any letters to Caranhall then. If you're still here I'm sure your stewards will forward them to you."

"Yes, I'm sure. Safe travels."

"And you. And good luck with your friend."

"Let's hope someone finds something soon or this investigation will never end."

7th of Thornfall, 24th Year of the 11th Rebirth
Golden Hall, Metalkin Province

"I didn't think I'd get to see you twice during your stay here!" Talia said as she welcomed Betha back into her home.

"I just couldn't stay away!" Betha said. "The suitors annoy me, the meetings bore me, you must rescue me!"

"Say no more. I have tea and snacks and a bright sunny room where we can sit and talk for the afternoon."

"That sounds like a dream come true."

"You've been busy, I take it?"

"Too busy. I never knew there were so many influential Animal People living in Golden Hall and the surrounding areas. Or that they had so many sons!"

Talia sighed. "You're so lucky. Everyone wants to meet you just because you're the princess. You have the pick of every young man. The rest of us have to struggle to be noticed!"

"I honestly find it surprising you struggle to be noticed. I thought you'd be fighting them away from the door."

"I think that's the problem. My father is very good at guarding the door, and his definition of a decent suitor is small, his definition of a good suitor even smaller!"

"Do you think he scared some of your suitors off?"

"Oh, most likely. But I've found someone new already, he's coming over this evening with his father. My father has a lot of meetings."

"Is that common for him?"

"Yes. Well, no, not when I was growing up, but this past year he's been busier than ever."

"Guild ties?"

"I actually don't know. He won't let me or Mother be in the room during the meeting, and if one of us does walk in with a letter or with refreshments the conversation stops cold until we leave. And they meet downstairs, in a special room off the pantry. There's no windows and the walls are eight-inch thick stone."

"I'm betting you tried eavesdropping more than once."

"To no avail," she said with a dramatic sigh. "I have snooped through some of his papers though. Which is how I knew to go visit that jeweller."

"I didn't know your family had ties to the Jeweller's Guild."

"Every noble Metalkin family has ties to the Jeweller's Guild somewhere, it's a matter of how influential those ties are."

"I see. Well, you're fortunate you saw that particular piece of correspondence. That necklace was amazing. Might I have another look at it? I'm considering stopping on my way back to the castle to have a look at his wares."

"Certainly." Talia rang for a serving girl and quickly instructed her to fetch the necklace down from her room. Once she had it she offered it to Betha for closer inspection.

"The colour of this stone is perfect you know. I've rarely seen so flawless." She turned the setting around in her fingers, examining the craftsmanship, paying close attention to the edges of the stone. She could see no sign that the stone had been in another setting; there was no damage at all.

"Did he tell you anything about the stone?" Betha said. "Where it came from?"

"A local mine," Talia said. "He didn't say which one."

"Well, I'm sure I could figure it out if I really needed to know, but I think that's probably a detailed enough answer for me to get one similar. I almost thought it was a stone taken from an old setting, with how low the price was."

"I know, I can't get over it either, but that stone has never been owned by anyone else before me."

"Well," Betha said, handing it back to Talia. "You're lucky to find such a beautiful piece for such a low price."

"Maybe he'll have one for you as well."

"Maybe."

After visiting a while longer Betha went out to her escort. "I need to make a stop at a jeweller's stall in the market. I have some questions for him, questions Mallory asked me to ask."

Sir Wild-Hart nodded. "Yes, Princess."

The stall was one of a dozen in a row down a narrow street. Betha was forced to climb down from her carriage and continue on foot with her guards surrounding her. She drew quite a few stares from the passing shoppers but her guards, in full armor, their swords sheathed but in plain sight, deterred anyone from approaching her.

There was a girl sitting at the stall calling to passing people about the necklaces and rings on display. When Betha stopped in front of her, her jaw dropped. "P-p-princess Jewel-Rose, it's an honour."

Betha laughed. "I'm Princess Living-Rose. I'm visiting Princess Jewel-Rose and a friend of mine recommended this shop."

"Yes. Sorry Princess Living-Rose. Welcome. Um, let me get my dad. You should speak with him."

"Hold on. Does your father make all these pieces?"

"Oh, yes Princess. He's one of the finest jewellers in the city."

"Do you know where he gets his gems from?"

"I don't know the names, Princess, I'm sorry. I assume they're all local gem cutters."

"Of course. I'll look while you fetch your father."

"Yes, Princess." The girl was off like a frightened rabbit.

The man who appeared in her place had the same dark eyes and the same black hair. He smiled and bowed. "Princess Living-Rose, this is an honour and a surprise."

"Your work comes highly recommended to me."

"Then I am twice as honoured. Is there anything here you like?"

"Quite a bit, actually. But I had a question for you. Do you ever reset old jewellery?"

"You mean, repairs?"

"No. I have some pieces that belong to the crown. The stones are lovely but the settings are not to my taste."

"Ah. No, sadly that is not something I do. I work with fresh cut stones and do some minor repairs."

"Then I'll have to find someone nearer to home. How much is this one?" She pointed to a brooch on display. The metal was burnished so the details were darker than the raised parts, and it was inlaid with small gem chips that made it glitter.

"A gift for you."

"No, you have a family to support. If I were Princess Jewel-Rose, and I could send customers your way, that would be different, but there are too many jewellers in my province for people to bother coming all this way for trinkets, even ones of this high quality."

"You've a shrewd business mind," he said. "You will bring prosperity to your people. If you were my princess I'd introduce you to my son!"

Betha chose to take that as a compliment and smiled. "Name your price."

"Fifty pieces of silver."

"I can hardly argue that. Sadly I don't have it with me."

"You would be foolish to carry so much with you in an open market. Here is my account information. Hand this to the Merchant's Bank and have them deposit the money." He handed her the slip of paper and then wrapped the brooch and handed that to her as well.

"I do have a few coppers. Give them to your daughter as a gift, for a job well done today. She'll make a fine merchant."

He accepted the coins with a bow. "My deepest thanks, Princess."

With the brooch in hand Betha walked back to her carriage and they returned to the castle where Mallory was waiting for them.

Betha unwrapped the brooch and set it on the table before her friend. "Fifty silver," she explained. "That's what he charged me."

"Even if he was giving you a bargain because of your social status, this should have cost half that again," Mallory said. "As near as I can tell. Your money is still a little strange to me."

"One hundred silver pieces is the same as a gold star, our smaller gold coin. Fifty gold stars are worth a gold sun."

"And this should be worth ...?"

"Probably a gold star. Even with the bargain, you're right, seventy-five silver pieces would still have been less than its value."

"So why price it so low? And why offer those prices to everyone?"

Before Betha could answer, Master Spirit-Light, Mallory's steward of religious affairs appeared at the door. "I'm sorry to disturb you. I must remind Princess Betha that she has dinner this evening with several suitors and her guests are beginning to arrive."

"I have to change," Betha said, looking down at her dusty day dress. "I'm sorry Mallory, we'll speak on this tomorrow."

"Of course. There's always some duty calling us."

12th of Thornfall, 24th Year of the 11th Rebirth
Golden Hall, Metalkin Province

"I'm sorry to intrude Princesses, but there is a letter here for Princess Betha. It's marked as urgent." The serving girl put the letter on the table and hurried out.

For a moment the two girls just stared at the letter then Betha wiped her hands on her napkin and picked it up.

Princess Betha,

Cloudfall has passed, and while I'm pleased you have kept us updated regarding your political endeavours in Golden Hall, we assumed you would be home days ago. As such, we've put off dealing with issues that must now be dealt with in haste and require your presence. Therefore, I am formally requesting you return to Caranhall.

There have been multiple reports in the last week of Dark Spirit attacks in some of the more remote villages and estates. The healers are doing what they can, but they do not have the space to house the possessed, especially if more attacks occur.

Among the victims are several hunters and two men who were scouting the rocky southeast corner for additional iron deposits.

News of these attacks is spreading quickly from wood camp to farm, from village to village, and we are concerned that the commoners will begin to panic if something is not done soon.

We need your guidance and assistance, and more importantly, the people need to see you, they need to know you are here and working towards keeping them safe. Your first duty is to your own people.

I know you are assisting in an investigation that affects all of us, but that is a vague thing to the commoners facing Dark Spirits each evening. For them, the most important thing is their immediate, day-to-day security and prosperity. And for that, we need you home.

Master Adalard Wise-Ranger

Betha calmly folded the letter, put it aside, and returned to her meal. "I need to soon," she said.

"Then I guess we'll have a busy couple of days ahead of us," Mallory said.

After dinner they retired to Mallory's room to discuss their plans. There was no way they could do everything before Betha was forced to leave, but at least they would have a solid plan of action for Mallory to follow in the days and weeks to come.

15th of Thornfall, 24th Year of the 11th Rebirth
Golden Hall, Metalkin Province

By the time Betha and Mallory finished their breakfast and made their way down to the courtyard, the carriage was already loaded and the horses saddled. The only people in the courtyard, aside from Betha's escort, were a handful of stable lads and Prince Kaelen.

"I didn't think you'd come to see me off," Betha said.

"I'll not let it be said that the Metalkin make poor hosts," he replied.

"I certainly never said, or even implied that it was all Metalkin who shirked their duties to their guests," Betha said. *Just you.* She left the last unsaid for Mallory's sake.

"It was nice to spend some time with you," Mallory said. "I wish we didn't live so far apart. I wish we had telephones."

"Invent them," Betha said.

"I wish I could. I certainly made use of them, but I don't understand them enough to make one!"

"That's too bad. I'll miss the sound of your voice." Betha embraced her friend. "Take care and write me if you need anything. Or if you find anything."

"I will. And the same goes for you, okay?"

"Of course." She turned to her carriage without bothering to say good-bye to Kaelen. Along the way she stopped one of the stable boys, speaking softly to him in hopes that Kaelen wouldn't hear. "Who saw to the carriage horses being harnessed?"

"I'm not sure, Princess."

"Have Master White-Hart double check them on whatever excuse he sees fit."

"Right away Princess."

Betha glanced back at Kaelen. He had one hand possessively on Mallory's shoulder and his face was set in a deep scowl. Mallory was smiling but Betha was sure some of the joy had already faded from her friend's eyes. *Something is not right here, and I hate to leave but things are worse at home and I am needed. Somehow, I think I will be back here before long.*

When the final check of the tack was complete, Betha and her escort headed for the main gates and the road west to Caranhall.

20th of Thornfall, 24th Year of the 11th Rebirth
Caranhall, Province of the Animal People

Riding into Caranhall the second time, Betha studied what she could see of it from her carriage windows as intently as she had that first time, a little over a month earlier. Until her wedding, she and Taeya would be the only princesses who had seen all five capital cities, and she had spent the most amount of time visiting the other capitals. She was coming to realize that comparing them on a simple scale of grandeur wasn't quite accurate.

The difference between Dinas Rhosyn and Caranhall wasn't one of grandness, but one of layout. Dinas Rhosyn sprawled. The castle was more of a palace than a fortress with terraces and gardens everywhere. The city too sprawled and blended almost seamlessly with the fields around it. Caranhall could not sprawl, not when it was built atop a great hill as it was, though the city did give way around the edges to pasture lands and farms the same way Dinas Rhosyn did.

Golden Hall was expansive, a palace like Dinas Rhosyn, but with fewer gardens. The city around it was dense with people and buildings which were all encased within the city walls. Stones Shore was a fortress within a walled city. The Sun Temple was a temple, a castle, and a university interlocked around a central courtyard. The city that sustained it, located just down the road, was bustling but not dense the way Golden Hall was, and was walled without being oppressive like Stones Shore.

Each capital has its own flavour, just like the people who live there, and the people who built them.

Her stewards were waiting for her as she climbed down from the carriage. She smiled as sweetly as she could but that didn't alter their somber demeanor one bit.

"So, you've decided to return," Adalard said.

"I was busy. I returned as soon as I was able."

"I hope it is soon enough," Adalard said. "Come. There is much we need to discuss." He half-turned away from her.

"I'd like to bathe first and eat."

"We have food waiting. Your bath can wait until we're finished."

She stopped walking and stared at him. His tone was firm, but not cruel, but it was the first time he'd directly contradicted her. "I'm covered in dust from the road …"

"The chair won't mind."

"I mind!"

He turned back to her. "Princess Betha, if you wanted a gracious and accommodating welcome to your arrival you should have returned earlier. I have dealt with the issues as best I can on your behalf for days now while you dallied about in Golden Hall, neglecting your duties. Your presence is required. NOW. Your bath can wait."

For a moment princess and steward stared at each other, Betha quickly debating her options and calculating the likelihood of any succeeding in getting her a bath before this meeting. The look in his eyes, solid, serious, absolutely humourless, shut down every idea she could come up with in the short time available to her.

"Fine. But I would ask at least for a basin so that I might wash my hands and face before I eat."

"We'll have one brought up. Come."

Through all this Dritan Bright-Star just watched quietly. Now he smiled and followed them up to the study.

When Betha had washed and they'd all settled around the table with their food, Master Wise-Ranger began. "While you were gone several issues were raised. First, the matter of your suitors grows ever more pressing. Keep in mind that the nobles were patiently waiting while Taeya took an extended trip to Dinas Rhosyn. For you to delay your return, and then leave so soon after arriving, it has made for some very noisy nobles."

"I can imagine," Betha said. "Are they angry at me for not being here, or you for telling them I'm not here."

"Both, I'm sure, but they're pointing it all at me since they don't see open hostility towards you as a wise decision."

"Then I'm sorry for putting you in that situation." They were the right words to say though at this point she wasn't sure how sincere they were. She *was* sorry that everyone was yelling at Master Wise-Ranger, she actually liked him, but she was still feeling miffed at his reprimand earlier.

"While your apology is nice, it doesn't solve the problem."

"I know I need to meet with people. I've just been feeling unsettled since this whole ordeal started."

"You haven't given yourself a chance to settle. You're barely studying, your teachers have been reporting on your progress, or lack thereof. You haven't visited the horses or the hawks, you haven't made arrangements to meet with the guilds beyond the one dinner."

"You're saying I'm not making an effort."

"I'm saying people aren't seeing an effort. You chose to travel to Golden Hall, you chose to stay there for an entire month. People see that. People see you turning your back on your people."

"I was serving our people in Golden Hall. I met with the guilds there. I was helping Mallory find the information she needed to put an end to the Academic Diplomats and the harm they are doing to other provinces, to *my* province and *my* people. And I was helping Mallory get her bearings, since *no one* else seems willing to. Maybe that doesn't seem like a benefit to us, but she can't be a strong ally if she can't be a strong leader, and she can't be a strong leader if she has no idea how our history or politics work."

"All noble claims that no one here cares much about when people are dying," Dritan said.

"Dying? What do you mean, 'people are dying'? What haven't you told me?"

Adalard glared at Dritan then cleared his throat. "Moving on, there has been an increase in Dark Spirit attacks since Taeya left for Vonica's wedding at the Sun Temple. We had hoped that her return and subsequent marriage would halt the attacks, but now she is not coming back. I did briefly mention this in my last letter to you while you were in Golden Hall."

"But why wasn't I told about these before I left for Golden Hall? I was here for an entire month!"

"We were waiting for reports to come in. We needed to know if your arrival had improved things. Since you were *only* here for a single month before leaving again, and since you were away for as long as you were here, your presence here has not improved the situation at all."

"In fact, reports suggest that it's worse, and spreading along the northern coast into Metalkin territory."

"Spreading into … has Mallory been made aware of this?"

"I don't know," Adalard admitted. "I know about it because it is affecting fishing villages along the coast. I'm not sure they've reported it to the Metalkin guards, or if the guards have reported it to the capital."

"I will write Mallory and inform her," Betha said. She turned to Master Bright-Star. "Write the priest in Golden Hall and make sure he does the rituals with her."

"I'm only a steward. I can make recommendations but not give orders, especially not to the priests."

"I'm sure you can impress upon him how important this is. You hail from the same province, you hold the same ideals."

"I'll do what I can," Dritan said, inclining his head.

"Thank-you. Now, I suppose you want me to undertake the ritual here as well."

"It would be a wise idea," Dritan said. "Your position was made official by High Priest Silver-Cloud but that ritual was performed in Dinas Rhosyn. No official ceremony has been held here. I don't think we need a full coronation, but it would be best if you stood in the temple and announced your allegiance to our spirit animals and to your new role in Airon's pact."

"Right. So, the protection ritual plus additional oaths. We'll need the better part of a day then."

"I'll make the arrangements," Dritan said.

21st of Thornfall, 24th Year of the 11th Rebirth
Caranhall, Province of the Animal People

There weren't many petitions to be heard, thankfully. Master Wise-Ranger had dutifully taken care of the small details in her absence, preventing a massive backlog of people waiting for assistance. The shortness of the list was its only saving grace as each case to be heard was tiresome, long-winded, and complicated.

The first complaint was presented by an older man in fine clothes. "My name is Gerald Sun-Stag and I have been selected to speak on behalf of most of the great families of our province. We are deeply concerned by the delays you continue to present in the search for your prince. It has been two full months since you were named the Carainhithe Princess by the High Priest of Airon and you've yet to meet with a single suitor!"

"I met one suitor while I was at the Sun Temple and almost a dozen while I was in Golden Hall," Betha said. He opened his mouth to protest but she raised a hand, silencing him. "I am meeting with four prominent young men today, and another four tomorrow. After which time I will be travelling …"

That one word stirred up grumbles and whispers from the gallery.

"I will be travelling around the province performing protection rituals and visiting with many of the great families. I'll be able to meet most of the suitors at or near their own estates. The rest I will meet when I return."

Gerald just stared at her.

"Weren't the families notified? I was told arrangements were made with the families already. I'll be staying at several estates in the next few weeks and meeting many suitors."

"Of course," Gerald stammered. "I'm sure all is in readiness for your arrival. Uh, thank-you for anticipating our concerns."

"I anticipate them because I share them. This province needs a prince. I'll hear the next petition please."

The others were guild matters, often relating to something Betha had requested for her investigation, or something one of the other princesses had requested. In each case Betha firmly insisted that every record, note, name, or testimony requested in connection with the various on-going investigations be provided, unaltered, and with all haste. After repeating the answer four times Betha was ready to scream.

Fortunately, Master Wise-Ranger chose that moment to announce, "That was the final petition. Princess Betha Living-Rose will return to court in two weeks time. Thank-you."

After court she met with Corin Sky-Fowl, the Captain of the Guard, to discuss increased security for both the capital city and the communities along the northern coast.

"That's all the men we have," he said. "And there is only so much they can do. They need to sleep and eat or they're useless as guards."

Betha sighed. "This would be easier if the outer walls were better."

"We've no evidence that walls stop Dark Spirits."

"We've no evidence of people being attacked in their homes."

"Homes and city walls are two different things. We have to make do with what we have."

"What is the quickest and safest option to increase our ability to fight these Dark Spirits?"

"Train more men. We don't need a permanent force, but if we trained some of the commoners to defend themselves …"

"They're not likely to rebel against the crown so I see no reason they shouldn't be taught to fight. But no younger that sixteen. I'll not have them saying that I'm throwing the children to the monsters."

"I'll make the necessary arrangements."

"Thank-you."

She didn't like any of the dresses in her closet. They were overwhelmingly brown, for one thing, and cut in simple, practical fashions. For day dresses they did well enough, but she could hardly tell the difference between her daily wear and her formal wear. The cinchers were nice and obviously flattering, but they were all leather. The workmanship was exquisite but that didn't change the fact that they, like the dresses, were brown. Even the hair combs were carved wood, gifts from the Evergrowth, or worked in brass, gifts from the Metalkin. The only ones that weren't brown were white, and those she shied away from after the serving girl explained they were carved from animal bone.

The cinchers and hair combs were all adorned with the images of hawks or horses. *At least it's not pigs,* she thought as the girls did her hair. She turned down the necklaces she was offered, choosing one from her personal collection instead. The gold chain and setting and the polished red stone stood out like a blazing sun but at least it made her feel more like herself.

With her chin held high she made her way to the dining hall where she had previously hosted the local guild representatives. Adalard was waiting for her outside the door.

"Are you here to threaten me into behaving my best?" she said.

His eyes widened. "I wasn't planning on it. Did your former stewards threaten you often?"

"All the time."

"Would you like me to threaten you? I'm sure I can think up some suitably horrible punishments."

"I'm sure you could but I'd rather you didn't."

"Then we're in agreement on that. No, I just came because I realized this would be your first official meeting with your potential suitors and thought you might need some ... guidance."

"What sort of guidance?"

"I'm sure you've noticed that the Evergrowth and the Carainhithe are similar in a lot of ways. They work with their hands and feel a strong connection to the land. Their farms are important to them, and even twice-named families still have wealth in herds. Prosperity here is measured differently than it is in say the Metalkin province."

"I'll keep that in mind," she said, though the thought of spending the entire meal discussing goats and sheep did not appeal to her.

"Don't worry, the Carainhithe are not nearly as reserved as the Evergrowth. They are more like you, blunt, honest, but playful. They are not at all shy."

The door opened, and Dritan appeared in the opening. "Ah, Princess Betha. I'm pleased to see you're here on time."

"If she's at all late, it's my fault," Adalard said. He bowed to the princess. "Good luck this evening."

"Thank-you." She smoothed her skirt, though she wasn't sure a wrinkle would do much to spoil so simple an outfit and smiled at Dritan. "I'm ready."

"Good. Your suitors are waiting. I will introduce you to them."

The four young men seated around the table stood as she and her steward approached. Back in Evergrowth she'd have been expected to appear demure, her eyes down, her hands neatly clasped, but Adalard's words comforted her and made her bold, so she openly studied the four men as she walked. They were well dressed, tall, and lean. They stood straight but without forced stiffness, their relaxed shoulders and easy smiles conveying comfortable confidence.

"Princess Betha, may I introduce to you Master Noah Hoof-Shield, he is a relative of the previous prince."

"Prince Logan Hoof-Shield was my father's uncle," Noah said with a bow.

Betha just smiled and nodded. He was the shortest of the four and had the roundest face. His voice didn't grate on her nerves but it was lacking the warm depth that she truly found appealing.

"This is Sebastian Fire-Hawk, Eli Ancient-Steed, and Corey Hound-Blaze," he went on. Each of the young men bowed in turn. They all had some varying shade of dirty blonde or light brown hair, all cut to a similar length. The only real way she could tell them apart was their clothing. Noah in brown, Sebastian in wine-red, Eli in grey with silver trimmings, and Corey in linen with gold trimmings.

They were all staring at her.

She cleared her throat. "It's a pleasure to meet all of you. I look forward to the beginning of a strong friendship with each of you. Even if none of you are my prince, you will all be leaders within our province and I look forward to a prosperous relationship with each of you and your families."

Next to her, Dritan smiled. He patted her shoulder. "I'll leave you then. They will bring the first course in immediately. Ring if you need anything." He nodded to the young men and went out.

Betha stiffly took her seat. She was seated between Noah and Sebastian whom she guessed were the most prominent of the suitors on her list, and likely had been among the first to meet Taeya too.

She turned to Noah. "I'm surprised I'm not meeting with an entire room full of your cousins and second cousins," she said. Servants brought in bowls of summer soup and a platter of thickly sliced, still-warm dark-brown bread.

"You could, if you'd like, but the room would be full of gossiping girls. I was the only boy born at an acceptable time to be considered. The others are either girls, too old, or too young."

"I see. Lucky for you."

"It didn't work out that way. I was turned down after my first meeting with Princess Taeya. Now, it seems, there's a chance for my luck to change."

His smile was making her uncomfortable, so she looked away, reaching for her glass and letting her gaze sweep her surroundings. Eli was sitting on the other side of Noah, looking bored. Corey sat across the table, intent on his soup.

Sebastian reached for his glass just as Betha's gaze passed that way. She gasped. "What happened to your hand?"

The back of Sebastian's hand was a scrawl of silvery-pink lines that disappeared beneath the cuff of his sleeve. He reached over and covered his hand with the other, drawing them both down onto his lap. His gaze dropped too. "It's nothing."

"It looks like it was painful," Betha said.

"It was a long time ago," he said. "The healer did a very good job. I'm lucky I have full use of the hand."

Corey was snickering into his hand. "Sebastian doesn't want to tell you that he was attacked by a hawk, not when his family are all famous austringers and have worked for generations with the Sun Hawks."

Sebastian kept his eyes down. Noah and Eli frowned but said nothing.

"How old were you when it happened?" she said.

"Ten years old."

"They must have been very deep to scar so badly. They remind me of Princess Vonica." And Corey's reaction reminded her of all the cruel children at the Sun Temple who had made Vonica miserable. Her usually blunt attitude softened, at least towards Sebastian.

"I'd heard she was badly scarred," Noah said.

Betha nodded. "She was in an accident as a child, she doesn't like to speak of it either. She was badly burned. I'm sure you often wear a glove to hide it."

He nodded.

"I wouldn't worry too much about it. And I'm sorry I brought attention to it."

"Most of the people I work with are used to them. If I'm going somewhere new, I cover them. That wasn't an option today though."

"Gloves at the dinner table would have been bad form," Corey agreed, still smirking. "Though I'm sure if you wore them to the next dance you'd look absolutely fetching. You could borrow a pair from your older sister."

Sebastian's cheeks turned a deep shade of pink.

Now Betha frowned. "You can lend a pair to Corey while you're at it. They might help disguise his boorish behaviour."

Next to her Noah nearly spit his drink back into his glass as he bit back a sudden laugh. Eli grinned openly as Corey scowled. Whatever clever retort Corey might have come up with was silenced by the appearance of the kitchen servants. Two worked to quickly clear the soup dishes while four others set out platters of smoked meats, sliced cheese, crusty bread, and fresh fruits, and placed a clean plate in front of each person. They worked quietly and efficiently, soon disappearing back through the side door.

"I suppose you and I will be working closely in the years to come if you work with the Sun Hawks," Betha said.

"I don't work directly with the hawks," Sebastian said. "I deal more with the accounting side of their upkeep and training. The guild here trains all of the Sun Hawks for all of the provinces."

"Then I am certain we will be working together." Betha smiled sweetly and turned to Corey. "And what is it that you do?"

"My family works with hounds," he said, puffing his chest up.

Betha gave a dismissive wave of her hand and reached for some fruit. "I have little interest in or use for hounds. I'm sure they're useful in their own way though."

"Yes, they are. We use them for …"

She waved again, silencing him. "And you, Eli? What does your family do?" From the corner of her eye she could see Corey's cheeks turning red.

"My family owns a large estate that manages multiple farms; goats, pigs, sheep. We work closely with the weaver's guild since they know what to do with all that wool the sheep keep growing."

"I like to see that," Betha said. "We need more cooperation between guilds."

"The weaver's guild is unique in that it employs people from three of the five provinces, and in that the majority of the guild workers are women."

"Three?" Betha said.

"Yes. Carainhithe to work with the wool, Evergrowth to work with the linen which is spun from flax cotton, and Metalkin to work the cloth of gold and cloth of silver."

"You say your family has close ties to the Weaver's Guild?"

Eli nodded.

"You must make arrangements for me to meet with them. I had a disastrous meeting with the local guild representatives earlier. If we're to start working together again I'm going to need help."

"I'll see what I can do," Eli said. His delight was evident in his eyes and smile.

"You sound like you're very concerned about the pact," Noah said.

Betha nodded. "With the mix up between myself and Princess Taeya, and the widespread corruption I think we all should be concerned with the state of things and the strength of the pact."

"So, what did happen in Evergrowth?" Corey said, leaning forward. "There have been all sorts of rumours."

"And it was very upsetting, and I don't wish to speak of it," Betha said.

"Rightly so," Noah said. "I could imagine that it was distressing and very personal." He shot a glare at Corey before smiling at Betha again. "My family was involved in the pact, right from the beginning."

"There he goes," Corey muttered.

"Has there been more than one prince in your family?" Betha asked.

"Oh, no, nothing quite so grand. We were among the first to train with the Sun Swords to stand guard against the Dark Spirits. One of my ancestors led the escort to the gate to find the first rebirth of the Carainhithe princess. Members of my family still serve in the royal guard."

"That's an honourable history," Betha said politely.

"When would you be interested in that meeting?" Eli said.

"Oh, it would have to wait until the end of Thornfall I'm afraid. As much as I want to start repairing relations between the guilds, I do have to travel around the province this month to perform rituals that will protect the people from Dark Spirit attacks."

"We've stopped four attacks since Taeya left for the Sun Temple," Noah said.

"And failed to stop a lot more," Corey said.

"We can't be everywhere at once. We need more guards, and more Sun Swords."

"We need to regain balance and harmony," Eli said. "We all know the Dark Spirits are drawn to chaos."

"And until then, someone has to protect us," Noah insisted.

"Are you trained?" Betha said.

"Who, me?" Noah said, a hand going to his chest.

"Yes. You've spoken at length about the achievements of your family, but what about you?"

"I know how to handle a sword," Noah said. "And I'm not afraid to stand against the Dark Spirits."

"Have you seen one?"

"N-no, Princess."

"Have any of you?"

They all shook their heads.

"Neither have I. I'm not sure I want to." They all looked relieved. "Not after I witnessed a possession first hand. That was terrifying enough. I don't want to see the thing that caused it."

"You've seen a possession?" Sebastian said. His eyes were wide.

"What was it like? Do they really turn wild?" Corey asked.

"Give the victim and his family some respect," Eli snapped. "Possession is a horrible thing, not entertainment for you."

"How are we supposed to recognize possession if no one will talk about it?" Corey snapped back.

"Enough," Betha said. "If you want to learn about possession, go speak with the healers. It's too horrible a subject to discuss in detail over dinner."

For a moment there was silence. Corey was stabbing angrily at the food on his plate and glowering at everyone. The others looked stiff and awkward.

"There is no easy answer," Betha said. "I need a prince. The island needs to regain balance and we need to root out the corruption that's taken hold. In the meanwhile, we do need to be able to defend ourselves. Master Sky-Fowl and I were discussing that very thing earlier today. I fear we'll all be needed for something, fighting or politics, before this is settled."

"Wise words," Eli said.

She wasn't surprised to find both Dritan and Adalard waiting for her in the study. Keren curtsied at the door then went on her way, leaving Betha to deal with her stewards alone.

"How was dinner?"

"Pleasant," Betha said. "I'm not sure that any of them are my prince, though."

"It was just a first meeting," Dritan said.

"Oh, I know. Don't make any rash decisions and all that. No, there's only the one that I'd rather not see again."

"Which one?"

"Corey Hound-Blaze."

Adalard chuckled and shook his head. "I warned you."

"He was at the top of the list with Taeya, there was no reason to exclude him now," Dritan said. "It would have been insulting to change the order."

"No reason," Adalard said. "Betha, why do you not want to meet with Master Hound-Blaze again?"

"He's arrogant, cruel, and not the least bit interesting."

"I'd think you'd be attracted to someone blunt and proud," Dritan said.

"I may be tactless on occasion and have little use for fools or little patience for the daily tedium of court, but I am not cruel. Eli and Noah were proud, and it is obvious they've been in competition before, but they are not cruel. Sebastian on the other hand is clever, if a little quiet. I doubt he's my prince either, but his family does work that is important to the crown so fostering a positive relationship with them is key. And at least I can stand speaking to him."

"See," Adalard said. "It wasn't just Taeya. I told you that boy was no good. Not the sort of person I would want to see ruling."

"It's not up to either of us," Dritan said.

"It's up to me," Betha said. "I will not rule out the other three, because it is my duty to give my suitors a fair chance and I really have very little to compare to. I will not meet with this Corey Hound-Blaze again."

"Well, one firm no out of four potential suitors isn't bad," Dritan said. "Taeya dismissed them all after the first meeting."

"I can see why. None of them have that down-to-earth simplicity she is so fond of in Francis. Not to speak ill of the man, of course."

"Of course," Adalard said, his expression obviously bemused. "Just an example of your barely tactful honesty. Your previous stewards did warn us."

She blushed. "Is everything ready for my trip? When the day arrives I want to leave early in the morning. I don't want any last-minute delays."

"You've done this sort of thing before, so we don't have to remind you to be careful and to listen to the advice of your guards."

She smiled sweetly at Adalard. "Of course not. The guards know this province better than I do." *And I'll listen right up until I need to escape.*

"Arrangements have been made with the necessary families. You will have safe places to sleep, and at the same time, you'll have the opportunity to meet several more of your suitors, and their families."

"Thank-you. I hope that will take care of some of the anger my visit to Golden Hall caused."

"The estate priests have been contacted as well and all have been supplied with the necessary prayers and rituals," Dritan added.

"Thank-you," Betha said again, less enthusiastically this time. "Is there anything else that needs my attention this evening? I'd like to turn in early so that I can get an early start tomorrow. I need to pack, and we have the ritual tomorrow morning."

"I think we will survive another week or so without you in the capital," Adalard said. "At least this time it's for a good reason."

"We made lots of progress while I was in Golden Hall," she said. "And I think Mallory benefitted greatly from my assistance."

"So you said upon your return," Adalard said. "Go, we will see you in the temple in the morning."

22nd of Thornfall, 24th Year of the 11th Rebirth
Caranhall, Province of the Animal People

    Betha was starting to hate ceremonies and rituals of all kinds but most especially the protection rituals. The dry, monotone voice of the priest, the heavy smell of incense, the standing around waiting for her turn to intone some repetitive reply, the expectation that she'd make some heartfelt plea to Airon every time, it had bored her at first but now that boredom had shifted into loathing. And she couldn't complain to anyone because the rituals were for the good of the island, part of her duty as a princess, something she was supposed to be fully supportive of.

    It's not that I want the island and everyone here to come to a horrible end, I'm just tired of standing in the middle of temples saying the same prayers over and over again.

    There was another option, she knew, and that was find her prince and uproot all of the corruption in the guilds and the bank. The latter was going to be a lot of hard work but even that was preferable to the meetings and dinners and dances with young men who smelled of horse and leather.

    She had yet another such dinner tonight with four more suitors, all of whom lived in the capital and came from politically influential families, and nothing short of making herself physically ill was going to get her out of it.

I should have invited Talia to come back with me for a visit, at least then dinner tonight would be interesting. Or Joseph. I'd rather have dinner with Joseph.

The priest was winding up the final prayer. He turned to Betha, his expression expectant.

She took a deep breath and began the speech she'd prepared that morning. "I stand here, a devoted servant of Airon, to renew my commitment to his sacred pact and to preserve the peace and prosperity of the Isle of Light. I pledge to do my duties to the best of my abilities and to be open to the guidance of the Sun God and the Spirits of my people. May Airon continue to guide and protect us."

"May his light shine upon us," the priest said. After a moment of silence acolytes began putting out the candles that had been placed around the room. The priest, an older man named Honourable Soul-Spark, limped over to her. "My thanks, Princess Living-Rose. I hope this ritual, and the ones you perform in the coming days, will stem the tide of attacks we've recently experienced along the northwestern coast."

His stuffy speech pattern made Betha grit her teeth. She missed Baraq and his more laid-back, normal way of dealing with people. "Yes, I hope so as well."

"I look forward to performing your wedding in the coming weeks."

"We would be fortunate to celebrate so soon," she said. "However, with my travels I don't foresee a wedding being possible before the end of the month."

"No, of course not. But sooner, rather than later, would be for the benefit of us all."

"No one is more aware of that than I am," Betha said. *And I'd appreciate it if everyone would stop reminding me about it.* "If you'll excuse me?"

"Of course, Princess." He bowed and took a step back allowing her to retreat to the relative safety of her rooms.

She had a quiet afternoon, for which she was thankful. She was supposed to be studying, and she'd even pulled out the book of Carainhithe words, but she wasn't reading it. Instead she was rereading the letters from Joseph and daydreaming about their time together in Golden Hall.

When the girls arrived to dress her for dinner, she scrambled to hide the letters before they came in.

The dull brown dresses put a damper on her happy mood and she went down to the dining room feeling no excitement for the meeting at hand.

Master Bright-Star introduced her to four more suitors: Edward Sun-Trout, Davon Mares-Grace, Charles Mares-Grace, and Lionel Horse-Spirit.

This dinner was far less interesting than the last. All four of these men were braggarts and spent the entire meal competing with each other with their outrageous tales of hunts and achievements, none of which impressed Betha in the slightest. All of these young men were first-born sons of first-born sons and were all heirs to their various estates and titles. Their sole job going forward would be to boss around a steward who would manage investments and workers on their behalf.

She could barely get a word in except when they invited her opinion on their grand tales. She merely gritted her teeth and smiled and nodded, keeping her true opinion to herself.

By the end of the meal she still didn't know how they felt about the pact of the corruption on the island or if any of them had been in contact with the Academic Diplomats. She didn't want to meet any of them again but she knew that wouldn't go over well with her stewards.

When she marched into the study later that evening to report she firmly said, "I want all four of those young men moved to the bottom of the list, and the next time I meet them, don't group them together."

Adalard and Dritan stared at her. Finally, Dritan coughed and said, "I take it the meal did not go well?"

"They are all four of them loud, arrogant, proud, and more interested in competing with each other than actually communicating with me. I couldn't stand any of them."

"You sound very sure," Dritan said.

"What I'm not sure of, is if it's just an act of bravado to fit in, or if that's how they really are."

"Hence, splitting them up."

"Precisely."

Dritan nodded and made some notes on a paper he produced from one of his many pockets. "Well, I must commend you on keeping an open mind, and for providing such specific feedback."

"They've exhausted me. I want to leave early so I'm turning in early. Do not disturb me until breakfast tomorrow."

"Of course," Adalard said. "Good-night."

When she'd gone Dritan let out a whoosh of breath. "That was, intense."

"Taeya was never so certain in her reasons," Adalard said. "Don't you remember? All the 'I don't know' and 'maybe not' and 'I'd prefer if I didn't have to'? It drove us both to the brink of insanity. We never knew what she wanted."

"Oh, Betha has no trouble making her desires known. I'm just not sure her desires have the best interest of this province at heart."

"She's undertaking a difficult journey for the good of her people, and she has met with eight suitors in two days. She'll be meeting with seven at the next dinner."

"She won't like that."

"She's the one who wanted to do the meetings this way. Besides, at least she can get it over and done with and appease all the nobles."

"Do we know what we'll do if she turns them all down?"

"Find an excuse for her to meet every eligible male of every social statues in five provinces, I guess," Adalard replied.

"Good heavens," Dritan said. "I can't imagine the paperwork."

"Then let's hope it doesn't come to that."

23rd of Thornfall, 24th Year of the 11th Rebirth
Caranhall, Province of the Animal People

Betha's trunks were loaded the night before and she was able to leave immediately after an early breakfast, as planned. She wished the windows of her carriage were larger so that she could see more of the city as they passed through it, but her sightseeing would have to wait now until she returned.

Once at the base of the hill they circled north, leaving the city through a different gate than on Betha's previous trip. They pushed north at a steady pace, pausing only to distribute food and water the horses. Their first destination was an estate on the coast, dangerously close to where the attacks had taken place.

Both Master Wise-Ranger and Master Bright-Star had argued against her travelling here, but she'd insisted. "This is where I am needed most. I will be safe within the estate walls."

In the end her stewards had given in, but had assigned two extra guards to her escort and had instructed everyone that she was to leave the estates as early as possible the day after each ritual so that she wouldn't be caught out in the dark at any time.

They arrived at the estate shortly before dinner and were unloaded and indoors well before dark.

Their host was an older couple, Lord and Lady Honour-Hoof. They and the Hoof-Shield family traced their family trees back to brothers, each of whom was honoured separately with a second name.

Betha smiled and nodded through the meal as Lord Honour-Hoof rambled on and on about the history of the two great houses.

Lady Honour-Hoof slipped into one of the rare pauses in her husband's stories and said, "Perhaps you can continue another time. I'm sure Princess Living-Rose is tired from her long journey. We've made the trip to the capital before and we both know it's a hard push to make it in a day. She must have left very early this morning."

"Yes, I did," Betha said.

"Of course," Lord Honour-Hoof said. "You've had enough to eat? Is there anything else we can get for you?"

"I'm fine, thank-you. Just a good night's rest, that's all I need."

"I'll show you to your room," Lady Honour-Hoof said. She patted her husband's shoulder and headed for the door with Betha hurrying after her. Out in the hall, Lady Honour-Hoof said, "I apologize for my husband. He thinks he's interesting."

"I'll admit, history was never my favourite subject."

"He only enjoys it because he gets to relive the glory of his forefathers. Hopefully tomorrow there will be enough other guests around to keep him occupied."

Betha smiled. At first glance, Betha had assumed Lady Honour-Hoof to be just another noble wife, quiet, agreeable, prone to saying, 'yes dear', while never speaking their mind. She was pleased to see the independence and sass beneath the polite social mask.

"Here's your room. If you need anything at all, just ring. And I'll have your breakfast tray sent up to you so that you can eat in peace in the morning."

"Thank-you. It would have been rude of me to ask."

"The way my husband gets on it would be rude of me not to offer. Good-night, Princess."

"Good-night."

24th of Thornfall, 24th Year of the 11th Rebirth
Honour-Hoof Estate, Province of the Animal People

Betha had been through all this before in Evergrowth. She ate breakfast in her room then dressed and went down to the waiting carriage. The chapel wasn't far from the manor house and she was quickly bustled inside before a group could form around her carriage.

The priest was old, older than the one in Caranhall, and walked with a frustratingly slow shuffle. Fortunately, he had a young acolyte who'd taken care of setting up the candles and incense earlier in the morning.

When the ritual was finally over Betha exited the chapel to find that most of the village was there to greet her. She smiled and waved as her guards helped her through the crowd to her carriage.

As she was stepping into the carriage one of her guards cleared his throat. "Maybe a brief word for them?" he said softly. "For many this will be the only time in their entire lives that they see a Princess of Airon."

Betha refrained from rolling her eyes, plastered a smile on her face, and turned to the crowd. "My thanks for the warm welcome," she said. "May Airon bless this village with prosperity and protection."

A cheer went up around her and she retreated into the dim interior of her carriage.

There were seven suitors, their parents, Betha's hosts, and three young noble born girls at dinner that evening. Betha had trouble keeping everyone's names straight and remembering which profession went with which family. Fortunately, two suitors were cousins of men she'd met at the capital and had the look of their kin, there were two other sets of cousins among the seven that made the matter at turns simpler and more complicated.

The young men dominated the conversation, at least the part that Betha could readily hear. The parents were wrapped up on their own discussion and the two only briefly and occasionally overlapped.

By the time Betha was able to turn in the only thing she felt was overwhelmed. No single suitor stood out to her, but at least she'd be able to report to her stewards that she wasn't planning to cross any of them off the list either.

She slipped into bed and into a restless sleep, her dreams a dance of faces she couldn't name and voices she didn't recognize.

25th of Thornfall, 24th Year of the 11th Rebirth
Northern Highway, Province of the Animal People

Fortunately, the need to leave early kept Lord Honour-Hoof relatively quiet at breakfast. He kept his conversation centered on the journey ahead: did they have enough food and water, did they need any other supplies, did they need additional guards or guides?

"Thank-you for the generous offers but we are ready to go and have no needs that need to be met at this time," Betha replied.

They made it out of the gates at a reasonable hour though they had to push the horses at a good pace for most of the day and only stopped for the midday meal.

The view to the north was rocky and open from what Betha could see as they bumped along the road. Somewhere off to her right was the coast, dotted with tiny fishing villages. She'd been able to see the water from the walls of the Honour-Hoof estate, but not from the road which had meandered southwards. They were headed west and somewhere ahead of them was more coast. To the south it was more treed, though not as heavy as the Great Forest between Evergrowth and the Sun Temple.

They stopped in a shady spot along the side of the road to eat. There was a narrow stream here, spilling out of the trees and gurgling happily towards the coast. Someone had built a crude wooden bridge over the place where the water cut through the road.

Betha sat on a small stool, eating alone, while the guards and servants ate their own meals and looked after the horses. When her food was gone she stood and stretched, wandering along the small roadside clearing. There was a path leading into the trees, probably a hunters' trail, it wasn't as worn as the road, the ground covered in leaves. The sunlight trickled through the leaves, casting dappled shadows on the forest floor. The dance of light kept her attention and she stood, staring into the spaces between the trees.

What is out there? Madam Olga said I should come here to find answers, but all I've found is more of the same. Maybe I'm looking in the wrong places. Maybe I should just walk off into the woods. Maybe the answers will be there.

She took a step towards the trees, the whispering wind calling to her, urging her closer.

"Princess?"

She almost ignored the voice but the touch at her elbow jolted her back into the here and now and she startled, turning to see who had called her.

"Princess?" the maid said again. "We're ready to go. We need to keep moving if we want to make it to the estate before dark."

"Of course," Betha said. "Let's go."

She walked calmly towards the carriage without looking back at the trees.

The horses were tired as they clattered into the courtyard of the Sun-Trout estate. Even more so than at the Honour-Hoof estate, the smell of the sea and of fish were strong here, so strong that Betha crinkled her nose upon exiting the carriage, bringing her hand to her face.

"Apologies," said the girl who waited for her. "The wind is from the west today. When the wind is from the south or east it's not so bad."

"I'll get used to it," Betha said through gritted teeth though she very much doubted it. "You work for the Sun-Trout family?"

"No, Princess. My name is Aubrey Sun-Trout. I'm Lord Sun-Trout's niece."

"Oh, my apologies." *It really is difficult to tell the nobles from the commoners; the way people dress here.*

"Not necessary. I'll show you to your room. We're having a bath drawn and you have to see these candles we have. The local healer makes them."

Betha didn't know what could be so exciting about candles but she was eager to get out of the courtyard. *Maybe the scent won't be as strong indoors.*

Inside the hall the scent of fish went from 'overpowering' to 'noticeable'. "Well, it's better at least," Betha muttered.

"I promise, it gets better still. Come on." Aubrey led the way at a quick pace, excitement lending her steps speed. She burst into the guest room with a grin. "Isn't it wonderful?"

Betha didn't have to ask what Aubrey was talking about. She stepped into the room and was immediately enveloped in the scent of roses. "How …?"

Aubrey laughed and clapped her hands. "I knew you'd love it. The healer started making them to help with my aunt's headaches."

"The candles are doing this?" Betha said, waving her hand vaguely at the room."

"Yes. Close the door so it stays in the room."

Betha was happy to oblige. "But how? I don't understand. Candles are just candles. They don't smell like anything, except a bit of smoke sometimes."

"That's the wick and these candles will smell that way too, especially when you blow them out. When the candles are still wet and setting, she mixes rose oil into the wax. When the candles burn it releases the smell."

"Rose oil?"

"Oh, I don't understand how she does it. She explained it to me. Something about pressing rosehips and soaking them in something and I lost interest and went out riding. But they work on my aunt's headaches like a dream. We thought you would like it because you wouldn't be used to the smell of the fish and the water."

"You were right on both counts. I'm not used to it and this is a hundred times better. Thank-you for this."

"You're very welcome. Oh, your bath is ready. I'll let the girls help you and I'll see you down at dinner."

Dinner that evening was casual, with just Lord and Lady Sun-Trout, their niece, Aubrey, and their two children, a young man who was on the suitor's list, and a girl Aubrey's age. To Betha's delight they didn't speak at all about suitors or princes. Unfortunately, the conversation centered mainly on fishing, something Betha knew nothing about and had no interest in.

As soon as it was polite she turned to Lady Sun-Trout and said, "Thank-you for the candles in my room. They are wonderful."

"Who knew such a thing was possible?" Lady Sun-Trout said. "I'm from an estate closer to the capital and I'm afraid the salt air and the fish have never agreed with me. I thought it was just something I'd have to live with, until this delightful healer came up with those candles."

"I would love to meet this healer before I go," Betha said. "Perhaps she can make me some to take along with me, or send instructions to the palace healer."

"You suffer headaches as well?"

"They smell like Dinas Rhosyn," Betha said. "The smell is one of the few things I miss." *And the smell of roses is preferable to horses, hawks, or fish, as far as I'm concerned.*

"I'll speak with her," Lady Sun-Trout said.

When the meal was over Aubrey said, "Can Annabelle and I go up to watch the sunset?"

Lord Sun-Trout nodded. "Stay out of the way of the guards."

"Yes Uncle. Princess Betha, would you like to come with us?"

Betha almost declined on account of the smell but Aubrey reminded her a little of Talia so she said, "I'd like that a lot. Thank-you."

The breeze had shifted a little but still, the smell of the fishing village below the wall was overwhelming. The girls didn't seem to notice at all so Betha didn't mention it and tried her hardest not to make faces.

"Why are you living here with your aunt and uncle?" Betha said.

"I have four brothers," Aubrey said. "You'll meet one of them at dinner tomorrow. Don't marry him, he's a jerk."

Betha laughed. "I hope he's not my prince then, but I actually have very little say in the matter. It's all pre-ordained by Airon. So, someone had pity on you with all those boys and sent you to live with your cousin?"

Annabelle nodded. "They thought it would be good for us to grow up together, since we're nearly the same age."

"I remember that from being a child, how nice it was to have the other princesses around. Tell me about the other young men coming tomorrow."

"You can't have Justin," Aubrey said. She clasped her hands to her chest. "Annabelle is in *love* with him."

Annabelle took a swing at her cousin and missed. "Oh, shut up!"

"Honestly, you should see her face, how red it gets when she sees him," Aubrey went on.

"It doesn't matter. Neither his mother or mine will let us court until someone is named as prince, just in case."

"Does he care about you too?" Betha said.

Annabelle looked down at her hands. "I think so."

"Something similar happened in the Stone Clan territory. Once I meet him, I can quietly speak to his mother and inform her that he's not my prince and that I recommend letting him follow his hear."

"What if he is your prince?"

"If he already feels so strong a connection with you, I doubt he will suddenly stop caring about you when he sees me."

Annabelle clasped Betha's hands. "Oh, thank-you!"

"Princess, ladies, the sun is nearly below the water line. I should send you all indoors now, for your own safety."

Betha glanced over the wall. The spectacular display of oranges and pinks in the western sky was indeed growing darker and overwhelmingly navy. She nodded to the guard. "All right, thank-you."

The girls went in together and spent the rest of the evening in Betha's room chatting about the other suitors who would be attending tomorrow's dinner.

26th of Thornfall, 24th Year of the 11th Rebirth
Sun-Trout Estate, Province of the Animal People

Betha stopped Lord Sun-Trout after breakfast: "Can I send a letter back to Caranhall?"

"Certainly. I can show you the way to the aviary, or I can take the letter there for you. I hope there's no emergency."

"No emergency, and no complaint, your hospitality has been wonderful. I just like to keep my stewards up to date about my progress and I had a question for Master Bright-Star." She handed him the scroll. "Thank-you. I would go with you to see the aviary but I'm expected at the chapel."

"You're very welcome. I'm glad to be of service in any way I can."

This dinner was far more comfortable for Betha than the one at the Honour-Hoof estate days earlier. For one thing, it was a slightly smaller group, and the information she'd gotten from Aubrey and Annabelle the night before helped Betha keep everyone's names straight.

It turned out Aubrey was not exaggerating, and her brother was, in fact, boorish, loud, and arrogant and Betha looked forward to removing him from her list. Justin, on the other hand, was kind and soft-spoken, but it was obvious he had eyes only for Annabelle.

After the meal, Betha went to Justin's parents and asked to speak to them privately. She could see the anticipation on their faces, but she didn't let that sway her.

"I'm not here to say what you want to hear," Betha started. She watched anticipation change to confusion. "Your son is not my prince."

"It was one meeting," his mother said. "You can't be sure."

"I can be. He didn't look twice at me tonight and I think you know why. Princess Rheeya encountered a similar thing. If my prince's identity is preordained by Airon, then he wouldn't let my prince fall in love with someone else."

"I knew that Annabelle Sun-Trout was no good," Justin's mother spluttered.

His father, on the other hand, was completely calm. He smiled at Betha even as he laid a restraining hand on his wife's shoulder. "Thank-you. Your honesty is refreshing and it's good to finally have a direct answer. I think Justin and Annabelle will be happy for the news."

"I wouldn't be surprised if they were engaged before the end of the week," Betha said.

"You can't be serious," Justin's mother said. "You're just going to stop pursuing this?"

"I have to," her husband replied. "I suppose if we tell them now, I'll never convince him to come home with me tonight."

"It might be better to speak to Lord Sun-Trout tonight and to Justin and Annabelle tomorrow," Betha agreed.

He bowed, "Thank-you for allowing my son to follow his heart." He led his red-faced wife back to the table where the other guests were still chatting over their wine.

Betha considered running away to her room since she knew that none of those men were her prince, but she knew that would be rude. She sighed, shoved her own desires deep inside of her, and tried to smile as she returned to the table.

Annabelle was watching her intently but said nothing so Betha smiled and nodded her head once then watched the smile light up the girl's shy face. She looked to Justin and their eyes met. No words were spoken but he caught the joy in her smile and looked from her to Betha to his parents who were speaking in hushed voices with Annabelle's parents and back to Annabelle.

She nodded, and his smile grew.

So much for waiting until tomorrow to tell them. They might just announce their engagement before I leave tomorrow.

27th of Thornfall, 24th Year of the 11th Rebirth
Western Coastal Road, Province of the Animal People

The winds were coming in off the water all day, but the prevailing scent was cool salt water, and not fish so Betha kept the carriage windows open. They were far enough from the shore line that Betha couldn't see or hear the water, but she could hear the gulls in the distance over the clatter of wheels and hooves.

They had a longer day on the road so Betha's midday meal was packed that morning and she ate it in the carriage. They stopped only briefly to water the horses and check harnesses. By the time they reached the next estate, Betha's legs were cramping and she needed to relieve her bladder badly.

The girl waiting in the courtyard to assist her was more than understanding and took her straight to her rooms by the shortest route, deflecting all questions and distractions.

"Lord and Lady Wise-Ranger have waited dinner for you," the girl said. "I'll take you down to the dining room as soon as you're ready."

"They didn't need to do that. I could have eaten here in my rooms."

"They're eager to meet you," the girl replied. "Honestly, the whole estate has been buzzing since the letter from your steward arrived."

"I see. Then it's best I don't keep them waiting."

Lord and Lady Wise-Ranger lived alone, their children were grown, ten years too old for the suitor's list, and lived in Caranhall where they worked for the guilds. Their grandchildren were twenty years too young to be suitors.

"But we don't mind hosting our nephews and a few other suitable young men tomorrow, and chaperoning your visit," Lady Wise-Ranger said. "It will be nice to have younger ones in the house again."

"Who will inherit the estate?" Betha said.

"Our eldest son," Lord Wise-Ranger said. "He works as a liaison between the Fishery guild and the Merchant's Bank. That sort of account keeping will serve him well when he takes over the estate."

"I'm sure I'll be meeting with him over the course of my investigation," Betha said. "And thank-you again for your hospitality."

"Thank you for travelling. We don't want to lose anyone else to those attacks."

"I didn't realize there had been a possession here."

"Two in the last five years," Lord Wise-Ranger said. "We've been lucky. But if nothing changes, we'll see more and more attacks, just like the northern coast has."

"I don't want that either," Betha said, honestly. She felt no affinity for these people, but that didn't mean she wanted to see them die horrible deaths with their souls ripped apart. "I hope this journey will help."

"We hope so too."

28th of Thornfall, 24th Year of the 11th Rebirth
Wise-Ranger Estate, Province of the Animal People

"Princess, a letter arrived for you from Caranhall," Lord Wise-Ranger said, scroll in hand. Though he shared the same last name as Betha's political steward, the two men were distantly related – third cousins on their father's side if she remembered correctly.

"Oh. Thank-you." She wiped her face on her napkin and accepted the scroll.

"I hope the news is good."

"So do I. I don't want to cut my travels short before completing all the rituals."

"If you need anything …"

"I'll let you know, thank-you." When he'd gone again, she set the scroll aside. She knew what it was, just a reply to the letter she'd sent from the Sun-Trout Estate, but it was a necessary piece of her plan. She couldn't claim to have received urgent news unless Lord Wise-Ranger could back up her statement and confirm that a hawk had come.

She finished her breakfast, dressed, and went down to inform her guards that she was ready to attend to the ritual.

The conversation over dinner was more pleasant than the evening before with no one mentioning Dark Spirits or the recent increase in the number of attacks. Instead they spoke of life in the village, the bountiful nets filled with fish that the fishermen were bringing in each day, and the prize-winning hawks that were being bred and trained in the region. At least one of Sebastian's cousins was at the table but he didn't share Sebastian's gentle nature.

Apparently, the arrogance is a class issue, not a provincial trait. I've met Metalkin men humbler than some of these suitors.

The stories of hawking and hunting bored her, and she longed to be back in Golden Hall with Joseph discussing the investigation or with Talia discussing court gossip.

But Joseph isn't in Golden Hall, he's in Stones Shore and you've already got your plans laid to escape these tedious duties.

"What do you think of the idea, Betha?"

All eyes were on her now and she blinked at them. "I'm sorry, I drifted into thought for a moment. What were you discussing?"

They exchanged looks. "Would you like to go hawking with us some time, when you're not in the middle of these rituals?"

"Oh. I'm sure it's a wonderful sport, but it could be years before I'm proficient enough with horse and hawk to keep up with you. You're all so good at hawking."

They visible preened at her words and the conversation, and the bragging, continued until Betha said. "I have to thank you all for your stories and your time. I've been travelling now for nearly a week and I'm exhausted. I'll be leaving early tomorrow so I really, regretfully, must turn in now."

The young men all stood and expressed their understanding and their regrets, their individual words lost in the jumble of voices.

Her "Good night" was met with a chorus of replies and she escaped to the tiny guest room to pack and finalize the next morning's plans.

29th of Thornfall, 24th Year of the 11th Rebirth
Wise-Ranger Estate, Province of the Animal People

The next morning after breakfast, Betha went out to speak with the head of her escort, the letter from her stewards in hand. "There's been a change of plans," she said.

The man frowned. "What sort of change?"

"We won't be heading to the next estate. We need to travel south."

"There's not much south of here except a small trade port."

"That's exactly where we're going."

"Were you summoned there by the village priest?"

"No. I was summoned to Stones Shore."

The poor man almost dropped his pack. "You want to ride to Stones Shore? We don't have the supplies."

"That's why we're going south and not southeast," she said. "We'll stop in the trade port, buy supplies, and hire someone to ferry us across the river. Then we can continue south to the capital."

"This is very sudden. We're already saddling the horses."

"Then I guess we won't have to wait long to be on our way. My things are packed and ready to be loaded. How soon can we leave?"

"We didn't bring a sun hawk."

"No. Why would we need to?"

"I'd like to write your stewards about this but that would mean waiting a full day for the letter to get there and the reply to get back."

"I already have a letter from my stewards," she said, waving the scroll. She tucked it back under her arm before he could reach for it. "We're going south. We're leaving today. I'm not turning my back on a friend in need."

He sighed. "Fine. We'll go south, Princess. We should be ready to leave within the hour."

"Thank-you," she said. She turned on her heal and marched back inside.

The estate's stable master paused at the guard's elbow. "An hour? You could leave in half that, and that wouldn't even be pushing my boys."

"I know that, but she doesn't, and I don't want her to. I want a little time to write a few letters and get them to the hawk master. I might not be able to wait for the reply, but I still need to send them."

"She's our princess," the stable master said. "Do you really think she'd lie about something like this?"

"I don't know. But something doesn't feel right about this."

34th of Thornfall, 24th Year of the 11th Rebirth
Stones Shore, Stone Clan Province

Betha had been to Stone Shore once before and found the castle overwhelming and intimidating. The heavy stone walls and narrow windows were bleak and grey and towered over everything. Inside the cold stone was warmed by carvings in the pillars but out here, where the stones had to withstand the weather, no such finery was wasted.

She could tell from the lack of surprise among the servants and stable hands that her arrival was expected. *And that means my stewards guessed where I was going.*

Rheeya appeared at one of the doors, her face serious. Betha took a deep breath, squared her shoulders, and approached her friend.

"I received a hawk from your stewards. It seems you changed your itinerary on the road and they are most upset."

"I know," Betha said.

"Come inside and we will talk away from curious ears."

Betha nodded and followed her inside. "How is James?" she asked while they walked.

"As well as the last time you saw him." She didn't elaborate.

The receiving room was small with simple furniture, but Rheeya had requested some light food and some tea at least.

"Betha, you should not be here," Rheeya said. "Your duty is at home."

"You did it," Betha said. "Everyone told you that your duty was here, and you still left."

"There was a crisis to attend to and I'd already met the suitors Evan intended to introduce me to, multiple times. Vonica was allowed to escape her duties because Johann spoke to Master Salazar Sun-Wise. And Taeya was following an emergency. What excuse are you using this time? Education? The investigation?"

Betha felt her cheeks going hot. "They weren't excuses."

"Why are you here?"

"Please, Rheeya, you have to understand. I don't belong in Caranhall. The horses stink, the birds stink, I've been biting my tongue trying to behave but at some point, I'm going to start snarling at everyone just like I did in Evergrowth, and then the people will hate me, just like they did before."

"I'm not sure you've been in Caranhall long enough to make those sorts of discoveries about yourself."

"It's been two months since I left Evergrowth."

"Right, a month and a half. You've spent over two weeks of that on the road. You spent half of Cloudfall and half of Thornfall in Golden Hall. And now you're here. You've spent all of a little over a month actually in Caranhall."

"Because I don't want to be there."

"I didn't want to be here either. I was twelve, alone, confused. This place was cold and dark and damp compared to the sunlit halls we grew up in. Evan was a hard man with no time for children or childish anything, and I was forced to grow up, to be elegant and regal all the time, to hide my emotions and my desires. Even before I left for the mine though I found things here that I liked. I was comfortable even if I wasn't completely happy."

"But you're the only one. Vonica never had to leave. Taeya and I were sent to the wrong places, and Mallory didn't grow up here."

"You just spent nearly a month with her. What did she say about all this?"

"That she doesn't feel like she fits."

"It's been less than a year for her, Betha. And less than two months for you, if you only count the time you were actually home. These things take time. But you won't settle in and find your place unless you're actually in Caranhall."

"It didn't take Taeya long at all," Betha countered.

"And maybe, if you gave it a chance, and made an effort to find your prince, it wouldn't take you long either."

"Please, Rheeya. I promise, I'll talk to guild representatives and meet with potential suitors who live here. I'm going to be trapped in Caranhall for the rest of my life. Please, just give me the chance to see a little more of our island before that happens."

"All right. But if you refuse to meet your suitors, or in any way shirk your duties while you're here, I'm sending you home."

"I understand."

"Good. You'll need to write your stewards, explain the situation to them, and request a list of suitors living in this province that you can meet with. You should also write to the guild halls in the city and begin making arrangements to meet with them."

"Now?"

"I wasn't exactly planning on company, so I have things I must tend to. And don't send for James either, he's in lessons until dinner."

"A bath at least. We were on the road …"

"Several days, I know, and judging by how quickly you got here I'd say you hardly stopped at all. It will take time to heat the water. You can start writing while you wait." Rheeya sighed and her shoulders relaxed as she shifted from princess to friend. "It is good to see you Betha, and I agree, it would be nicer if we could see each other more often but we all have duties to tend to."

"I know. It's just I'm not ready to be locked away yet. At twelve I couldn't protest, couldn't make demands this large and be listened to. Didn't you ever demand or beg to see me? Or Vonica? Or Taeya?"

Rheeya nodded. "All the time, for about half a year. And then I learned it would do me no good."

"We're not children anymore."

"That doesn't mean we can just do what we want whenever we want."

"It also means we don't have to do *just* what is expected of us all the time."

"You have work to do and so do I. I will see you at dinner tonight."

Betha managed to have her bath and still get all the required letters written before dinner. When she breezed into the dining room James grinned and waved at her. "You're sitting with me," he said.

"On Rheeya's orders, or yours?" Betha said.

"Tell me about Caranhall. And Golden Hall. I never get to go anywhere."

"I know how that feels. Give it time. You'll have the chance to explore when you're older."

"That's years from now. Tell me everything."

Betha started with Golden Hall, describing everything she loved about the buildings and the artwork while James listened with rapt attention.

While they were talking, Rheeya and Tomas came in, busy with their own conversation. Quick 'hellos' were exchanged, and the two conversations continued.

After a moment Betha said, "Is dinner late?"

"No, but one of our guests appears to be," Rheeya said. She flagged down a servant. "We'll start with soup while we wait," she said.

"Yes Princess."

"Another guest?" Betha said. "You told me that you weren't expecting company."

"I wasn't expecting more company than I already had," Rheeya clarified. "And while our current guest is here on business and requires little of my attention, he does have a habit of joining us late for dinner." The corner of Rheeya's mouth quirked up in a little smile as she spoke. "But he's polite about it."

As if on cue the door opened, accompanied by, "I'm sorry, I'm late again, these guild masters know how to keep a person talking. Oh." He stopped short about halfway to the table. "I didn't know you had other guests. I'm doubly sorry."

"It's not a problem," Rheeya said and shot Betha a 'you see what I mean' smirk.

But Betha wasn't looking at Rheeya, she was looking at Joseph. "I wasn't sure you'd still be in the capital," she said.

"Actually, I did a lot of the mines on my way here," he replied.

Rheeya and Tomas kept glancing from Joseph to Betha, back and forth. It was James who spoke up. "Guess you two have met."

"Yes, a few times," Joseph said, pulling out the seat next to Tomas. "Our paths keep crossing in unexpected places."

"Ah, just in time for soup," Tomas said as the servants came out.

The conversation over dinner remained light – the weather, the roads, a little about the guilds without conversation turning overly political, how James was doing with his lessons, and so on.

As they were finishing the meal Rheeya turned to Joseph. "Have you found anything?"

"Some," he replied.

"Do you have time to talk about it in the morning," Rheeya pressed.

"Aww, you can talk about it now," James said. "I won't interrupt or tell anyone."

"James, this has nothing to do with you and everything to do with me being too tired to want to talk about anything serious for the rest of the day."

"Oh, okay."

"May I join you tomorrow," Betha said. "Mallory and I were working on the problem and I could fill you in on what we discovered."

"All right," Rheeya said. She turned to James. "Go wash up and get ready for bed. Captain Honour-Shield is expecting you in line early tomorrow morning for drills."

"That's right," James said, popping out of his chair. He stuttered to a halt and bowed in the direction of the table. "G'night Princess, g'night Master Rose-Gold."

"Good night James," Joseph said.

"Good night, and we will talk more tomorrow," Betha said, smiling.

The boy dashed off.

"We can speak now if you wish," Joseph said once James had gone.

"Honestly, I am too tired this evening," Rheeya said. "I try not to lie to James if I don't have to. We can speak over breakfast since James will be eating late because of his training."

"Well then, I suppose I will retire to my room. I have letters to write. Princess Betha, I can walk with you if you're headed that way."

"All right," Betha said, pushing her chair back. "Unless you still need me for something this evening?" Both she and Joseph glanced expectantly at Rheeya.

"No, I'm turning in too. Good night, both of you."

"I'm happy you're still here," Betha said. "I mean, I'm happy I have this brief chance to see you again, not that your task is taking so long. Have you had any word about your father?"

"After your visit he actually improved, if only marginally. In my mother's last letter she claims he asks after you often. I get the impression it's bothering her immensely."

"I'm sorry. I should have met you elsewhere. It seems I've caused quite a mess for you at home."

"I'm not sorry. You didn't cause the mess. I'm sure my mother would like to blame you for that as well though."

"And your sister? How goes her courtship?"

"They are getting married. My mother is furious. My sister is smug. I wrote back and told them that if it was convenient to hold the ceremony before I returned, not to wait on my account. I hope the next letter I receive will be an accounting of their wedding."

"You don't wish to attend?"

"I don't wish to be a part of the drama and scandal that I'm sure will surround the event."

"How is your younger sister?"

"She doesn't write to me directly and my mother's last few letters have been so full of complaint that she hasn't had the space to say more than 'your sister is well' in any of them."

"That must be frustrating."

"It is. She and I were close as children."

"This is my room," Betha said. She stopped walking but made no move towards the door.

"I'll be here a few more days," Joseph said. "But I'll be busy with the guilds."

"I'll be busy most of the day as well," Betha said, refusing to mention the word 'suitors' in front of Joseph. *This moment is too nice to spoil that way.*

"Hopefully I'll get to spend a little time with you. I'd like to know more about your visit to Golden Hall after I left."

"Yes, we'll have to make time to get caught up," she agreed.

He reached out and took her hand. "Good night Princess." He smiled and kissed the back of her hand then bowed and continued down the hallway, disappearing around a corner.

Her heart fluttered, and she took a few deep breaths. "He kissed me," she whispered.

35th of Thornfall, 24th Year of the 11th Rebirth
Stones Shore, Stone Clan Province

Betha walked into the dining room in the morning eager to see James again. When she didn't see him waiting, she remembered he was off training somewhere. She bit back a sigh and made her way to the table. She was soon joined by Rheeya, Tomas, and Joseph. Servants brought out tea, pan fried potatoes, fried eggs, and sliced ham.

Their conversation centered on the ongoing investigation surrounding the Academic Diplomats. Joseph had discovered whispers in the mines that pointed towards a connection with the gems seen at the Sun-Song Estate. Rheeya had uncovered several closed accounts that shouldn't have been closed, and several accounts that shouldn't exist at all, tying into the corruption Vonica had found at the banks. Betha filled them in on the developments with the foals in Golden Hall.

"The only pattern I'm seeing here is that these men are suddenly showing interest in everything they once snubbed their noses at," Tomas said. "Wait, you said something about gems missing from mines."

"I did," Joseph said. "But only rumours, nothing they could prove."

"Do you remember," Tomas started.

"Of course, I do," Rheeya said. "It's still on my bedside table."

"What are we remembering?" Betha said.

"When we'd finished rescuing the miners Tomas took me into the mine to look around. We found a freshly unearthed patch of gems, right near the outer wall. Tomas, you said no one had reported the find."

"I assumed it was found so soon before the collapse that there wasn't time to report it. What if …"

"What if the Metalkin ignored the order to stop digging because of the gems?" Rheeya said. "We thought it was Jared's fault, that he cancelled the lumber, but what if they were digging when and where they shouldn't have been?"

"All gems found in a mine are supposed to be handed over to the Stone Clan," Joseph said. "It's in all the guild agreements."

"The Iron Guild isn't fond of following guild agreements or contracts," Rheeya muttered. "Still, to make an accusation of theft and interference at this scale, even I would require proof before I'd be believed."

"They'll fight you tooth and nail to deny it," Joseph agreed. "But the question remains. Why? Why would they steal the gems? Why would they steal the foals?"

"Where are they hiding everything? And who is behind this?" Betha said. "The who is tied into why they are going out of their way to hide behind these cultural lessons, I'm sure of it. And why they are going to Caranhall to learn about mining and Evergrowth to learn about horses."

"I will record everything we've discussed and everything we suspect and send it to Vonica and Taeya," Rheeya said.

"Not Mallory?" Betha said. "She's not a part of this. She has no idea what's going on either."

"I trust her," Rheeya said. "But I assume Master Rose-Gold will fill her in upon his return to Golden Hall."

"I will," Joseph said.

"Then that's settled. Please, take your time if you're not done eating. I need to get to court. Rheeya, Master Alessandro will be here shortly with an itinerary for your day."

"Oh, yes. Thank-you. And I'll be sure to thank him as well." She smiled and kept on smiling until Rheeya and Tomas were out of the room. As the smile dropped from her face her whole body relaxed. "Joy," she muttered. "A full day of boring meetings with boring people whom I don't want to deal with."

"I was going to say, you seemed awfully cheerful. I was wondering where the scowling was."

She blushed. "I'm sorry. I …"

"No, don't worry about it. I find most nobles, especially the women, are so polite all the time, too polite. They sound fake, never voicing displeasure. Except for my sister, as you saw, but she's only that honest around family, and you, apparently. When she's with potential husbands she's so sweet. She can't keep that up forever and what happens when her husband finds out there's sour wine beneath that sweetness."

"Sour wine?" Betha said, laughing. "Oh, I like that. Your sister wouldn't like it at all, but I like it!"

"Ah, Princess Living Rose, it's nice to see you in a good mood this morning." Master Alessandro Hearth-Glow came in with a handful of papers. "Do you mind if I join you?"

Betha reined in her laughter. "When Rheeya said you'd be along shortly I didn't realize you'd be quite so prompt, but please, join us. We're just finishing our meal."

"Thank-you. Master Rose-Gold, it's good to see you again. How fares your investigation?"

"Slow, if I'm to be honest. I'm not sure I'll find many answers in Stones Shore. There are a few places I still want to look, a few people I still want to talk to, and then I'll have to return home."

"We certainly appreciate the work you are doing on Princess Jewel-Rose's behalf."

"And I should get to it. I will see you later, Princess."

When he'd gone, Alessandro said, "He's a good man, as far as I can tell. Mallory is fortunate to have someone like that working for her."

"Yes," Betha said. "What adventures do you have planned for me today?"

"Nothing too extravagant today. I'm still waiting to hear back from some of the local Animal People nobles. I expect they'll be very excited to be moved so far up your list of suitors and there will be no shortage of meetings in the next few days."

"You make it sound like I have time to myself today."

"You might. But in the meanwhile, there's the hawk master here at the castle, and the stable master."

"That reminds me, I need to speak to the Equine Guild while I'm here. I came across something concerning while I was in Golden Hall that I should pass along to them."

"I'll make a note of it, though I'm sure they'd be delighted to host you, bad news aside. After lunch I will need your signature on some letters, to some of the more difficult guilds. And the local historian would like to speak with you. Apparently Rheeya told him something about a different name for the Animal People and he's immensely interested."

"I can tell him what I know. I'm still learning myself."

"Excellent. Dinner will be with Rheeya and her family."

"And Master Rose-Gold?"

"Yes, he is likely to attend, unless business keeps him away. After that I'm sure young James would like a few hours of your time."

"Thank-you for thinking of that. I would like to spend a few hours with him as well."

"Then, that is your day for today. As soon as you're finished, we can begin."

She didn't want to visit either the hawk master or the stable master since they would insist on showing her the animals and she'd be expected to touch them and praise their lovely breeding, all while not making a face at the smell, but she knew that any time she wasted now would be taken off her time with James at the end of the day. *The Stone Clan are certainly a 'work first, play later' people.*

"I'm ready now."

"Excellent. This way please."

The aviary was, as usual, located in one of the castle's towers. The small space was made more appealing by a wide balcony that completely encircled the tower.

It smelled of bird and corn and dead animal but Betha was able to refrain from making a face, except when the hawk master took a dead mouse from a container and fed it whole to one of the hawks.

The man laughed. "It's not an easy sight, is it? Takes a lot of getting used to, handling the dead animals for feeding them."

"I don't think I could ever do it," Betha said.

"No, it's not for everyone."

"I'm glad there are people like you around to take care of these – fine – animals. It's so important, the work that you do."

"Thank-you Princess."

"Have you noticed anything odd lately? Odd requests from people, concerning the birds? Birds not returning? That sort of thing?"

"There's always a chance a bird won't make it to their destination, or won't return home. It's dangerous for them out there. But no, we haven't had any more missing than in a usual year. And no, I haven't had anyone come around asking questions."

"Good. Could you talk to the guild and the other breeders and trainers? I need to know if any of them were approached by young Metalkin nobles who were asking questions about breeding or training or purchasing hawks."

"I will. If I hear anything at all I will send word to you at once."

"My thanks."

After the aviary they went down to the stables, in the courtyard. The smell of horses and hay and leather was becoming a familiar one to Betha but she hadn't developed any fondness for it. And to be honest, the snorting and stamping of the animals in their stalls made her nervous.

"We brought one of the sun mares round back for a good brushing, to show her off," the stable master said.

"Of course," Betha said, forcing a smile and following him through the long, low building.

The sun mares weren't much larger than a normal horse, but they were compact animals, dense with muscle, and they came with an attitude to match. This one seemed calm enough as Betha stepped out of the stables again but as she approached the horse tossed its head and stamped loudly against the stones.

Betha took a step back.

"It's okay," the stable master said. "She's tied up. She's not going to charge you."

"I'm sorry. I'm not used to them yet. They're so big."

"Yes, but they're darlings, for the most part. Here." He handed her half a carrot."

"What's this for?"

"For the mare. Offer it to her. She likes them, and if you give her one, she'll like you too."

She took the offered vegetable gingerly and approached the Sun Mare with quick, nervous steps. Two arm-lengths from the horse she stopped and thrust out her hand, carrot extended to the horse. The horse just stood and stared at her. She took a few deep breaths and took another careful step forward, and then another.

The horse didn't move until the end of the carrot was an inch in front of her nose. Then she reached out and took it from Betha's hand with surprising gentleness.

Betha wanted nothing more than to retreat to the safety of the castle. She looked over her shoulder.

"You can pet her," the stable master said. "Her neck, or her nose, but stay away from her ears."

Betha nodded and turned back to the horse. They weren't going to let her leave until she'd made an effort. The horse was soft, especially the velvet end of her grey and cream coloured nose.

A few pats was enough for Betha to admit that the horse was a lovely beast, but she still didn't want to be here, staring at it and touching it. She wiped her hands against each other but her palms stayed dusty.

She retreated to where the stable master stood talking to Master Hearth-Glow.

"Thank-you for that," she said.

"The more time you spend around them the less intimidating they become," he said. "But you did well for someone who hasn't spent much time around horses yet."

"I'm not sure I'll ever be fully comfortable around them. They're just so big."

"There are other animals," the stable master said, kindly. "Hounds, cats, farm animals. I hear the sheep are nice and spinning and weaving is what my wife does."

"When I return home I'll have to acquaint myself with all of the animals and the associated jobs," Betha said. "For now, can you tell me if you've had any Metalkin visitors interested in the horses?"

"Nothing outside of when can I have them harnessed so they can leave," he said.

"Thank-you. I'll be speaking to the Equine Guild later this week so I won't pester you with political questions. Your stables are impressive. You should be proud."

"My thanks, Princess. From you that means everything," he said with a deep bow.

Betha nodded and headed back towards the castle with Master Hearth-Glow.

"You have a meeting with the historian next," he was saying. "Which will give me a chance to check for correspondence from the noble families. I'll walk you to the study."

"I need a book from my room, something I brought with me. I think it will be of interest to the scholar."

"Then we will make a detour. We have plenty of time. Do you want tea or food sent up?"

"Maybe later," Betha said. The smell of the birds and horses had left her stomach a little unsettled.

"All right, just ring if you need anything. Master Quill-Song will be along shortly to speak with you," Master Hearth-Glow said, leaving her in a small study with heavy stone walls and a very narrow window.

The closeness of the room didn't bother Betha as much as it should have and she settled into the plush chair to wait.

The meeting with the scholar dragged on most of the afternoon partly because Master Quill-Song was late, and partly because he spoke slowly and at great length. Betha rang down for lunch part way through, asking the serving girl to pass along her apologies to Princess Betha.

Master Quill-Song seemed to have a story for every one of Betha's answers and he took notes even slower than he spoke. By the time their session was wrapping up Betha was speaking through gritted teeth to keep from yelling.

Master Hearth-Glow finally arrived to rescue her and to her delight informed her, "You have a few hours free until dinner, and after dinner …"

"James."

"Yes. He's looking forward to seeing you."

Betha hid in her room until dinner. Boredom was preferable to visiting at this point. She was tired of the drone of voices and persistent questioning.

She was looking forward to dinner, however, and waited impatiently as the soup was served for Joseph to arrive. Instead a boy came in with a note for Betha.

"It seems our other guest is dining at one of the guilds this evening." She waved down one of the servants and had them clear the last place setting away.

"Did you find out anything about the cheap jewelry in Golden Hall?" Betha said.

"No, but I have my suspicions," Rheeya said.

Tomas nodded. "I've been speaking with some of the miners from the Black-Mountain mine and none of them knew anything about those gems we found after the rescue."

"Wasn't that cave-in caused by reckless digging on the part of the iron miners?"

"Partly. When some of the Stone Clan workers refused to dig, Jared ordered the Metalkin workers to do it. They're not supposed to dig, that's our job. But if the iron workers found the gems …"

"Isn't gem mining your job as well?"

"Yes," Tomas said. "But it would explain gems being transported by the Metalkin without our knowledge."

"Do you think this is happening in other mines?" Betha said.

"It's possible," Rheeya said.

"The iron workers are refusing to talk. They've made it quite clear that we have to address all of our questions to the guild reps."

"Maybe your father needs to get some of the long-time iron workers in the village drunk," Rheeya said. "Maybe they'd be more talkative then."

"I'll mention it to him the next time I write," Tomas said.

James was quiet through the entire conversation. Every time Betha looked at him he was frantically shovelling food into his mouth. She chuckled softly at it and went on with her meal and the conversation with Rheeya.

When dinner was done and everyone pushed their plates back, James leapt out of his chair. "Is it my turn now?"

Tomas frowned and looked ready to scold the boy but Rheeya just laughed. "Yes, yes. You two can go visit. Don't fill his head with too many stories or I'll never hear the end of it," she added.

"I make no promises," Betha said. She stood and held out her hand to the boy. "Come on James. I've missed you too."

**3rd of Daggerfall, 24th Year of the 11th Rebirth
Stones Shore, Stone Clan Province**

Master Hearth-Glow had been right when he'd said that her days were going to get very busy. Between guild representatives, meetings with Rheeya, and meetings with her suitors, Betha hardly had a moment's peace. The only highlights of her days were dinner with Joseph, though Rheeya, Tomas, and James were always present, and visiting with James.

When she was with her suitors she spent the time mostly lost in thought, thinking about Joseph and his family, or about Golden Hall and the political drama that was playing out there while she was stuck in Stones Shore entertaining suitors.

Stuck here or stuck in Caranhall and I'm not sure which is worse. At least here I have James to talk to. And Rheeya. When she's not being a serious princess she's wonderful.

Today had been all suitors and Betha was exhausted from smiling and pretending to be interested in their hobbies. She'd almost skipped dinner but she hadn't seen James since the first and she wanted friendly conversation for a change.

Unfortunately, James was not available to visit after the meal, something about lessons not being completed. James sulked off to finish whatever work he'd been assigned, dragging his feet along the stone floors.

"I suppose I should set a good example," Betha said. "I brought some texts that I'm supposed to be reviewing and all these meetings and visits have prevented me from spending much time on them."

"All right," Rheeya said.

"I'll walk back with you," Joseph said. "I should begin packing."

"Are you leaving tomorrow?" Rheeya said.

"No, but I may have to leave soon. And I like to keep my things neat and orderly. Good-night. Thank you for another delicious meal."

"I enjoyed it as much as you did," Rheeya said. "Good-night, both of you."

"Do you really need to pack?" Betha said as they walked.

"I'd like to get some of my things sorted, yes. And I have a letter to write."

"Do you have a few moments to spare?"

"Of course."

They stopped in a lovely sitting room just down the hall from Rheeya's room. There was a padded bench in one corner with a view from one of the rare windows that was more than a slit in the stone. They settled there, side-by-side.

Joseph took a deep breath. "I told Rheeya the truth. I must leave for Golden Hall soon. Princess Jewel Rose may have other duties for me and there is little more I can learn here."

"You're really finished your job here?"

"Yes. Unless I find something new I cannot justify staying longer."

An idea popped into Betha's mind. She'd imagined it a hundred times, but to consider actually following through with it? No, she couldn't, and yet she found the words tumbling from hesitant lips. "If I give you a good reason, would you stay?"

"Yes."

205

She leaned into him quickly, fearful he would stop her before she could kiss him, fearful he would push her away. Her lips met his and her eyes closed. Instead of pushing her away he touched her face with gentle fingers. The kiss was sweet and lingering, and it calmed the restlessness within her in a way nothing else had.

When he pulled away his eyes were sad. "It's impossible," he said. "Excuse me." He stood and walked away.

Betha was too stunned to call after him. *He let me kiss him. He kissed me back.* Her heart leapt in her chest. *Impossible, yes, but still the first thing in a very long time that has made me happy.*

4th of Daggerfall, 24th Year of the 11th Rebirth
Stone Shore, Stone Clan Province

It would have been inappropriate for Betha to be alone with Joseph in his room but he hadn't joined them for breakfast and there was no guarantee he would seek her out to say good-bye before he left. *And I need to stop him from leaving.* So, Betha went to the one person in Stones Shore whom she could trust. James Quarry.

Joseph set the shirt in his trunk before crossing the room to respond to the sharp knock. He was tired from a restless night and the dim prospect of returning home. He didn't want help or breakfast, he just wanted to be left alone to pack.

He opened the door, his gaze falling upon the boy Rheeya had adopted. He was a sharp lad, eager and full of energy. "Can I help you?" Joseph said as politely as he could manage. A servant would not have faired so well but Joseph couldn't bring himself to yell at a child for simply being there.

"Not me," James said. "I'm just the messenger."

"Not just the messenger," Betha said. She'd been hovering next to the door, just out of Joseph's direct line of sight. "You're my escort as well."

Joseph stood a little straighter. "Princess Living Rose, I didn't see you there."

"Princess Living Rose now? When did we go back to being so formal with one another?"

"After yesterday I thought it was for the best. I'm just in the middle of packing."

"I know. That's why I must speak with you now, before you call for your horse and guard."

"I don't know that allowing you into my room would be proper …"

"Nonsense. I have an escort, don't I?"

James beamed up at him, his smile nearly reaching his ears.

Joseph sighed. "Of course. Won't you both come in? Shall I ring for tea?"

Before James could answer Betha said, "No need. Besides, I don't want anyone but James to know I was here."

"You trust him?"

Betha nodded sharply. "Wait by the door James. If anyone knocks you answer and stall them. Tell them you're here to assist Master Rose-Gold with some tasks. He sent for you after breakfast."

"Not a problem," James said. He produced an apple from a pouch at his waist and settled onto a stool by the door.

"All this secrecy but you bring him?" Joseph said as Betha crossed the room and settled herself in one of the chairs.

"Yes. And you'd best learn to trust him. We'll likely need his help."

"Help with what exactly?" He dropped into the other chair.

Betha leaned forward. "I don't want you to return to Golden Hall."

"I know."

"Do you want to go back?"

"I'm needed there."

"That's not the same thing."

Joseph sighed. "No. No, I don't want to return to Golden Hall. I don't want to think about my father being gone. I don't want to deal with my mother and sisters grieving, or not grieving as the case may be. My eldest sister and my father did not always see eye-to-eye, so I don't know how she's handling his passing. And I don't want to leave you."

"I was hoping you'd say that."

"Betha, what happened yesterday ..."

"That's why I'm here."

"It's impossible, you know that."

"Taeya and Francis was impossible."

"Evergrowth didn't have a prince yet. Mallory, she's found her prince already. There can't be more than one Metalkin Princess."

"Maybe you're adopted."

"There were days I felt like it," Joseph said. "But you only saw my father after the disease had crippled him. Everyone says I'm the spitting image of him in his younger years. There's no doubt he's my father."

"Your mother ..?"

"No. He was devoted to her. There was no way he'd have an affair. And even if he did, why would they take me in? My mother never would have stood for that."

"There has to be an explanation."

"Betha, as much as I care about you, we cannot be involved. It's impossible."

"You keep saying that. Are you trying to convince me or you?"

"You," he said though 'both of us' may have been a more accurate answer. He didn't want to give Betha the slightest hint that his resolve in this matter was wobbly at best.

"Why did you take this job for Mallory?"

"She asked me to go so I went. I'm loyal to the crown."

"Did you ever feel a restlessness? A sense that something in your life was out of place? Did you ever feel like something was missing? Did you ever feel a driving need to go out and find it?"

As Betha spoke Joseph felt an old, familiar sense of panic rising inside of him. His heart rate sped up and his hands began to tremble. He swallowed the lump in his throat and said, "I did feel that way, a long time ago, when I was a very young man. The first time I walked into the castle in Golden Hall I felt like I was home. Something settled inside of me. I knew that was where I belonged. When they said they were going on one last expedition to find the missing Metalkin Princess, I was ecstatic. I wanted to meet her so badly."

"And?"

"And then Mallory returned and announced she was engaged to Kaelen Iron-Heart. I would have been devastated but when I met Mallory myself I knew I wasn't meant to marry her. I convinced myself that I was destined only to serve, and I swore an oath of loyalty to the crown."

"Did it go away?"

"What?"

"That restlessness?"

"For a time. It started to come back when they found Mallory."

"That's why you took this job. That's why you agreed to leave your home and your ailing father to travel the entire island and talk to people who probably didn't want to talk to you and sleep in strange places. Because as much as Golden Hall felt like home you couldn't stand to be there anymore."

"How could you possibly know that?"

"I tried to adjust to Dinas Rhosyn. I told myself I was being a baby. I was twelve, I had to grow up and accept that I couldn't go back to the Sun Temple, I couldn't go back to Madam Olga, the woman who raised us. I told myself once I got used to it, that it would feel like home. It never did. Everyone told me Caranhall would feel like home. It doesn't either. Twelve years I waited for Everygrowth to feel like home and it never did. I don't think waiting twelve years is going to make Caranhall feel like home either. That's why I stopped at the Sun Temple. That's why I visited Golden Hall. That's why I'm here. Because anywhere is better than being trapped in that castle pretending I belong there."

"I was so sure, you know? But I could never love Mallory. I will serve her, but I do not love her. I'm not her prince. Once I realized that I became lost."

"Detached, adrift, like you're falling."

"Exactly, yes."

"All that went away yesterday."

Joseph closed his eyes and turned his face away.

"For the first time in twelve years everything quieted. I didn't feel like running. I didn't feel like I was falling anymore." She waited for several heart-pounding moments, but he said nothing. "Joseph?"

"I know what you want to hear. You want me to tell you that I felt the same thing. You want me to be in love with you."

She felt like her heart had just dropped into her stomach. She nodded, her body strangely numb.

There was a knock at the door and Betha jolted in her seat. A wild panic gripped her.

"Play along," Joseph muttered, heading for the door even as James was pulling it open. He looked back and hissed, "Come on."

She stumbled out of the chair and followed him.

"I know this is Master Rose-Gold's room," James was saying. "I was just …"

"He was escorting Princess Living Rose," Joseph said. "Thank-you James. And thank-you Princess. That information will prove most valuable to my investigation." He turned to the servant. "Please inform Princess Stone Rose that I'll be staying several more days to investigate this new information." He held the door open and let

James and Betha out. "Thank-you again, Princess. I look forward to joining you at lunch."

"Of course, Master Rose-Gold," Betha said. "Anything to help." She nodded and then followed James down the hallway, not waiting to hear why the servant had come to the door in the first place.

When they'd rounded the first corner James said, "Where to next?"

"I want to go back to my room," Betha said. "I need to be alone."

"I'll walk you there, since I am your escort."

Betha nodded, not trusting herself to speak, she was too close to tears. At her door she said, "Thank-you James."

"I'll come fetch you for the midday meal."

"I don't know that I'm all that hungry."

"But you have to. Master Rose-Gold said he'd see you then. Don't you want to talk to him again?"

"I don't know that it would be a good idea."

"Why not?"

"There's nothing left for us to talk about." She sighed. "I made a mistake. I shouldn't have bothered him. I should have just let him go."

James stared at her. "But he lied so he could stay here longer. Didn't he do that for you?"

She returned his stare.

"I really couldn't help hearing most of what you said, and you're right, you can trust me, I won't tell. He wants to talk to you again, today. Shouldn't you try talking to him again? Don't you want to know what he would have said if that servant hadn't interrupted?"

Betha took a deep, shuddering breath. She didn't like this swell of hope that was rising inside of her because she didn't want to feel the bitter disappointment that would follow, but she couldn't stop it. "Okay. I'll dine with him."

"It would probably be best if you dined alone, just the two of you," James said. "Leave the kitchen staff to me. And Rheeya too."

"James, you don't have to do this. I don't want you getting into trouble."

He grinned. "I'm in trouble all the time. At least this time it'll be really fun. Don't worry about me. I guess if I'm taking care of Rheeya I can't fetch you for lunch, but someone will be along to tell you where your meal is being served."

"All right. Just this one meal. And that's it. No more sneaking around after that."

"Sure thing! Anything to help. I'll come by for tea after my lessons this afternoon, okay?"

"I look forward to it."

As promised a servant appeared at her door to summon her to her midday meal, being served in a little used study in the guest wing. Joseph was already there, pouring cider into glasses. He smiled at the servant. "Thank-you. Leave the door open please."

"Open?" Betha said when they were alone. "But anyone could walk by."

"That's right. And if anyone could just walk by and see us then there's no chance of either of us doing anything to make people talk."

"Of course," Betha said. She turned her attention to the table. "The meal looks good."

"Come, sit, we'll eat. We can talk about the investigation."

Betha nodded and let him seat her. She served herself, focusing on the simple, concrete task at hand while trying to get her emotions under control.

"We're far enough in the corner that a casual passerby won't see us," Joseph said in a hushed voice. "Someone would have to stick their head in the door. And as long as we're not shouting …"

Betha glanced at the doorway and smiled. "So we are." She relaxed a little. "What did you want to speak about?"

He fussed with his fork and knife, suddenly feeling awkward. "We were interrupted earlier, and I just thought you'd want to finish talking."

"I do, yes," she said. "But I'm afraid of what you're going to say."

"You're afraid it won't be what you want to hear."

"Yes."

"You're not afraid of being in love with me? We could bring the whole island to ruin."

"Do you believe that?"

"Yes. The Metalkin have a princess and she found her prince. This is impossible. But, there is no denying that I feel something for you, something I shouldn't feel, something we shouldn't indulge."

"Then why tell the servant you were staying a few more days? Why not leave as planned?"

"I wanted to share this meal with you, wanted to tell you how I felt. I saw the hurt in your eyes earlier."

She blushed.

"And honestly, it's just what popped out of my mouth in the moment. I could easily join Rheeya for dinner tonight, tell her it was a false lead, and that I'm leaving in the morning. One more night is not a big deal, and with the complicated nature of these investigations no one would even bat an eye."

"Then you'll leave in the morning."

"I should leave in the morning." He reached out and touched her hand. "But I don't think I'm going to."

She felt her heart flutter and a shiver went through her. "You have a duty to Princess Mallory."

"I know I do. But that doesn't change the fact that when you kissed me I felt everything fall into place, just as you did. I don't know what it means because it's impossible for us to fall in love. But I think we need a few days together to figure it out."

"Are you always so logical?" she said, the corner of her mouth twisting up in a smirk.

"Why?"

"Can't you just say ..." She stopped talking when he cleared his throat. She looked over her shoulder and smiled at the servant who had come in.

"I'm sorry, I was just putting something away. I didn't realize you were dining here." He arranged a few books on the shelf, bowed, and went out again.

"Will he tell?" Betha asked.

"Tell what? The door is open. We're not doing anything wrong."

"And yet, we'll have to keep it a secret if we continue to meet alone."

He nodded. "But, you were saying?"

"Do you always have to add all these logical statements to what you're feeling? Can't you just tell me that you love me?"

"I can't love you."

"I'm not asking what you're allowed to feel. Feelings don't always follow the rules you know."

"You're very forward."

"And difficult and lacking in tact. Does that bother you?"

"No, not at all. It's refreshing because I talk around things too much."

"You really do."

"This will never work."

"Then let's enjoy it while we can."

"It could be disastrous."

"You're doing it again. This isn't logical. It doesn't make sense, not even to me, but it feels right. Can you at least admit that?"

"It feels right."

Betha stood and walked across the room. She glanced out the door, first one way down the corridor than the other, then closed the door.

"What are you doing?" he asked as she walked back.

"The impossible," she said. She touched his cheek then bent and kissed him.

Betha had never seen James eat a meal that quickly. Usually he lingered at the table and had to be sent away, generally with food in his pockets, hand, and cheeks. This time he was done and out of his seat before Betha had finished her last few bites.

Even Rheeya laughed. "Slow down, James. What's got you so excited?"

"Princess Betha is going to teach me about the Animal People this evening."

"I've never seen you this excited about studying," Tomas said.

"The teachers probably don't order dessert or let him sit in the bed," Betha said.

"You spoil him," Rheeya said.

"I hardly see him," Betha replied. She wiped her mouth and set her napkin on her plate. "Let's go then. Joseph, you'll have to let me know if anything comes of that new information."

"I will. And thank-you again for bringing it to my attention."

Betha resisted the urge to look back as she followed James out of the room.

"What happened?" James said as Betha closed her bedroom door. "He's staying, right?"

"James, you know this is dangerous, right?"

"This is so exciting. A secret affair."

"We could destroy the entire island."

"You'll have to sneak around. I could help!"

"Are you listening to me?" she said, her voice sharper than usual, at least her usual for speaking to James.

James stopped bouncing and pacing and stared at her with wide eyes. He blinked a few times. "You are going to meet with him again, aren't you?"

"Yes, most likely. We'll meet to talk about the investigation, probably with Rheeya, and we'll have a few more meals together."

"What about meeting alone? You can't talk about being together if Rheeya is there."

"James, we're both guests here. Master Hearth-Glow has all sorts of activities and meetings planned for me every day. I know what you're suggesting and it's impossible." Even as the last two words escaped her lips she knew who she sounded like.

It's all impossible. Why ask him to stay and not spend time with him?

Maybe James could see the wheels turning in her mind because he stayed quiet, waiting, staring expectantly at each other.

She let out an exasperated sigh. "Fine, I will see him. But you will not be involved."

"Tomorrow morning is too soon," James said, going off at full speed again. "What does Master Hearth-Glow have planned for you tomorrow?"

"Lunch with suitors. No, James, you're not listening."

"All right, after lunch you say you need to lie down for a bit. I'll come find you and escort you to Joseph. Then I'll keep watch for you and let you know if anyone is coming and …"

"James!" Betha said, unable to contain a laugh. "Stop!"

"What? I don't think dinner together would be a good idea. Do you? I could talk to the cooks."

Betha sighed. "No, no dinner. That would be too difficult and raise too many suspicions."

"Then after lunch is best. Trust me on this. I'll find the best spot for the two of you to meet. A new spot each day would be best. I'll need to really look around."

Betha crouched in front of James and took his face in her hands. "This is a very bad idea."

He just grinned at her. "I know."

5th of Daggerfall, 24th Year of the 11th Rebirth
Stone Shore, Stone Clan Province

Betha was pacing just inside her bedroom door, twisting her fingers and fussing with her skirt and hair, when James arrived to fetch her. Lunch had dragged on and on and she'd been too nervous to eat much.

"Come on, quickly. I don't know when the maids will be up with the fresh linens." He took her hand and they hurried down the hall together.

They must have looked odd, James a step ahead, his arm back, clutching her hand, while she was bent forward to accommodate his short stature, being pulled around corners at his whim. Luckily no one actually saw them. She nearly ran into him when he stopped in front of a door down a hallway Betha had never explored.

"Are you sure this is safe?"

"Safe enough. I'll stay out here in the hallway."

"What about …" But before she could ask, James opened the door, ushered her inside, and closed the door behind her.

"He's quite the child," Joseph said.

Betha whirled around. "Oh, it's you. He found you then."

"Yes, and explained everything to me, I think. He's excitable."

"Yes, he is." She glanced around. The room must have been a study at some point, or an office, but now it seemed to be mostly storage.

"He said he couldn't have food sent up without arousing suspicions."

"That's all right, I already ate."

"Yes," Joseph said, his voice tight. "Your suitors. James mentioned that." Joseph sat on the arm of the nearest chair. "How did it go?"

She pulled the other chair closer to his and sat. "I don't want to talk about them. Tell me stories of growing up in Golden Hall. Tell me about your adventures working for Mallory, just don't bring up suitors."

He nodded, his features softening again. "All right."

They had no interruptions that first meeting and James only knocked to tell them that Betha had to go or she'd be late for a meeting with a guild representative.

"I'll see you soon," Joseph said at the door. He kissed her softly and it warmed her from her lips to her toes.

"I can arrange something for after dinner, if Betha will 'help me with my studies' again," James said, reminding them that he was standing right there.

Betha blushed. "James, that's not …"

"Leave it to me," he said. He took Betha's hand. "You don't' want to be late or people will start asking questions."

She smiled at Joseph over her shoulder and let James drag her away.

9th of Daggerfall, 24th Year of the 11th Rebirth
Stone Shore, Stone Clan Province

Betha and Joseph sat by the fireplace, their high-backed chairs moved close together so they could hold hands. Across the room, James was picking over the remains of lunch.

"I have to return to Golden Hall sooner rather than later," Joseph was saying in a hushed voice. "These have been the best few days of my life, but I can't stay here with you."

"I can't stay either. Rheeya will send me home soon. I have duties in Caranhall."

"When I'm finished in Golden Hall, perhaps I can come to visit you in Caranhall?"

"On what errand?"

"Do I need a job? We're friends, aren't we? I could simply come to visit you."

"And it would be like now all over again, you and I sneaking about, stealing moments between my other duties, between meeting my official suitors. You don't like it that I still have to meet all those young men."

"No, I don't. I didn't want to believe it, Betha, but every moment I spend with you I become more and more certain. We were meant to be together. I don't know what's going on, I don't know what went wrong or where, but you are my soulmate."

"I love you too."

He smiled. "I love how easily you say that."

"It's the truth."

"It's impossible, and we both know it."

"You're not back to that, are you?"

"Betha, you're the Princess of the Carainhithe and I'm a Metalkin noble. There is no possible future in which they will allow us to be together."

"I don't believe that. I can't." She sighed. "We don't have much time left together."

"No, we don't."

"We need to do something," she said. "I don't want to live the rest of my life and never see you again."

"We don't have a lot of choices."

"No, we don't. But I think I know what we need to do, what I have to do."

"Do I want to know?"

"Probably not. I have to go now. I'm supposed to have a meeting this afternoon. I promise, by dinner I will have some answers."

"All right." He leaned forward and she responded in kind. He kissed her gently and they touched foreheads, staying there a moment before she leaned back and stood up.

"Come James."

"Just a minute," he said, stuffing apple into his mouth.

Betha laughed. "Do you ever stop?"

His answer was muffled by the food in his mouth and he hurried out the door after her, pausing to wave to Joseph on his way out.

"Enter."

Betha took a deep breath and opened the door to Rheeya's private rooms. "I've never been in here," she said, looking around. The room was large but with the heavy walls, small window, and solid furniture it felt smaller.

Rheeya looked up. "Oh, it's you. Come sit. I'm just finishing a letter."

"Don't rush on my account," Betha said. She settled herself in a chair near the hearth and poked through the pile of books on the side table while she waited. They appeared to be reports and records, for the most part – nothing interesting.

Rheeya finished her letter and went to the hallway. She flagged down a passing servant and sent them off to the Hawk Master with the letter. She joined Betha with a sigh. "There always seems to be one more thing to do around here. You need to find your prince so that I can take a vacation to Caranhall."

"About that …"

Rheeya sat up straighter in her chair. Betha had her full attention now. "You found someone."

"Don't get too excited," Betha muttered. She sank lower in the chair.

"You're not?"

"No. I'm terrified."

"I don't understand. Betha, this is a good thing, isn't it?"

"I don't know."

"Okay, you'd better explain everything to me because I don't like the way this is sounding." The excitement in her voice had been replaced with wariness.

"You're not going to like it any better after I explain. You see I did meet someone, I met him months ago, before I found out about Taeya and Francis, and I figured it would be impossible, what with me being the Evergrowth Princess."

"But then you weren't the Evergrowth Princess anymore."

"That's right. But I didn't really think I'd see him again."

"Why not? Wait a minute."

Betha nodded.

"Betha, no."

"Every time I saw Joseph Rose-Gold there was an instant and undeniable connection. We both knew it was impossible. A few days ago, I did something foolish. I was afraid. I thought I'd have to settle for someone who didn't make me feel as wonderful as Joseph did and that once Joseph returned to Golden Hall that I'd never see him again."

"What happened?"

"I kissed him. I just wanted to know how it would feel. He said it was impossible. He was going to leave. But we talked, and he stayed."

"There was no new development in the investigation?"

"No."

"Did you kiss him again?"

"Yes."

"Why are you telling me this?"

"Because I love him, and I don't know what to do."

Rheeya leaned back in her chair and folded her hands in her lap. Her face was serene, but her mind was churning with questions and possibilities. Across from her Betha waited quietly if impatiently.

Finally, Rheeya leaned forward again. "I have some questions for you."

"Anything. I will try my best to answer."

"Did you meet with any of your suitors while you were here?"

"Yes. Master Hearth-Glow set up several meetings. I met with some suitors in Golden Hall too."

"Did you feel a connection to any of them?"

"No. But then, I haven't met with any of the suitors in Caranhall yet."

Rheeya nodded. "Meeting your suitors, what did it feel like?"

"Like ice in my stomach. Imagining myself with a man like any of them made me cringe."

"Did you really try while you were in Caranhall?"

"To the point where I thought I was losing myself," Betha replied. "I felt like I was drowning."

"Tell me honestly, what did it feel like when you spoke to Joseph Rose-Gold for the first time?"

"I felt a deep curiosity."

"And when you kissed him?"

"I felt connected for the first time in years. I didn't feel adrift any longer. I didn't feel like running anymore. I felt that there was no need to run anymore."

"Come with me."

Since Rheeya had yet to raise her voice or use the word "impossible" Betha decided it was in her best interested to follow. They went to the private chapel down the hall from Rheeya's room. Rheeya lit several candles on the altar and instructed Betha to sit on the bench in the center of the room. Then Rheeya moved the candles until they were positioned on the floor around Betha, one in the location of each capital city as though Betha was at the center of the island facing north.

"I don't know if this will work," Rheeya said. "I've tried similar things before and the spirits never answer me, not the spirits of stone, and not Airon. But I saw them answer when Tomas was in the chapel in South Bay with me, and I saw them answer for Taeya and Francis in Dinas Rhosyn."

"What are you going to do?"

"Maybe Airon will be willing to point us in the right direction."

"You're not a priest."

"This isn't something we can trust with a priest," Rheeya said.

"Okay, go ahead. But what if nothing happens?"

"Then we try something else. Sit still."

Rheeya stood behind Betha and put her hands on her friend's shoulders. She took several deep breaths and imagined her feet becoming one with the stone floor. When she felt solid and connected to the stone she said, "Airon, chief among the spirits, we come to you for guidance. I know we're supposed to figure this out on our own, but this hasn't been a normal rebirth. If you can help us, we'd be grateful." It didn't sound official and stuffy, but she didn't have time to think off all the official stuffy-sounding words right now.

"What now?" Betha said.

"Don't move. Don't take any deep breaths. Don't sigh. Don't talk."

Betha nodded.

"Rheeya," Rheeya said. To her left a candle flickered and went out. "Taeya." The candle on her right did the same. "Vonica." The second candle on the right went out leaving two candles lit, the one for Caranhall and the one for Golden Hall.

"It's actually working," Betha said.

"He hasn't told us anything we don't know," Rheeya replied. She took a deep breath. "Where does Princess Betha belong?"

Both candles wavered and danced as though something, or someone was blowing gently on them. Betha held her breath and watched. She felt Rheeya's hands tighten on her shoulders. Before their eyes the Caranhall flame steadied and the Golden Hall flame went out.

Almost in a whisper Rheeya said, "Mallory Brock."

The last candle went out as though pinched between two unseen fingers and only a lazy line of smoke remained, drifting up from the wick.

Back in Rheeya's room the girls sat sipping tea, the silence between them heavy. Both were deep in thought and both startled in their chairs when the door opened.

"I just spoke with the history tutor and James is …" Tomas stopped when he spotted Betha. "I'm sorry. Am I interrupting."

"At the moment, no," Rheeya said. She set her cup down. "Tell me about James."

"He's doing well. He remembers the events, though he's not as accurate with the dates as his teacher would like him to be."

"That will come with time," Rheeya said.

"Did we figure out where he was the last few days?"

"That was me," Betha said. "I required an escort."

Rheeya's eyes narrowed and her friend blushed.

Tomas took a step backwards. "And now I am interrupting. I will see the two of you at dinner tonight."

"You'll see one of us for certain," Rheeya said.

Tomas nodded once and fled.

"You involved James in this?"

"I needed an escort," Betha said again.

"You needed someone to lie for you and watch for anyone who might interrupt your irresponsible meetings with a man who could not have been your prince."

"But that's not true now, is it?"

"You didn't know that when you asked James to help you!"

"I only asked him to accompany me the first time I went to speak to Joseph because it would have been inappropriate for me to visit his rooms alone and James was the only one I trusted. He volunteered for the rest."

"You're the adult. You should have told him no."

"You're his guardian, how often does telling him no work for you?"

Rheeya growled in frustration. She felt like throwing a tea cup against the wall, but this was her favourite set.

"I'm sorry. I'm sorry for all of this. I'm sorry for putting you and your family in the middle of this. It was irresponsible of me, just as it was irresponsible of Taeya. And yet, both times, we discovered another thing that was out of place. Everything is a mess and following the rules and traditions is just letting it stay messed up. I followed my heart, just like Taeya told me to, and now we know something new, something that might help us set everything right."

"What about Prince Kaelen?"

"I don't know. There was no sign of glowing hair when he and Mallory met, or when he and Mallory were married."

"But there was no controversy either, no stubborn stewards to persuade, no traditions being bucked. And rarely in the history of the pact has Airon been this obvious about his will."

"So, no one was expecting glowing hair, just two people to say 'yes, we want to marry each other'. And that's what they got."

"Kaelen is twice-named, on the suitor's list, exactly the sort of man Metalkin Princesses have married ever since the pact. There was no reason to doubt the truth of his claim."

"No reason except some candles in a chapel," Betha said.

"And your insistence that you've fallen in love with a Metalkin man."

"Who is also twice-named and on the suitor's list."

"This is beyond me. I honestly don't know how to solve this. I don't know how this could even be possible. All I can say now is that you need to write to Baraq Silver-Cloud. He's the high priest of Airon. He's vowed to sort out this mess. He can't do that without all the pieces."

"It could be worse. I could be writing to Honourable Balder Gold-Spark."

"Yes, that is one bright side. Betha, be honest in your letter, please."

"I will."

"It's probably best if you don't linger here much longer. You may want to talk to the stewards at Caranhall in person."

"Joseph needs to return to Golden Hall to make his report anyways."

"Send the letter today. You'll leave on the eleventh."

"All right."

"And we will see you for dinner tonight, you and Joseph both."

"So that you can keep an eye on us?"

"Exactly."

11th of Daggerfall, 24th Year of the 11th Rebirth
Stone Shore, Stone Clan Province

The hardest good-bye was James. "You're his favourite, you know," Rheeya said after Tomas took the boy back inside. "He'll mope about for days now."

"I'm sorry I got him involved."

"I'm pretty sure you were right, you wouldn't have been able to keep him out of it. He once lamented that he wished to be older just so that he could marry you." Rheeya placed a hand on Betha's shoulder. "Take care. I don't want to hear about you coming to an ugly end on the road somewhere."

"I'll be fine. As soon as I hear anything I will write you."

"Same."

Joseph Rose-Gold appeared beside them. "Princess Stone-Rose, thank you for your hospitality. I'm sorry that I abused it."

"Save your apologies. I'm certain this is not over yet. Which road do you plan to take?"

"We'll travel north together to the river," Joseph said. "I will ride with Betha's guards."

"I'll be taking the boat back across the river and then straight to Caranhall," Betha said.

"And I'll be heading east through the northern most pass and then northeast to Golden Hall."

"Keep all this quiet," Rheeya said. "Tell no one aside from Mallory and the stewards in Caranhall. I would advice Mallory not to inform her stewards of this either."

"What of the other princesses?" Betha said. "I want to write to Taeya, there are things I need to say …"

"Wait. Somehow I think we won't have to wait long."

Betha bit her lip but nodded.

"Safe journey, both of you."

Betha and Rheeya embraced and then Joseph escorted her to her carriage and helped her inside.

She didn't see much of him on the journey north except when they stopped to water the horses and have a quick meal themselves. It was strangely lonely, even if there was a girl with her. She could picture Joseph astride his horse only a few feet away and she longed to speak with him, to hold his hand and listen to his stories, but that was impossible. Not even her guards knew the truth and until they heard back from High Priest Silver-Cloud no one could know.

She sighed, not for the first time that day.

"Is everything all right, Princess?" the girl asked.

Her name was Robin or something like that, Betha had never been good with names. She forced a tight smile. "Fine. Everything is fine. The sooner we return to Caranhall the better." *The sooner I return to Caranhall the sooner we can sort this mess out and the sooner I can be reunited with Joseph.*

12th of Daggerfall, 24th Year of the 11th Rebirth
Sun Temple Complex, Sun Temple Province

When Baraq Silver-Cloud had joined the Order of Airon as a young man he'd been wide-eyed and full of optimistic naivety. His schooling had dulled that somewhat, but he'd been elevated to the position of chief priest of a royal temple at a young enough age that he'd held out hope he could make some real changes. In Dinas Rhosyn he had made changes, reinforcing some traditions and lifting other restrictions, trying to shed the classist elitist structure the church had been building since The Pact.

These past two months as the High Priest of Airon had opened his eyes to how deeply engrained these elitist attitudes had become. There would be no easy fix, just years of fighting against old men who were content with their positions and had no interest in change, especially change that threatened their personal comfort.

Reluctantly he'd set his personal crusade of reform aside without really starting on it because he knew he needed assistance from as many people as possible if he was going to sort out what had happened to send two young girls to the wrong provinces. *And it's the old men who will have answers, the ones who were already priests when the girls were first brought here. They're the ones I need to talk to. I need their cooperation.*

Because in the last two months things had not gotten easier. If the letters sitting open on his desk, one from Betha and one from Mallory, were any indication, things had gotten more complicated. *I'd never have thought that possible, and yet, here we are.*

It was nearly mid-Thornfall, only a month and a half from the onset of Holy Week, a five-day celebration of the changing of the year. Ordinarily the princesses were required to be home at their own temples for Holy Week as there were blessings that needed to be done to renew their oaths to Airon.

Another thing I'll have to change.

He pulled out a stack of parchment and a pen and started writing five nearly identical letters "requesting" the princesses' presence at the Sun Temple for Holy Week.

He set Rheeya's aside, then Taeya's, then Vonica's which explained that they would have company for that week. When he got to the end of Betha's he added a post-script.

~Bring this young man with you. We will get to the truth of this matter. ~

At the bottom of Mallory's he added a different post-script.

~Betha claims to have found her prince, a Metalkin man. You and I have one month, give or take, to figure this out. Bring records of whatever you find when you come for Holy Week. We must set this right. ~

He signed and sealed all five letters, marking each with a ribbon coloured to match the five provinces, silver for Rheeya, gold for Vonica, green for Taeya, copper for Betha, and black for Mallory. He rang for a servant and instructed the boy to deliver four of the scrolls to the aviary, and the fifth directly to Vonica.

With that done he sat back and studied the two letters again, Betha's first.

~I believe I've found my prince; his name is Joseph Rose-Gold. He is a Metalkin noble. I know this is impossible, but I also know what I feel. What I don't know is what to do next. ~

If Betha's was disturbing, Mallory's was even more so.

~I regret to inform you that there has been a tragic accident in the city and Prince Kaelen Jewel-Rose of the house Iron-Heart was killed. ~

Bonus Story
The Roses of Airon: The First Princesses of the Pact

The Isle of Light was changing. More often people were coming over the Narrow Water to the island, and in ever greater numbers. They were different, these people, they did not worship Airon, the god of the sun, nor were they blessed by any of the five great spirits of the world. At first, they had been merely a curiosity, but their presence soon brought much concern to Aden, the High Priest of Airon.

For the first time in two hundred years, Airon's High Priest called the five kings of the Isle of Light, to the Great Temple for a meeting of the High Council. King Adam of the Stone Clan, King Kenneth of the Metalkin, King Gavin of the Animal People, King Florence of the Evergrowth, and King Celio of the Sun Temple, were not happy about the summons, but all answered.

~Excerpt from *A History of Airon's Pact* by Master Scholar Julianus Winter-Sun

Princess Vonica of the Sun Temple rolled out of bed with a groan. The serving girl had roused her early and was preparing one of the fancy dresses. Dragging her feet the whole time, Vonica allowed the girls to dress her and style her blonde hair. She joined her mother for a quick breakfast, looking around the mostly empty room in disappointment. "Where are all the guests?"

Queen Sera said, "They're eating in their rooms this morning. They've all had long journeys."

"But some of them have been here for days already and I haven't seen any of them yet."

"You'll meet them today."

Vonica wasn't all that eager to actually *meet* the royal families from the other provinces, but she was interested in seeing all of them. She was certain she could guess each one's name without introduction.

As soon as their meal was complete, they joined Vonica's father and High Priest Aden in the temple.

"After the prayers are complete, I will invite you and the other kings to join me for the meeting," Aden was explaining. "Did you see to refreshments and entertainment?"

"Yes," King Celio said. "My wife saw to the details."

"Everything is prepared in the gardens," Sera said.

"Good. I suspect they will join us shortly. You should take your places in the temple proper."

From her place next to her mother, Vonica watched the other four royal families arrive and take their places around the room. The first to enter were the Metalkin family, with their black hair, cloth of gold clothes, and fine jewelry. The Stone Clan family was next and Vonica couldn't help but crinkle her nose at their clothes. Though finely cut and perfectly fitted, the fabric was plain and the styles simple. The Evergrowth and Animal People families entered together, the two kings deep in conversation. They had to part ways, however, as their provinces were in opposite corners of the island so their seats were at opposite ends of the temple.

When everyone had arrived and settled into their seats, Aden thanked them all for coming and started on the prayers, first of welcome, then of thanksgiving, and then prosperity. Vonica wasn't paying attention. She never paid attention at temple.

Instead she spent the hours staring at her guests, examining their faces and their clothes, watching for who was paying attention to Aden and who was letting their minds wander. From the number of people cleaning their fingernails, fussing with their clothes, and staring at the décor and other guests, she guessed no one was actually paying full attention to the old priest's ramblings.

Finally, Aden said, "And all this we ask in Airon's name, he who is protector, and light."

"May his light shine upon us," everyone responded, the words jumbling as people started at different times and spoke at different speeds.

Aden nodded and said, "If the queens and princesses would like to make their way to the gardens, I'm told Queen Sera has seen to refreshments and entertainment. I'll ask the Kings of the Isle of Light to join me. We have much to discuss."

The five queens and their adolescent daughters filed out leaving the men to their politics. The garden was in full bloom and alive with vivid colours and smells. Birds sang in the ornamental trees and tall hedges provided shade in the small flagstone courtyard. In one corner a table had been set with delicate sandwiches and sliced vegetables, in the other corner stood four young men with instruments. As the ladies entered they struck up a soft but cheerful tune.

Out in the gardens Sera watched her guests with distress. They had helped themselves to food and found shady seats, but they were seated mother with daughter, each pair separate and not looking at the others.

Sera nudged her daughter. "You should go speak with the other princesses."

"I don't want anything to do with them. They follow other Spirits besides the Great Airon." She shook back a wave of sun-blonde hair. "I don't like them."

"You've never met them, and they've never met you. Someday the five of you will be ruling together. You must learn to get along. And besides, you've been asking about them for days."

"And now I've seen them. We don't need them."

"Vonica, you are the hostess. You must learn to entertain guests, even guests you don't think you like. Now go. Take them on a tour and get them talking."

Vonica crinkled her nose and paused to smooth her skirts before making her way to the first pair of guests. Princess Rheeya of the Stone Clan sat near the garden wall with her mother, Queen Georgia. Her dress was grey but finely embroidered, her hair was dark, and her shoulders were broad. Even with her fancy clothes and hair pin Vonica thought the other princess looked more like the peasants out in the fields than a member of a royal family. Still, she put on her polite smile and said, "Princess Rheeya, would you like to join me for a tour of the temple complex?"

"I don't know," she replied, staring at her shoes.

Her mother nudged her. "You should go. Many great masons and sculptors worked on the temple. Consider it part of your cultural education."

"Yes Mother."

Vonica smiled. "Let me just ask the others." She made her way over to the next pair of guests who were seated by a flowering hedge. They were gently handling the blooms and talking softly. "Princess Betha, I am doing a tour of the temple complex, would you like to come?"

"It's so nice out here. I don't really like being indoors," said the willowy girl. Her lighter brown hair was tied back in a plain and practical braid.

"That's too bad …" Vonica started but Celyn, the Evergrowth queen cut in.

"Now Betha, you can spare the time. Princess Vonica is being very kind, offering to take you on a tour. I'm sure you'll find it interesting. It will be rare that you get to return to the Great Temple."

"Yes, of course Mother," Betha replied.

Vonica's cheeks were starting to hurt from smiling. "We'll begin shortly." She moved on.

The next princess at least looked like a princess. Her silky black hair was adorned with a jewelled hair clip and her dress was trimmed with cloth-of-gold. Her mother, Queen Orabel, was dressed all in cloth-of-gold and her hair, also a silky black, was twisted up with gold and jewelled pins. "Good afternoon Princess Ashlyn, you look lovely today."

Ashlyn smiled back but Vonica could see the same forced tightness that she felt in her own cheeks. "Thank-you, Princess Vonica. You look, er, lovely too."

Vonica's mother always said the Metalkin were a vain clan and Vonica could hear the haughtiness in the other girl's voice. "I'm leading a tour of the temple complex and I hoped you would join us."

Ashlyn feigned a yawn, covering it daintily with her hand. "There's nothing else to do so I guess I might as well."

"We'll meet by the archway in just a moment."

Vonica made her way to the final princess, Taeya of the Animal People. Like Rheeya, Taeya didn't look much the part of a princess but the soft leather cincher she wore over her dress was exquisitely worked with finely detailed horses. "Princess Taeya, would you care to join us for a tour of the temples?"

Taeya smiled. "I would love to. I am so tired of just standing around."

Vonica fought not to roll her eyes. "If you'd come with me?" Vonica led the way to the arch that led into the gardens. The other girls made their way over, eyeing each other with open curiosity. Vonica could see her mother rounding up the queens, starting with Taeya's mother, Queen Karnia. "You've already seen the Great Temple of Airon," Vonica said, "So why don't we start in the scholarly wing?"

She caught Ashlyn's eye-roll but smiled and led the way down one of the many winding garden paths.

The scholarly wing housed the library, the scholars' dorms, and the professors' dorms as well as classrooms and study halls.

"This is the heart of our people," Vonica said proudly as they stood in the foyer of the library. "It was the Spirits of Knowledge who favoured our people and we are proud to store the knowledge, history, and legends of all the provinces here."

Vonica expected the other girls to marvel at the sheer size of the room and the shelves that stretched, row after row, from one end of the great room to the other. The shelves stretched to the height of four men and nearly every one of them was full from top to bottom and from end to end.

Rheeya wasn't looking at the books at all; she was studying the pillars on either side of the doorway. The Stone Clan Princess's fingers traced the carved vines as high as she could reach. The other three girls just looked bored.

Vonica forced a diplomatic smile. "Moving on, you can see that the scholarly wing connects to the central temple building through there." As she walked through the foyer she gestured to a set of wide doors further down a side hallway. "The dorms are through there," she gestured down another side hallway, "The scholars' on the lower levels and the professors' on the upper levels. And this last hallway leads to the classrooms, conference rooms, and the illuminators' workrooms."

The only indication Vonica had that the other princesses were still following her was the sound of their shoes on the stone. There were no gasps of amazement at the vaulted ceilings or the books or anything that Vonica's suitors had found so fascinating when she gave them the same tour. Occasionally she'd hear a sigh and then a set of hurried steps as Rheeya scampered to catch up, a sign the Stone Princess was lingering over the pillars that lined the room.

Vonica led the way through an ornate set of doors and down a wide set of steps. "Through here is the Chapel of the Guardians where we house the shrines to the Spirit Guides from all five provinces."

The girls spread out around the room, each drawn to their own shrine.

"Pilgrims who come to seek out the wisdom of Airon at the High Temple stop here to make offerings to their Spirit Guides," Vonica explained.

Before each shrine was a large altar and each altar was piled with gifts: pottery and pretty stones on the Stone Clan altar; hawk feathers, braids of horse hair, and smoked meats on the Animal People's altar; fresh and dried flowers, shafts of wheat, and a bowl of fruits on the Evergrowth's altar, books and scrolls on the Sun Temple's altar, and fist sized chunks of iron ore, jewelry, gold coins, knives, and shields on the Metal Kin's altar.

Ashlyn flipped her hair back over her shoulder with a haughty shake of her head. "It certainly shows you where the truth wealth of the Island lies."

"What's that supposed to mean?" Vonica snapped.

"Just look at what our people have to offer compared to the rest of you," Ashlyn replied.

Rheeya was poking around the Metal Kin offer and came up with a dusty iron horse shoe. "Yes, because farm implements are so glamourous."

Taeya snickered as Ashlyn went red in the face.

"Knowledge is just as important as wealth. Without the knowledge of my people the whole Island would be doomed to these strangers," Vonica said.

Betha rolled her eyes. "You can't read a book after you've died of starvation. No farms means no food and that means no knowledge and no crafting."

"That's right," Taeya said, stepping up beside the slender princess of Evergrowth. "You need farmers and hunters to survive."

"And you're all going to live in grass huts now?" Rheeya snapped. "I think you'll very quickly miss your stone walls."

An acolyte stuck his head through the doorway of the chapel. "Is everything all right?"

Vonica smiled as sweetly as possible. "Yes, everything is fine. It was just a heated theological debate but I think it's settled now. We're on our way outside now."

The acolyte nodded and retreated. The girls exchanged hostile glances and followed Vonica out of the chapel.

"The chapel and the main Temple Complex both open onto the main courtyard," Vonica continued, gesturing to the oversized, ornate doors. "Those are used for festivals and processions. There's a door here to the side that the pilgrims and acolytes use for their day-to-day comings and goings."

Now it was Betha's turn to linger as her fingers traced the elaborate tree that had been carved into the dark wood.

Vonica rolled her eyes. "Really, what is it with the two of you that you have to stop and finger every crack in the stone or wood?"

Rheeya and Betha exchanged a look and Rheeya said, "They're not 'cracks', they're carvings. They're art, and they were done by the great artists of our provinces."

Vonica snorted. "That's not art; it's just a poor attempt to pretty up a boring piece of stone or wood."

"Like the pictures in books are just poor attempts at prettying up a boring piece of paper?" Ashlyn said. "At least when the Metal Kin make art we aren't prettying up something, we're creating something beautiful that stands on its own."

"It takes a lot of effort to make a beautiful diamond into beautiful 'art'," Taeya said, rolling her eyes. "Not like making a plain piece of leather into something beautiful." She carefully smoothed her cincher and skirt, drawing attention to the horses worked in the leather.

Rheeya nodded. "She's right, it doesn't take any talent to make a pretty thing pretty. It takes real talent to make clay into something pretty."

"Let me know when they succeed in making clay into something pretty," Ashlyn said with a false smile.

Before the fight could gain any more volume a pageboy darted into the courtyard. He stopped just short of the princesses, quickly composed himself, and said, "Your Royal Highnesses, your presence is requested in the Temple of Airon."

"They must have come to a decision," Vonica said.

The girls straightened their skirts and smoothed their hair as they hurried across the courtyard to the temple doors.

High Priest Aden stood before the kings and their families. As his eyes drifted from one family to the next he could see the differences in the five kingdoms that made up their island, differences of facial features, clothing, and body type, and yet every king wore the exact same expression of misery.

Aden took a deep breath and began. "After much deliberation between us, and after much conversing with the gods, Airon, the God of the Sun, and the protector of our Island, with the help of the five clans of Spirit Guides, has agreed to move our Island without moving the island."

Everyone began talking at once, some to Aden, some amongst themselves. All the noise boiled down to a single question, *How is that possible?*

Aden raised his hands and silence slowly returned to the room. "Our people are content to remain here on our Island, living a simple life. Here we are close to our Spirit Guides. Here we are safe. But beyond our Island, across the Narrow Waters, is another Island. And beyond that there are other lands, in every direction."

"But why do they come here? What do they want?" asked Queen Karnia. The Province of the Animal Clan was in the northern corner of the Island and furthest from the onslaught of the Strangers.

King Florence of the Evergrowth frowned. "They come for wood and fish to take away with them across the waters."

King Adam nodded. "At first we thought they were Evergrowth, for some of them spoke of spirits in the trees. None of them knew what a Spirit Guide was. They believe in different gods, and in strange creatures they call faeries and in men who can perform magic. They are looking to settle here, to make a life here. They want to stay. They'll spread north as more of them come and they'll upset the balance."

"Let them come," King Kenneth of the Metalkin asserted, not for the first time that day, his arms crossed over his broad chest. "We relish the chance to trade."

Florence shook his head. "They want to work the mines but they want to take the iron away with them. They do not understand that the iron belongs to the Iron Guilds. They have never heard of such a thing. They were very angry when the Iron Guild in our province would not let them take the ore away. Their anger will spread with them. They do not understand our way of life."

Kenneth gave an indignant snort but said nothing so Aden continued.

"We've spent all morning discussing the benefits and problems of these new comers, there is no point in having the *discussion* again. Airon will move the island and we will separate ourselves from these people who do not respect our way of life. When Airon is done his magic there will still be an island in that place in the bigger world but everyone bound to the Spirit Guides, all their possessions, homes, and animals, will not be in that bigger world any longer. Our Island will float, alone, tethered to the big world but no longer able to communicate or trade with those off the island."

Now Kenneth did speak out. "No trade? You never mentioned that during the meeting. How do you expect us to get the things we need?"

"From each other," Aden replied. "We will be completely dependent on each other from now on – if we choose to accept his offer and if his price is acceptable to us."

Aden watched the five royal families eye each other with suspicion and even contempt. *How have we come to this? 200 years ago the five clans were as close as kin. Now we are haughty and hateful.*

"What does Airon ask of us?" Queen Orabel of Metalkin asked, her chin raised.

"The Spirit Guides of every province must be tied to the pact or the people of that land will be left behind with the strangers. The pact must be upheld by a member of each province."

"Our husbands?" asked Queen Celyn of Evergrowth.

"No," Aden said, watching displeasure and misery turn to anger in the eyes of the other kings. He'd had trouble convincing them of this part of the pact and he didn't think it would be any easier to convince the queens. "Your daughters. Their souls will be the keys to the pact. When they die, they will be reborn so their souls will forever tie the magic to our land. They will have no heirs but will be the eternal rulers of our Island."

The shouting erupted as everyone leapt to their feet. Fists were shaken, and fingers pointed as the volume continued to climb.

Gavin was arguing that he'd never even met one of these strangers so how could he know if they posed a big enough threat to sacrifice his daughter? Florence insisted that they were decimated the forest in the south of his province and hunting on his lands. Adam was arguing with his wife over suitors and bloodlines and the loss of support from the noble houses if they let their daughter be a part of the pact. Kenneth and his wife were storming on about the lack of trade opportunities and Aden stepped in, trying to explain that they could be self-sufficient, just as they had been before the strangers' appearance.

"We're passing up a great opportunity!" Kenneth bellowed.

"All you care about is money," said Florence's wife, Celyn, turning on Kenneth.

"You don't know anything about money and trade and the progress of commerce," Kenneth retorted. "You're no better than an uneducated peasant!"

"Better an uneducated peasant than a puffed up wind-bag," muttered Adam's wife, Georgia.

"What did you call my husband?"

Soon the Metalkin queen, Orabel, and the Stoneclan queen, Georgia, were bickering as the other arguments raged on around them.

"I'll do it."

Betha's voice was almost lost in the din. The easily over-looked girl crossed to the altar and took her place on the seal of the Evergrowth. The five seals were arranged around the altar to correspond to the geographical positions of the provinces. Betha stood southeast of the great table. "I'll do it, even if I have to do it alone."

Her mother turned away from Kenneth and said, "Betha! What do you think you're doing!?"

"What needs to be done." Betha turned to Aden. "Start the ritual."

"I ... I can't. It won't work with just one."

Princess Vonica stepped out from behind her mother, her head held high with pride. "Airon is my spirit guide, as well as my chief god, if he has asked this of me how can I say no?" She stepped onto the Sun Temple seal next to Betha, directly east of the altar.

King Celio was spluttering and Queen Sera glared at Aden. "This is all your doing. We allowed you to educate our daughter and you've brainwashed her. What about her duties to her bloodline?"

High Priest Aden was solemn as he said, "She understands her true duties."

While they were arguing Rheeya silently took her place on the Stone Clan seal on the other side of Betha, the Southwest corner. When her mother noticed her she said, "Rheeya! What are you doing? What about the suitors waiting for you at home? What about our family bloodlines?"

"This is about the good of my people, not satisfying the noble houses and their quest for power."

"We're leaving now," King Gavin snarled and stormed towards the doors. Karnia looked bewildered but hurried after him.

"I'm not," Taeya said, standing her ground.

Her father stomped back and grabbed her arm. "You'll do as you're told, young lady."

"That's exactly what I'm doing," she said, trying to pull her arm free. "This needs to be done."

"You've never met these strangers, you don't know if they're a threat. Why should we sacrifice you because these fools are afraid?"

"Sacrifice? My soul will live forever."

"So they tell us."

"Do you not believe in the words of your high god?" Aden asked. "Your daughter shows more wisdom than you or your wife. Release her now so she can take her place around the altar or I will have to call the guards."

"You'll do no such thing!" King Celio bellowed but Gavin had already released his daughter who moved to the Northwest corner.

Everyone was staring at Ashlyn who was busy examining her nails. She glanced up, her eyes moving across the gathered faces and she shrugged. "I guess we're doing this," she said.

"Ashlyn," her father said, menacingly.

She smiled sweetly at him. "We're outnumbered, Father. Besides, I think I like the idea of being an eternal ruler." She took her place between Taeya and Vonica.

When all five girls were standing on the seal of their province Aden turned to the gathered monarchs. "I must ask all of you to step back. This pact is between Airon and your daughters. There is nothing for you to say or do as part of this ceremony except bear witness to the event."

Before any of them could argue further a large gong sounded and men began filing into the room. Acolytes, priests, scholars, and students, anyone who had been within the temple complex took their places in neat rows until the great room was nearly filled with bodies.

Aden stood on the raised dais with the altar and raised his hands to the elaborate mosaic of the sun which had been carefully laid into the domed ceiling. "Airon!" he called. "Your chosen five stand before you, ready to take the oath and seal the pact that will save their people. Show your blessing and consent! Let your presence be known to us."

"Let your presence be known to us," the hundreds of gathered men and women echoed, their voices filling the air.

The mosaic began to glow with a radiant light that soon neared a blinding intensity.

"Spirit Guides, your chosen five stand on the symbols of your ancient unity to the high god Airon, ready to take the oath that will bind all the people together. Show your blessings and consent. Let your presence be known to us."

"Let your presence be known to us," came the resounding echo.

The five seals began to glow, softer than the sun overhead, but enough to set each girl awash with light.

"The chosen five, the princesses of the five provinces of the Island of Light, you stand here before your Spirit Guides and the High God, the God of the Sun. Are you ready to take your oaths?"

"We are ready," the girls responded, their voices almost in perfect unison.

The light beneath Rheeya's feet began to glow almost violently. A thought suddenly filled her, coming from nowhere and everywhere. *This is for our people. You stand for our people. We are proud of you.*

And then the words began to form and she spoke them as though she had known them her whole life. "I, Princess Rheeya of the Stone Clan, daughter of King Adam and Queen Georgia, stand before Airon and my Spirit Guides, ready to place my soul in the hands of the Sun God that he may save our Island from the Strangers. I am ready to protect my people, our way of life, and our means of survival, by whatever means Airon deems worthy. I entrust my soul to Airon. I swear an oath to uphold this pact, to honour it all the days of my life, and all the days of my future lives."

Pride filled her momentarily and then faded like the light beneath her feet.

Taeya could hardly stand still. The waiting was hard but just being a part of the ceremony had her heart racing. Doing things filled her with excitement, it always had, and this was the biggest thing she'd ever get to do in her life. The light at her feet flared and, like Rheeya, she found the words to the oath simply coming to her.

"I, Princess Taeya of the Animal People, daughter of King Gavin and Queen Karnia, stand before Airon and my Spirit Guides, ready to place my soul in the hands of the Sun God that he may move our island to safety. I am ready to move, ready to do whatever I am asked to do. I entrust my soul to Airon. I swear an oath to uphold this pact, to honour it all the days of my life, and all the days of my future lives."

Though Betha had been the first to step up she now felt all her courage and conviction slipping away. She watched the lights grow and wane, she listened to the words of commitment, and she trembled. *"I am insignificant,"* she thought.

So is a single grain of wheat, answered a voice inside her. *So is an acorn. You feel bent in the winds of change but this will not break you. You are Evergrowth.*

"I, Princess Betha of the Evergrowth, daughter of King Florence and Queen Celyn, stand before Airon and my Spirit Guides, ready to place my soul in the hands of the Sun God that our lands may continue to prosper and flourish. I am ready to cultivate an age of peace and prosperity. I entrust my soul to Airon. I swear an oath to uphold this pact, to honour it all the days of my life, and all the days of my future lives."

Vonica stood staring in wonder at the lights around her. Never had she seen the temple looking like this. With eyes too wide she turned a full circle, slow and deliberate, taking in every possible detail as the other girls said their oaths. When she faced the altar again her own seal flared to life and she spoke, her voice carrying great dignity.

"I, Princess Vonica of the Sun Temple, daughter of King Cecil and Queen Sera, stand before Airon and my Spirit Guides, ready to place my soul in the hands of the Sun God that he may bring light and wisdom to the people. I am ready to learn what is needed to aid in whatever way I can, to preserve the events of this day and to spread the knowledge of our people. I entrust my soul to Airon. I swear an oath to uphold this pact, to honour it all the days of my life, and all the days of my future lives."

Throughout the entire ordeal, from the time they had set foot in the temple complex that morning, until this very moment, Ashlyn had been bored almost to the point of tears. The fighting had been entertaining for a short while and defying her father in front of everyone had been fun, but now she stood bored once more as the other girls droned on about duty, action, prosperity, and wisdom. As the last words left Princess Vonica's mouth everyone turned to look at Ashlyn. She stared back, her face blank.

Moments passed.

King Kenneth cleared his throat audibly.

Ashlyn sighed and in that half heartbeat that her body relaxed she felt something grip her. The light from her seal blazed and the words came unbidden to her mind and flowed unwanted from her lips.

"I, Princess Ashlyn of the Metalkin, daughter of King Kenneth and Queen Orabel, stand before Airon and my Spirit Guides, ready to place my soul in the hands of the Sun God that wealth may bless our people. I am ready to stand as sword and shield. I entrust my soul to Airon. I swear an oath to uphold this pact, to honour it all the days of my life, and all the days of my future lives."

The room filled with light so heavy that every person there could feel it weighing on their bodies until it was harder to breathe than it was to see. A great wind howled around the room, but not one candle flickered out and though all five girls felt their skirts twisting around their ankles their hair stayed out of their faces. The entire room, and later they would learn the entire Island, shuddered, like the last heaving breath of a dying man. Twice – three times – the shuddering came and then all was still and quiet and the light faded away.

Everyone had dropped to the floor, some kneeling in prayer, others clutching their neighbour or a bit of furniture, for fear of being blown or tossed away. Only the five princesses remained standing and as the light faded and everyone staggered to their feet they saw the first sign that Airon's magic had worked.

All five girls had hair the colour of roses.

Aden looked at the reports on his desk and sighed. The meetings he'd had with 'Queen' Vonica these last few months had done nothing to ease his mind.

"The strangers are gone, as promised, but what are these dark creatures? Where did they come from? What are they doing to my people?" wrote Gavin.

Kenneth's letter read, *"No one on this island knows a damn thing about trade. Why did you drive away the other people? How am I ever going to turn a profit?"*

The other news was just as bad: fights between the Iron Guild and the farmers in Evergrowth; fights between healers and miners in Stone Clan Province; charges of fraudulent trading laid against a horse farmer in the Animal People's territory; and always the reports of dark creatures, or spirits, no one knew what they were. They had appeared after the pact and were attacking people across the island.

Aden sighed again. True the Strangers were gone but at what cost? Fishermen were reporting that they could only go an hour out to sea before they hit riptides so strong it sent them spinning back to shore. The Big World was gone. *And our troubles are only beginning, it seems.*

The older man pushed away from his desk and shuffled out of his study. *I won't find any answers here.*

Airon's Chapel was much smaller than the Great Temple. The room was round with a small round altar at the center. An acolyte was just refilling the incense bowl when Aden came in. Aden nodded in response to the boy's bow and said, "Close the door behind you, I am not to be disturbed."

"Yes, High Priest."

The order was easy to obey for the first several hours. A cleaning lady almost walked in at sun down and would have broken Aden's meditation if an acolyte hadn't stopped her. By the next morning acolytes and scholars were hovering in the hallway outside the chapel – some were waiting to pray, others were waiting to see what was keeping Aden.

When Aden hadn't come out by dawn the *next* day King Celio himself came down to the temple complex to see what was happening. Of course, no one in the hallway had any idea and Celio returned to the palace empty-handed.

At the third dawn an acolyte found the doors to the chapel open and the room empty. A maid reported receiving a summons for food from Aden's study. At sundown an acolyte was summoned to Aden's study and given five scrolls, four to be taken to the aviary, one to be delivered to the palace.

At last Aden slept.

The Sun Temple was as centrally located on the island as was possible with a mountain range running down the center, stretching from the southern coast to within sight of the northern coast. Still, it took the Metalkin royal family and the Evergrowth royal family less time to make the journey than it did the Stone Clan and Animal People royal families.

King Celio, Queen Sera, and Princess Vonica found themselves suddenly playing host to the visiting royals, as well as the guests Aden had requested each family bring, as they waited for the stragglers to arrive. The week was tense as trade relations had all but broken down between the provinces and each was blaming the others for the current hardships. In that time Aden was unreachable, never answering a summons or responding to knocks on his study door.

Finally, when King Adam and his family had finally arrived, scant days behind King Gavin, Aden called for all of them to join him in the Great Temple.

The sun mosaic on the ceiling looked faded, that was the first thing Vonica noticed when she walked in. It was strange seeing the other princesses – though they were still dressed so differently they all had the red hair now and it made them look strangely similar, almost interchangeable. The thought made Ashlyn shiver.

Aden was waiting by the altar as the five kings, five queens, five princesses, and their servants and guests gathered into the temple. "Airon is not pleased," he said by way of greeting.

"Is that why we had to drag all this with us?" Kenneth asked, gesturing to the guards, servants, and escorts behind him.

"Yes," Aden said. The simplicity and force of his answer startled everyone. "The pact worked. The Island is moved. But your discourse has caused complications. What you have brought with you are the bandages that will repair the pact."

"Nobles and trinkets?" King Adam asked. "How are these things going to repair the pact?"

"And why does it need repair?" asked King Gavin. "Didn't you do the ceremony right?"

"The ceremony was done correctly, but which of you has held up the pact?" Aden didn't give them a chance to argue. "Which of you has put aside your distrust, or your hostility, or your hatred? Which of you has made any effort to sustain the others? Which of you have stepped down and allowed your daughters, the chosen ones of Airon himself, to rule as the pact entitles them to rule?"

"You expect us to allow fourteen-year-old, unmarried, females to rule?" Kenneth's eyes were wide, but his mouth was twisted in a sneer.

Ashlyn's eyes hardened but she said nothing.

Celio had the good sense to look ashamed. "We did not feel they were ready to rule, not with the upheaval."

Florence nodded. "With so many changes in recent days, surely a stable government …"

Aden shook his head. "I may be old and grey and nearing the end of my days but even I know better than to argue with Airon." He gestured over another elderly priest. "This is Mikael; he will show you how to set up for the ceremony. The princesses and I have something to discuss. In private."

All five girls appeared subdued; even Ashlyn's usually haughty expression was missing. They stood in the small side chamber in a semi-circle, facing Aden but each one looking at either their hands or their feet.

Aden studied them. Even with the red hair they were still so different, especially in dress. *They're supposed to be different,* he thought. *As different as animals are from plants and stone is from metal. But the world lives in harmony and so must we.*

"You will not have an easy task," Aden said. The gentleness of his voice after the ranting he'd done in the temple startled the girls into looking up. "You are young and inexperienced. Our life here has changed very suddenly. And now these Dark Spirits threaten the people."

"But what are they?" asked Vonica.

"They exist on the edges and when our island was moved we were no longer protected by the rest of the Big World. The edges got closer and so did the Dark Spirits. They are drawn to chaos, and to discourse. The squabbling between the provinces invited them in."

"I saw a man who had been taken over by one of these spirits," whispered Betha. "They had brought him to the healer who is one of my teachers. The healer could do nothing and all the while the man cursed and swore and threatened us with horrible things. His wife was sobbing and apologizing. 'That's not my husband' she kept saying." She shuddered.

The other girls had gone pale.

Aden frowned. "They are possessing people and devouring their souls. As time passes the possessed person becomes wild, their darkest side starts to appear. They will say and do things no one thought possible of them."

"How do we stop it?" asked Taeya, her hands balled into fists. "What do we do?"

"Didn't you hear him?" Ashlyn snapped. "Our fathers keep fighting and that's what's making them come here in the first place. What do you think needs to be done?"

Aden could see tempers rising but he said nothing.

"Leave her alone," Rheeya said. "She's at least looking for a way to help."

"And I'm not?" Ashlyn said.

"No," Rheeya said. "You're picking fights, just like your dad does."

"But I'm surrounded by idiots!"

"Better an idiot than a fool," muttered Vonica.

Ashlyn turned on Vonica. "What did you call me?"

Vonica's eyes went innocent-wide. "I didn't call you anything; I was just voicing my preference. I'd rather be an idiot than a fool. I wasn't saying that anyone here was necessarily a fool …"

"But if the shoe fits …" Taeya added, almost under her breath.

"Your fathers are not the only ones to blame, I see," Aden said. "Perhaps this was all for naught. Perhaps the pact will fall and our Island will drift so far from the Big World that it will be lost in the darkness and the Dark Spirits will devour us all." He shuffled from the room leaving five very ashamed young girls behind him.

In a soft voice Ashlyn said, "When I was young I found a tea set in the market. It was the most beautiful thing I had ever seen, made especially for little girls with a little teapot and little cups. The colours were like nothing I had ever seen. Everything in the palace that can be metal is metal, so our dishes are pewter or brass or even silver. These were the most amazing sea green colour with swirls of blue and flecks of black."

"Sea clay," Rheeya said. "They add salt to the clay when they fire it in the kiln, that's what makes the sea colours."

Ashlyn went on. "I bought them because the servants who were with me couldn't stop me. I carefully unwrapped each piece. They were a marvel to me, so fragile and yet so heavy. When my father discovered them, he was angry. No, he was furious. He told me only the craft of the Metalkin was worth anything. He took me out to the courtyard and he smashed every single piece of that tea set. He wouldn't even let me take a single shard back inside with me. The next day I had a little brass tea set. They were so cold in my hands, but I smiled and I played with them and I forgot about the beautiful clay tea set for years."

"I had a pet rabbit once," said Rheeya. "My parents gave it to the local huntsman when I started school. They said pets were a waste of time, that I had important duties to tend to, and that my people needed a strong queen."

Taeya nodded. "I used to sit and stare at the clouds and look at picture books, but my parents said I needed to get out and see and do and be active, that our people worked, they didn't daydream."

"There are still days that I'd rather spend in the gardens than in the library," Vonica confessed.

"It was a nice library," Taeya whispered.

Betha pulled at her braid. "I think the wrought iron fences around our gardens at home are beautiful. I know gold and silver are supposed to be the pretty metals, but those strong black fences make me feel safe and at the same time they're beautiful."

"Did they curve the tops or point them?" Ashlyn asked.

"Curved, like vines," Betha said.

The girls looked at each other with new eyes and for the first time they saw girls, their own age, scared and now very alone. Except for each other.

"I guess we'd better go fix things," Vonica said. The others nodded.

The altar was piled with the items the five royal families had brought with them. There were five swords, five ornate clay jars with lids, five roses, five large leather-bound books, five horse shoes, and five hawking gloves. On each seal where the girls had stood only a few months prior now stood five young men dressed in the clothes of nobles. The kings and queens stood off to the side, all looking upset.

The princesses hesitated in the doorway until Aden beckoned them over. "The pact must be strengthened. These items will strengthen the bond between Airon and the Spirit Guides. The swords from the Metalkin will be blessed so that they might kill the Dark Spirits. The jars from the Stone Clan will become Soul Vessels to protect our princesses during their transition from one life to the next so that the Dark Spirits will not find and devour their souls. These books, provided by the Sun Temple, contain a complete record of the pact, and space to fill in every meaningful encounter and the date of each rebirth. The horse shoes and gloves represent the mares and hawks from the Animal People waiting outside. They will be blessed with speed to be used for emergencies – to send messengers and guards, or messages. And the roses from Evergrowth will be transformed into a new rose, the sacred sign of the pact. This was decided by Airon.

"The first part of the ceremony will involve blessing these items. The second will be the marriage and soul-binding of the princesses to these suitors you have brought."

There was instant outcry from the kings and queens but a stern look from Aden silenced them.

"The princesses will be vulnerable during their time of rebirth. By joining their souls to their husbands, the Dark Spirits will be confused and will not find the souls of the princesses. With each rebirth of the princesses the Sun Princes will also be reborn. The princesses will not be complete without their soul mates. The joining of each prince and princess in each rebirth will keep the pact strong.

"The final part of the ceremony is the coronation. The princesses were selected by Airon to rule, and he will make their rule official. When you leave here today the princesses will be the true rulers of each province. Is the Captain of the Guard from each province present?"

Five men in varying styles of armour stepped forward.

"Once the ceremony is complete you will be taking your oaths of service to the princesses."

"Won't we be queens now?" Ashlyn asked.

Aden shook his head. "You shall remain princesses. Without each other you cannot rule. No one of you is supreme or best. You are the Princesses of Airon, the Guardians of the Pact, and the Protectors of the People."

"That's easy for you to say," Celio said, stepping forward. "You get to remain High Priest. You get to keep your power even as you strip away ours. What if we won't step down?"

"Then your daughters may have to have you arrested."

Celio laughed. "I'm leaving, and Vonica is coming with me. You didn't do your job right and now everything is falling apart. You want us to step down and let you mess up again. I won't allow it. We will set to rights what you have broken. Sera, Vonica, we're leaving."

"Celio," Vonica said, calling her father by name for the first time in her life. "You will remain and stand witness, as Airon requests of you. You will not bring further shame on my people. Airon is your

True God, your High God, and your Spirit Guide. You will obey him. And if not, you will obey me."

Celio strode across the room and struck his daughter across the face. "How dare you speak to me this way?! I am your father! I am your king!"

"You will be under arrest as soon as the ceremony is over," Vonica replied calmly. "Return to your place."

There was fire in Vonica's eyes, fire that looked too much like the light that had shone from the mosaic. Celio swallowed hard and stumbled back to where the other kings waited.

"Let us begin," Aden said.

The first part of the ceremony was simple and short. While the former rulers of the five provinces stood off to one side, the princesses stood off to the other, and the soon to be princes stood on the five seals, Aden prayed over each offered symbol, asking for blessings and a strengthening of the pact. In turn each item glowed with intense sunlight even though the day was cloudy.

Presently he turned to the girls and beckoned them over. "Please stand at your seals; it is time for the soul binding."

The girls had started meeting suitors months before the first ceremony and each was familiar with the young man who now stood with them. Shy smiles were exchanged as Aden instructed them to join hands. The seals beneath their feet began to glow as Aden began the blessing.

"Airon, God of Light, Protector of the Island, shower your blessings down on your chosen daughters and their husbands. Geralt Iron-Shield, Sheldon Sun-Dome, Samuel Wide-Field, Darrin Fair-Clay, Jonas Wild-Hound, the five of you have been called upon to stand before Airon as the shields that protect his roses. Your souls will defend the souls of our princesses in this life and in every following life. Do you five swear to uphold the pact, to protect your soul mate, and to honour Airon and the Spirit Guides?"

"We do," the young men answered.

"Airon, God of Light, Protector of the Island, bless your chosen daughters with wisdom, strength, determination, faith, and compassion. Bring stability and prosperity to your Island once more. Bring strength to the pact; protect us from Dark Spirits that threaten your people. "

Aden turned away from the altar and approached Ashlyn and Garret. "Today you shall be joined, not your bloodlines or your families or your wealth but your souls. From this day forth your souls shall call out to each other, seeking each other beyond death and into your new lives. Do you accept this blessing and burden?"

"We do," they said.

"Then receive the blessings of Airon, Princess Ashlyn Jewel-Rose and ..."

Kenneth barreled forward. "Jewel-Rose? What nonsense is that? She's an Iron-Blood! The last eight kings were Iron-Blood! There is no Jewel-Rose family in our province!"

A priest and two guards stepped forward to restrain him.

"You can't just erase our bloodline like this!"

Aden's attention remained on the ceremony and once Kenneth had been removed from the temple he continued. "Receive the blessings of Airon, Princess Ashlyn Jewel-Rose and Prince Gavin." He moved to the second couple, naming them Princess Vonica Bright-Rose and Prince Sheldon, then Princess Betha Rose of Roses and Prince Shawn, Princess Rheeya Stone-Rose and Prince Darcy, and lastly Princess Taeya Living Rose and Prince Jonathan.

"All that remains is to make your positions formal," Aden stated. The great gong rang out and acolytes filed in, two coming to rest behind each couple. In their hands rested golden pillows and on each pillow was a crown.

Starting with Ashlyn and working his way around the altar he crowned each couple. He then stepped back. "As decreed by Airon, and as witnessed by those here, so shall you five rule until the end of your natural days and again when your souls are reborn. Long live the Roses of Airon!"

Everyone in the room, some more enthusiastically than others, echoed, "Long live the Roses of Airon."

The final part of the ceremony was very short as the Captain of the Guard from each province swore their oath of service. Celio was led away to the palace where Vonica would deal with him. The other former rulers were escorted out of the temple to their waiting carriages.

The girls lingered in the temple.

"What happens now?" Betha asked.

"We go home and rule as best we can," Ashlyn said, placing a reassuring hand on Betha's arm. "We have those special hawks now, right? If there's any problems we can get word to each other quickly."

The other girls nodded. "What about later, when we die? What happens when we are too young to rule?" Rheeya asked.

The heavy silence was broken by Vonica. "We'll just have to have stewards. We'll train them and then they can help us rule when we are children. They can be a sort of bridge."

The others nodded.

"The rest I will take care of," Aden said, joining them. "Your souls will return to the Island in the Big World but Airon has shown me the gate and the signs to find you by. This knowledge shall be passed down to each High Priest so that we never lose you. We will survive."

"No," Taeya said. "We will prosper."

Above them the sun mosaic glowed.

Coming Spring 2019
The Exciting Conclusion to the Rose Garden Series

Mallory Brock's life was anything but ordinary from the beginning. The daughter of an English politician and an Irish lass, she'd grown up at the embassy in India where her father worked as a diplomat. Not wanting to follow in her father's political footsteps she returned to Ireland to attend university. There her life took a twist that made a childhood in India in the 1970s look boring.

She thought the men were crazy, thought maybe she was going crazy. Their story made no sense! How could she possibly be a lost princess, destined to rule one-fifth of some magical island? And yet, there was a portal in the middle of the sidewalk, one that no one else seemed to see, one that seemed to have no affect at all on anyone walking past it or through it.

So, she agreed to step through it, figuring nothing would happen. She figured wrong.

On the Isle of Light things have not been easy, and the return of the Metalkin Princess did not set things to rights as many hoped and believed. Instead things seem to be worsening as more and more corruption is uncovered.

High Priest Baraq Silver-Cloud is at his wits' end. Time is running out, he can feel it, but there is no answer in sight and the riddle gets more complicated at each turn. No history lecture or theology lesson prepared him for this.

Now, it is up to Mallory to figure out where things went wrong in a world she barely understands.

She may not understand magical pacts or Dark Spirits, but she understands politics and she's not about to let an entire island of people perish.

Upcoming Titles

Rose Garden

<u>Rose at the End</u> – Mallory Brock Jewel-Rose is tasked with unravelling a mystery before the choices of a few break the Pact and send the Isle of Light hurtling into oblivion.

Underground

<u>Turn Coats</u> – Shawna is in danger, but is help closer than she thinks? Ethan knows time is running short, for his sister, and for himself. He needs proof of what he saw, and he needs it now, but at what risk?

<u>Sunlight</u> – Shawna, Ethan, and their friends face off against the Complex Government in the thrilling conclusion to the Underground Series.

<u>Cheyanne</u> – There's more to the world than a few underground cities. Meet Cheyanne and discover what Ethan and Shawna's world looks like from the other side.

And look for the Underground Graphic Novels coming soon!

More Books by Casia Schreyer

Rose in the Dark
Rose from the Ash
Rose without Thorns

Nelly-Bean and the Kid Eating Garbage Can Monster
Nelly-Bean and the Adventures of Nibbles
Janelle et le Monstre de la Poubelle Mangeur d'Enfants

Complex 48
Separation
Reunion
Training
Rebels

Nothing Everything Nothing
Pieces

ReImagined
The Ultimate World Building Book
The Ultimate World Building Book Companion Worksheets

By Yvonne Ediger
Recipes and Memories

About the Author & Cover Artist

Casia Schreyer lives in Southeastern Manitoba with her husband and two children. She is the author of over a dozen titles, including the first three books in the Rose Garden series. Most of her time is spent being a writer and a mother.

Sara Gratton lives in Southeastern Manitoba with her husband and three children. She works as a photographer and graphic designer. She is the creative mind behind the Rose Garden covers, her first book cover project. She also took many of the photos Casia uses for her author photos in books and other promotional materials.